Worse Happen at Sea

A Clara Fitzgerald Mystery
Book 24

By
Evelyn James

Red Raven Publications
2021

© Evelyn James 2021

First published 2021
Red Raven Publications

The right of Evelyn James to be identified as the Author of this work has been asserted in accordance with the Copyrights, Designs and Patents Act 1988.

All rights reserved. No part of this book may be reprinted or reproduced or utilised in any form or by any electronic, mechanical or other means, now known or hereafter invented, including photocopying and recording, or in any information storage or retrieval system without the permission in writing from the author

Worse Things Happen at Sea is the twenty-fourth book in the Clara Fitzgerald series

Other titles in the Series:
Memories of the Dead
Flight of Fancy
Murder in Mink
Carnival of Criminals
Mistletoe and Murder
The Poisoned Pen
Grave Suspicions of Murder
The Woman Died Thrice
Murder and Mascara
The Green Jade Dragon
The Monster at the Window
Murder on the Mary Jane
The Missing Wife
The Traitor's Bones
The Fossil Murder
Mr Lynch's Prophecy
Death at the Pantomime
The Cowboy's Crime
The Trouble with Tortoises
The Valentine Murder
A Body Out of Time
The Dog Show Affair
The Unlucky Wedding Guest

Chapter One

There is no finer way to spend a Saturday afternoon in the late summer than by sitting in a comfortable chair, consuming strawberries and cream, sipping a pleasantly sharp and cold glass of lemonade, and vaguely paying attention to a cricket match occurring a few feet away.

At least, this was the opinion of Clara Fitzgerald, private detective, currently taking an afternoon off as she had no immediate case to investigate, and it was a very warm and muggy day in August. The sort of day when a person's brain feels like it is gently melting, and it is best not to try to undertake anything particularly taxing.

She also very much liked strawberries with cream, and the lemonade at the cricket club was rather special, though she made absolutely sure never to allow Annie to become aware of her feelings. Annie was her housekeeper, friend and, to complicate matters, now her sister-in-law. Clara had quietly raised the topic of Annie still undertaking housekeeping duties now she was officially one of the family. She had even suggested hiring in some help, as they could afford it and it seemed slightly wrong to continue allowing Annie to do everything.

Her suggestion had been greeted with the sort of hard

stare one commonly associates with tigers or similar wild animals who are about to eat the hunter that has pointed a gun at them. Clara pretended she had not said anything at all and allowed the situation to revert to the way it had always been, which suited Annie perfectly.

However, one thing she had been insistent on was Annie spending more time out of the house with Clara and Tommy on leisurely activities. So it was she had dragged Annie (and dragged was not too farfetched a word for the ordeal it had been to persuade Annie to leave her kitchen) along to a local cricket match between the Brighton Badgers (among whose players was Tommy, Clara's brother, and Annie's new husband) and the Hove Cricket Bats. Tommy and most of his fellow players, were still sporting the limps and awkward gaits war service had left them with. One of Hove's star bowlers was minus a hand, though he had a special artificial one he wore when fielding. It looked like a leather mitt, and he was very good with it. There had been soft mutters of cheating among the Badgers, who were now wishing their own bowler had lost a hand. Since Tommy happened to be that bowler, Clara was rather unimpressed by their chatter.

Annie shuffled in her deckchair, restless at being kept still for so long. Annie was the sort of person who was always moving, always doing something. Sitting around felt like a waste of her time.

"Tommy is up next at the stumps," Clara informed her, trying to distract her. "It is good to see him back playing, isn't it?"

"Very," Annie said firmly, while also suggesting it would be just as good if she had not been dragged along to watch. "Do you want more strawberries?"

"I am quite full of strawberries," Clara replied. "Just sit and enjoy the sunshine."

Annie frowned at the sun; it had personally offended her when she had discovered it brought out freckles on her cheeks. She had discovered this as a child and now had an ongoing grudge against the glowing gaseous orb. She was wearing a large summer hat as a result and was wishing she could go indoors. The sun had never appealed to her, though it did help dry her washing.

Clara had returned to the game in time to see Tommy strike the lobbed cricket ball with a satisfying thwack. He then started his runs, going as fast as ever, to Clara's eyes, even if he did have a noticeable limp.

"I think he is going to get all his runs," she said, offering Annie her limited cricket knowledge.

The ball had sailed through the air and there was excitement among the Badgers, but then the artificial mitt of the Hove team's bowler came up and the ball seemed to be sucked into it. Tommy was turning to return to the stumps, frantically trying to reach it before the ball. He put on a good sprint, but he was pipped at the very last and with triumph the Hove team cheered as he was declared out.

"Oh," Clara said, disappointed.

"Something is amiss with that," Annie's ire had been inflamed. "I do not believe that ball could have possibly made it to those stumps in that space of time."

"I watched it, and I think it could, and more to the point, it did," Clara replied.

Annie glared across the cricket pitch.

"Look how despondent Tommy is. He was running his heart out! They should not have called him out, whatever that means."

"It is the rules of the game Annie," Clara informed her.

"There is something up with that mitt the other team's bowler wears, did you see how the ball was sucked into it?"

"Look, he is just a good catcher," Clara said in her best placating voice. "It is unfortunate, but this is how things go in cricket."

Annie was far from satisfied and spent the rest of the game glaring at the Hove Cricket Bats' one-handed bowler. If it were possible for a person's gaze to be felt by another, it would be the sort of gaze Annie was giving him, and once or twice the bowler seemed to rub uneasily at the back of his neck.

The game now started to swing away from the Badgers, and Clara was regretting getting Annie to come as it looked very likely the Badgers were going to lose with their star bowler out. Tempers were fraying in the team as they were soundly thrashed by their rivals, the Hove's bowler time and time again seeming to have an unerring ability to catch the ball. The afternoon was rapidly turning into a disaster for the home team.

There was a pause halfway through the game. Time to regroup and discuss tactics. Clara excused herself to use the ladies' bathroom in the clubhouse. Annie was still venomously scowling at the Hove team and barely noticed her leave.

"I should have left her in the kitchen," Clara groaned to herself.

The bathroom was busy – a lot of lemonade had been consumed. It was also refreshingly cool after the heat of the day outside. Clara splashed water on her face when it was her turn and then wiped it off with a tissue. As much as she loved summer, she did find this clagging heat rather draining. She exited the bathroom to allow another lady to take her place and was just preparing to go back out and try to tame Annie's temper, when she heard a polite cough behind her. It was the sort of cough that indicated someone wanted your attention.

Clara turned and found herself facing a gentleman in a smart naval style uniform. Not quite Royal Navy, but certainly something nautical. He nodded his head to her and removed his cap.

"Are you Miss Fitzgerald, the private detective?"

"I am," Clara said.

"My apologies for tracking you down like this, but we have a rather difficult situation and desperately need the help of fresh eyes. We are told you are the best at these sorts of things."

Clara endeavoured not to preen at the praise. She certainly did try hard, and she was doggedly determined to get at the truth, whether that made her best was always open for debate.

"Precisely who is 'we'?" she asked.

"I am Lieutenant Harper of the King Edward luxury liner," the gentleman explained. "We have had to drop anchor off the Brighton coastline due to a mishap that occurred to one of our crew. Due to its nature, we were asked by the police to remain where we are until they can investigate the matter. It is something of a grey area, being at sea when something occurs. My captain rather hoped he could continue his journey and dock to unload the passengers before the police needed to become involved."

"This all sounds rather serious," Clara said, her brow puckering as she considered the information being given to her.

"It is serious. There are a number of prestigious passengers aboard who are upset by the delay," Lieutenant Harper shook his head.

"That was not quite what I meant," Clara tried not to sigh at his mixed priorities. "I take it someone has been badly hurt or worse?"

"A crew member is dead," Lieutenant Harper whispered. "It was probably just an accident, but the captain felt it best he telegraph to the authorities to get advice on what to do. He contacted the maritime authorities and they in turn felt it necessary to contact Scotland Yard. We were still sailing at the time, but the message came back that we must stop wherever we were and report to the local police. We happened to be off the coast of Brighton."

"Have the police been aboard?" Clara asked.

"Yes," Lieutenant Harper looked morose. "They say we must remain where we are until they have resolved the matter to their satisfaction. The captain has tried to persuade them to let us carry on, but they insist we remain. He was quite beside himself because our employers look dimly on delays. It will throw off the entire schedule."

"If someone has been murdered, it is necessary," Clara

told him gently.

"We are not denying that," Lieutenant Harper said firmly. "But the whole matter was an accident, clearly. We just need someone to prove that to the police so we can move on."

"Which is why you have come to see me," Clara extrapolated.

"One of the crew is from Brighton and recalled your name. He said you might help us. Again, I am very sorry to have hunted you down like this. If it were not so urgent, I should have waited."

Clara held up a hand to pause him as it looked likely he would continue to apologise for several minutes if she let him.

"I understand," she said calmly. "I shall certainly help you, but might we wait until the cricket match is concluded?"

As she spoke, she heard a groan from the crowd outside and a joyful cry of 'out.' It did not appear things were going well for the Badgers.

"Of course," Lieutenant Harper agreed keenly. "I cannot drag you away just like that."

Clara glanced out the clubhouse door and saw that Annie was now marching determinedly across the cricket pitch, bringing the game to an abrupt halt.

"Oh dear," Clara said. "Please excuse me, Lieutenant Harper, I shall just be a moment."

Clara dashed outside hoping to catch Annie before she unleashed her temper upon someone. She was too late.

"There is cheating afoot!" Annie declared hotly to the team captain of the Hove Cricket Bats. "You are not playing fairly!"

"Annie, this is not the time," Tommy said, hurrying over as swiftly as Clara.

"I have watched that bowler," Annie declared to her husband. "There is something wrong with his glove. The way the ball falls into it makes no sense. More than once, I swear he should have dropped the ball from his mitt, instead it stuck there."

"Annie, he is just a very good catch," Tommy persisted.

Annie gave him a hurt look.

"I have eyes Tommy, and I am not a fool. I saw what I saw."

Clara had reached them by now.

"Annie, I appreciate you are upset, but we should not interrupt the game."

"It is not a game when someone is cheating," Annie said firmly. "I see you do not believe me. Had you decided someone was cheating, Clara, you would have not hesitated to do the same and we should all have backed you up. Just because it is me who is saying these things, you think I must be wrong."

Annie was obviously hurt at their lack of faith, and she was utterly right. Had Clara thought she saw cheating afoot, she would not have paused to consider the consequences, but would have stood up and declared she thought something was amiss. Instead, because it was Annie saying these things, they doubted her. Clara felt a pang of guilt and realised she did not have as much trust in Annie's judgement as she should. Of all of them, Annie was the one with the sharpest eyes and a good dollop of common sense.

"Annie…" Tommy began.

Clara interjected swiftly.

"Annie has a fair concern to make," she said. "If she has seen things that did not look right, then she has a duty to speak up and address the matter."

"What is this?" demanded the captain of the Hove team. "We are not cheats!"

"Then it is imperative we demonstrate that at once," Clara informed him. "So no one shall harbour any doubts."

"This is just because we are winning!" someone else shouted, and now there were murmurs of protest from the spectators. Those favouring Hove were furious at the interruption, those supporting Brighton were listening with interest and cheering on Annie.

Things looked likely to get messy swiftly. Fortunately, the chairman of the Brighton Cricket Club came over at that point.

"People have been saying things," he said quietly but forcefully. "Not just this young lady, others too, about the bowler's mitt."

"He is a war veteran!" Hove's captain snapped. "People need to show some respect!"

"This has nothing to do with respect," the chairman said calmly. "It is about assessing whether an artificial device is offering your team an unfair advantage. We are all sportsmen here and we should take pride in proving ourselves honourable in our game. It is what makes us British, after all."

There were mumbles and mutterings, but the chairman was right. A lot of people were concerned about that strange mitt and its magical ability to snatch balls from the air. It was probably nothing, but until it could be proved the Hove team did not have an advantage, there would continue to be rumours and the game could not carry on.

"I suggest we return to the clubhouse and discuss all this in a sensible and private fashion," the chairman carried on.

"I agree," Annie said forcefully. "People who play fair do not fear being examined."

She gave a sharp look to Hove's captain, who scowled back.

"We shall discuss it," the chairman persisted. "In the clubhouse."

They began to move away, Annie was right among them, not going to be left out of this. Clara took her brother's arm just before he left the pitch.

"I have been asked to assist on a passenger liner where there has been a suspicious death," she said quickly. "I have to go."

"Do you want me to come?" Tommy asked.

Clara glanced over at Annie.

"No. I need you here to make sure Annie doesn't start a

war."

Chapter Two

Lieutenant Harper had secured a carriage in his search for Clara. It was a two-seater affair with a driver who looked positively ancient and was wrapped up in a thick coat despite the heat. Though all the other components of the carriage looked old, the horse itself was a sprightly young thing, that was restless in the shafts and had the sort of tilt to its head that suggested it might just do something stupid, such as bolting off a bridge.

Clara rarely rode in carriages, preferring public transport, walking, cycling or, when it was possible, borrowing Captain O'Harris' car. She gave the horse a warning look as Lieutenant Harper held the door open for her.

"Lieutenant, you best explain this situation to me," she said once inside.

Harper pulled the door firmly shut and tapped the roof to inform the driver to head off.

"By all accounts, it was an unfortunate accident," Harper began. "The problem we have is no one is quite sure how it occurred. It should not have been possible, you see, and no one witnessed it. Yet, a man is dead under peculiar circumstances."

"How did he die?" Clara asked, she sensed Harper was reluctant to talk about that portion of the affair.

The lieutenant winced as he prepared himself to explain to a lady the grim reality of what had occurred. Despite being advised that Clara was a professional private detective, far from easily shocked, and the best person to assist with the situation, he still had an inherent reluctance to talk to her about the matter.

"Lieutenant Harper, sooner or later I must be told what has happened," Clara reminded him.

"Yes, yes, you are quite right. It is not something I have been wanting to dwell on, that is all. Quite simply a man was crushed to death in one of the watertight doors in the early hours of the morning."

He waited to see Clara's reaction. She did not flinch or frown, she accepted the information with a nod.

"That seems like a straightforward accident," she replied. "The poor man did not get out of the way of the door as it closed."

"It is not quite as plain as that," Harper explained. "These doors, they close relatively slowly for the very purpose to enable people to get out of the way. He had to just be standing there, waiting for the door to shut upon him."

"Or there was some reason he could not get out of the way," Clara suggested.

"Exactly, and you have come upon the reason the police are so reluctant to just declare it an accident. It is a mystery, for sure."

"Who was the poor man in the door?" Clara asked.

"His name was Alf Matlock, an apprentice engineer. He joined us a couple of months ago. Our voyage out was his first."

"Where were you headed?"

"America," Harper said. "Docking at New York to be precise. Then returning to Dover, with a stopover at

Belfast along the way."

"You were nearly at the end of your voyage," Clara remarked.

"Yes," Harper said. "We would not have had to sail far to reach our port and the matter could have been dealt with there. The passengers and the shipping line would have been happy, or should I say, happier. Instead, we are stuck off the coast, under orders not to move."

"The police cannot detain you forever," Clara consoled him.

"They can detain us long enough to cause a sizeable problem for my captain and the crew. The passengers are already restless and complaining, yet we cannot tell them what has occurred and why we are stopped. We have made up some story about engine trouble, though that has not prevented questions being asked about why the police came aboard."

"A trying situation for you all," Clara agreed. "However, I think Mr Matlock's circumstances even more trying."

"I do not deny that," Harper said swiftly, concerned she had thought him unsympathetic to the death of a crew member in such unpleasant circumstances. "We obviously want to know what occurred. It is just we cannot imagine how it was anything but an accident. To suppose anything sinister, well… it defies belief."

"You said yourself the circumstances were peculiar," Clara reminded him.

"Peculiar, but not suspicious," Harper corrected firmly. "We just need you to find the answer for us, and then we can prove to the police it was just a terrible misfortune and be on our way."

Clara opted not to burst his bubble. If it were so simple to prove the matter an accident, she was sure Inspector Park-Coombs would have done so already.

Clara and Park-Coombs had worked together often, and they trusted one another. Admittedly sometimes the inspector let his common sense slip away from him when he got an idea into his head, but that merely proved him human. Clara was sure he would not be detaining the liner and dealing with all the administrative problems that would lead to if the death had obviously been an accident.

"Why was Mr Matlock near the watertight door?" she asked.

"He was doing an inspection of the area for leaks and so forth. The liner is vast and its underbelly enormous with many corridors and rooms. The pipework is extensive, as you may imagine, water, gas, and of course the steam power from the engine is all channelled through pipes. These have to be routinely inspected to ensure there are no problems. Matlock was on the early morning inspection."

"Would the watertight door be open or closed during these inspections?"

"Closed," Harper assured her. "Unless someone was going through it, the watertight doors are always closed in case of flooding. It is their purpose."

"Of course," Clara nodded. "I see why you cannot fathom how Matlock ended up crushed in one."

Harper gave her a look of relief that she understood.

They were approaching the pier, Clara could see its struts out of the window of the carriage, even though she had to look past Harper in his bright white uniform.

"There is a small boat waiting for us, to take us over to the liner," Harper told her. "We have even considered transporting the passengers off the liner by such a boat and then providing road transport to get them to Dover."

"That sounds quite an undertaking," Clara considered how many passengers they must be talking about, including a sizeable quantity of luggage.

"If it saves complaints, we would do it," Harper said. "However, the police do not want anyone leaving the liner. I am taking quite a chance coming to see you."

Clara thought it might have been less of a hazard if he had taken off his uniform and dressed in ordinary clothes. She suspected that Harper was the sort of man who felt incomplete without his dress whites and would not have even contemplated the idea of removing them.

The carriage deposited them at the end of the pier and Clara had to admit the horse had been perfectly amenable and had not taken them to their doom. She had misjudged the fellow. Though, as they were walking along the wooden pier she heard a commotion, turned her head, and saw that the horse had taken a dislike to a lamppost and had backed the carriage sideways across the road in its panic. It was bucking its head and refusing to move, while traffic was held up either side of it.

"Oh dear," Clara said under her breath, relieved at least to know her instincts were still up to scratch.

She found herself being ushered into a fishing smack; a tiny thing that remarkably housed a crew of five when it was out working. Today there was just the captain and first mate. They kept their distance from Harper and Clara, happy to get on with their work undisturbed. The smack was unhitched from the line holding it to the pier and its engines started to chug them across the water. Clara was not used to travel by fishing smack, and she watched the water swirling against the wooden sides, wondering how such an ungainly boat managed to move forward at all.

"I am very grateful for your assistance," Harper told her. "The captain will be very grateful too."

Clara hoped they would not expect results swiftly, as so often was the case when she was hired. She could only work at the pace the clues and evidence allowed.

"Tell me about Matlock," she said as a large luxury liner loomed ahead.

Sitting on the flat horizon, it looked at first as if someone had taken a tiny ship and stuck it on top of a cake, only as you drew closer did it seem to become real.

"I am afraid I cannot tell you much," Harper replied. "I had nothing to do with him, at least, not until after his death."

"Who found him?"

"Another engineer, Stan Barnes. He was heading to the engine room to begin his shift and found Matlock in the doorway. I happened to be on duty at the time. There is always someone in command of the ship, day and night."

"Naturally, in case of emergencies," Clara understood.

"I had just completed a walk around the deck to see that all was well. When I came back to the bridge I was informed of a message from engineering. Barnes had told the bridge crew there had been an accident and a senior officer was needed, also someone in a medical capacity. On my way down below, I collected our night nurse and we proceeded down together.

"I was not sure what to expect, though I was thinking someone had fallen or cut their hand open in machinery. I had a dozen different notions running through my head, but none of them came close. When I saw Matlock crushed in that doorway it was awful. Barnes was trying to release him, but the door had seized shut for some reason. He was working at it with a wrench.

"I helped him, and we managed to release the door enough that Matlock fell forward and the night nurse, Miss Nettles, caught him and laid him out on the ground. We thought he was still alive at that point. He was blue in the face, but Miss Nettles was sure she could feel a faint pulse. She gave him morphine and then we hurried to carry him to the medical bay. We summoned the ship's doctor from his bed, and he pronounced Matlock dead. There was nothing we could do for him."

Harper was morose at the memory. It had been a horrible night and the vision of Matlock wedged in that doorway was going to haunt him for a long time. He had not slept since the incident, and exhaustion was starting to weigh on him too.

"This has been a trying time," Clara sympathised. "No one expects to see such a thing on a civilian liner."

"No," Harper agreed. "I am still trying to get my head around it all. It is a terrible thing, but all this police nonsense is making it a dozen times worse."

Clara did not comment on whether it was nonsense or not. The situation was obviously peculiar, and questions had naturally been raised. Perhaps it was just a terrible tragedy, one of those weird flukes of life that snatch away a man's future remorselessly.

"I shall find the truth for you," she told Harper.

Harper relaxed a fraction.

"That is all we ask. The crew has been briefed to provide all the help you need, but I must make it plain that you are not to bother any of the passengers."

Clara was not happy about that.

"What if I need to ask them questions?"

"The passengers were not involved," Harper said firmly. "Of that I am certain."

Chapter Three

The cricket teams had regrouped in the clubhouse, with the chairman, umpires, and some of the senior club members. Annie and Tommy were also present. The Hove Cricket Bats were fuming, feeling they had been cheated of an imminent victory. The Brighton Badgers were casting scowls at them, angry in turn that their rivals might not have been playing fair.

The chairman, Mr Percival Hardcastle, looked upon the collected people and tried not to groan at the inconvenience of a pleasant afternoon ruined by accusations of misconduct on the cricket pitch. It was all very un-British.

"Now we are all here, we ought to begin by asking the young lady who has made these declarations of cheating what precisely she believes she saw," he said.

All eyes turned to Annie. Some were eager, wanting to hear her suspicions, others were angry and were trying to pour forth that emotion upon her so she would not be able to speak up. Annie was not so easily swayed, not when it was a matter of principle and also her new husband was involved. Annie met the angry gazes with calm composure. She had folded her arms across her chest and was ready to take them all on.

"It was just like the Easter fair of 1919," she told the room. "Where something was wrong with the Best Daffodil displays. The flowers had all gone in looking perky, but by the time judging came around most appeared to be wilting. Only one bunch remained upright and stunning. People blamed the unseasonal heat, and the way the sun had been allowed to fall into the tent, but I was sure it was something more sinister than that. I had this feeling, and I was right. When we looked further, all but one bunch of daffodils had had their water contaminated with weed killer.

"The natural assumption was that the person who had presented the unaffected daffodils was responsible, but she denied it and if you knew her, well, you would not think she was the sort to do such a thing. In the end, it turned out the culprit was another contestant who had been set on vengeance but had not realised her own vase of daffodils had been moved and switched earlier in the day. She poisoned her own flowers along with the others by mistake."

There was a pause after Annie had finished speaking.

"As interesting as that is," Mr Hardcastle said, "how does it relate to today?"

"I had an instinct that day, not only about the flowers being tampered with deliberately, but also that the culprit was not as obvious as everyone made out. I have that same instinct today. I was watching that cricket match intently and I am convinced there was cheating afoot."

There was an eruption of protests from the Hove team, matched by an outcry of indignation from the Brighton Badgers.

Mr Hardcastle put out his hands and made a pressing down gesture to calm everyone.

"Now, now, the lady has not finished. Perhaps she could explain what she believes she saw," he said when silence returned.

Annie straightened up. It was not a question of what

she believed she had seen; it was a matter of what she knew to be the case.

"I watched the Hove bowler when he was acting as a fielder," she began. "One might say what a remarkable fielder he was. I think he caught nearly every ball that was batted in his direction and some of them were truly extraordinary catches. You would have thought, watching them, that he should have missed them entirely as they should have sailed over his head. Yet he did not, it was as if the ball was attracted to his special mitt."

Annie's statement caused a commotion once more. The Badgers were furious, declaring there had been foul play, the Hove Cricket Bats were voicing sharp denials. Mr Hardcastle had a difficult time calming things down again.

"You are suggesting, Mrs Fitzgerald, that the mitt was somehow rigged to bring the ball to it," he clarified.

Annie nodded.

"That is precisely what I am saying. There were several times when it almost looked as if the ball changed trajectory to reach the mitt."

"That is preposterous!" Jim Reed declared, he was the one-handed bowler for Hove and the man at the centre of this fiasco. He was feeling very hurt and hard done by right in that moment.

"We can deal with this in a couple of ways," Mr Hardcastle said in his best placating tone of voice. "First, we should examine the cricket ball used in the game to see if it has been tampered with in any way. Who has it?"

There was an awkward pause.

"I believe it was left where it last fell," an umpire explained. "In the commotion, it was quite forgotten."

"It should be retrieved," Mr Hardcastle said pointedly to the umpire, who hastened to head outside and find the ball.

"Secondly, if we could see your special mitt, Mr Reed?" Hardcastle turned to the bowler.

"It is in the changing rooms, in my bag," Reed said sharply. "I only wear it when I am fielding. The thing cuts into my wrist like a demon. I took it off and put it back in my bag the moment we came in here."

Hardcastle tried not to sigh at this secondary inconvenience.

"Perhaps someone might fetch this bag? Our second umpire, preferably, to keep everything fair."

The second umpire agreed and, having been told what Reed's bag looked like, he went to fetch it. They all waited impatiently, Annie now starting to feel the first elation of triumph. They would find the ball had been tampered with and the mitt would have some sort of device in it that gave Hove an unfair advantage. She was trying not to smile.

The first umpire returned and placed an inoffensive looking cricket ball before the chairman. Mr Hardcastle picked it up and examined it carefully. An experienced cricketer himself, he should be able to spot any sort of defect in the ball. He ran his fingers over the surface, pressed the ball to see if it was softer than it should be, felt its weight and lastly examined the stitching.

"I see nothing wrong with this ball," he said at last.

He asked the umpire to offer a second opinion. The same careful examination was carried out; if anything, the umpire was even more intense in his work than Hardcastle. When he was done, he simply shook his head.

"I can find nothing wrong."

The ball was passed back to Hardcastle. He turned it in his hand and then offered it to the Brighton Badgers' team captain. Accepting it, he conducted his own examination, his team looking over his shoulder and occasionally asking him to turn it so they could look at something. They were hopeful at first, but as the ball turned in his hands and they found nothing amiss, their faces fell.

For a while they had really been convinced they had been cheated of victory, that the Hove team had used an unfair advantage. Now it seemed they would have to accept that they were simply not as good as Hove.

"It seems fine," the captain said at last, the words bitter

in his mouth.

Annie felt that awful moment when certainty becomes doubt. She lowered her arms and stared at the ball, feeling sure they had to be wrong. She looked so despondent; Tommy came to her aid with a suggestion.

"Perhaps the outside of the ball is perfectly fine, but what about inside?" he said.

There was renewed hope among his teammates, though the chairman gave a groan. He took back the cricket ball, removed a penknife from his pocket and started the destructive task of cutting open the ball. For the devoted cricketers, the sacrifice of the ball, its stitches sliced, and its perfect covering peeled back, made them cringe. Internally the ball contained a core of cork, to provide the necessary bounce. This was covered by tightly woven strings, before the red leather covering was placed upon it and stitched up. The disembowelled cricket ball sat in the chairman's hand, looking a sorry thing.

Annie plucked it from his palm and looked it over. She could see nothing suspicious, but then she was not a cricketing aficionado. She passed the ball to Tommy who spun it in his fingers, desperately hoping to find something to prove her concerns correct. All he saw was a perfectly normal cricket ball.

The Hove Cricket Bats were beginning to preen and smirk. Annie wanted to run away and hide, feeling a fool. She had been so sure, so utterly sure. Tommy reached out for her shoulder, but she shrugged him off. She did not want to be consoled, she wanted to be proven right.

"Are we satisfied the ball has not been tampered with?" the chairman asked them carefully.

The Brighton Badgers had no option but to nod their heads. Mr Hardcastle was sorry things had come to this, sorry that his cricket club had been the site of these nasty accusations and drama. It was going to put a taint on the place, that was for sure.

"Mrs Fitzgerald, I believe you owe the Hove Cricket

Bats an apology," Hardcastle said to Annie.

"Steady on!" Tommy declared at once. "Annie was only being honest about what she saw. If things had been different, we would be slapping her on the back!"

He glanced at his teammates for support, but they all turned their heads from him. Tommy bitterly realised he was on his own.

"The fact remains, Mr Fitzgerald, that this accusation was false."

"But made in good faith," Tommy insisted. "If we punish people who come forth believing a crime has occurred and are incorrect, then people will never report anything. It was not maliciously done."

"Oh, I am not so sure," Jim Reed stepped into the fray. "After all, it was the wife of Brighton's star bowler who made the accusation. She has cost us a victory today, and was it merely because she could not bear to see her husband lose?"

"What rot!" Tommy snapped at him. "You would not say that if you knew Annie!"

"Gentlemen," Mr Hardcastle interceded. "The matter has been dealt with, let us not make this into more than it needs to be. If the young lady will do the right thing and apologise to the Hove players then we can move on from this and schedule a rematch, say, for three weeks' time?"

Annie was stony silent. She had been so sure, but now the facts were set before her, and she had clearly been mistaken. She felt hollow and hurt, as if her mistake made her something less than she had been before. How could she ever trust her instincts again after this?

"Mrs Fitzgerald?" Mr Hardcastle said quietly. "You do owe these gentlemen an apology. You called into question their honour as sportsmen. It is a very serious matter."

Annie looked into his eyes, feeling suddenly very alone in the room.

"I did not say it because I felt bad for Tommy," she insisted, though she was beginning to doubt herself over that as well now. "I really thought something looked amiss."

"We all make mistakes," Mr Hardcastle consoled her. "We also have to own up to them."

Annie glanced at the Brighton Badgers, who would not meet her eye. She had given them false hope and they resented that almost as much as they resented being cheated. Annie could not look at Tommy, even though she knew he was desperate to give her his support. He would back her to the very end, but how could she let him when she had been so foolish?

Maybe she had allowed her love for Tommy to blind her? Maybe she had been so horrified to imagine him losing, and doing so in such a dramatic style with a landslide victory for the opposition, that she could not bear it? Had she allowed her emotions to overrule her common sense?

She wished Clara were there. Clara always knew what to say and how to see things from a different angle. Clara had tried to stop her making these claims, she had wanted her to leave it alone. Well, it seemed she was right, but she was not there to make things better again. Annie tried not to feel angry about that.

She wasn't angry at Clara; she was angry at herself. She had allowed her pride to rule her, had thrown out accusations that were obviously wrong. She did owe the Hove players an apology for calling into question their integrity.

She finally turned in their direction, even though her stubbornness really, really wanted to refuse, wanted her to just leave without backing down. Annie hated apologising, because apologising meant she had been wrong, and Annie abhorred being wrong. She studied the Hove players, who were casting her fearsome looks. Earlier these had not bother her, now she felt the power of their stares and wanted to cry.

"I suppose I made a mistake," she said, her voice tight with tears. "I honestly believed I was witnessing something peculiar. I did not mean to belittle your honour as cricketers, at least, not without cause. It was not done simply out of sour grapes. Will you accept my apology on this matter?"

Hove's captain, an arrogant fellow at the best of times, had a smile on his face that made Tommy want to punch his lights out. He was revelling in Annie's apology. Tommy nearly growled at the sight of his face.

"Well, I suppose, seeing as you are not a cricketer the mistake is understandable," the captain began. "Seeing men who are in their top form might seem like something magical and impossible. I can understand you have not witnessed players of our calibre before…"

"Hey!" the Brighton Badgers' captain interrupted him. "Mind what you are saying!"

"Captain Rhodes, please just accept the apology without all this unnecessary aggravation," Hardcastle told the Hove captain.

Captain Rhodes sneered at him, and Annie felt even worse that she was wrong and had allowed such a man to get the chance to lord it over them.

It was that moment the second umpire returned.

"Chairman Hardcastle, I am sorry I took so long," he said as he entered, not realising what he was interrupting.

"It is no matter," Hardcastle informed him. "We have examined the cricket ball and it had not been tampered with."

The second umpire did not seem interested in that.

"That may be so, but we have another problem. I cannot find Mr Reed's mitt. In fact, his whole bag is missing."

Chapter Four

Captain Blowers was a professional fellow who ran his ship with naval precision. He had actually served with the Navy during the last war, valiantly commanding an old liner as a troop carrier. He was very proud of this fact and had taken on board many of the naval traditions he had encountered during this time, even if he was only ever part of the Naval Reserve. He believed in punctuality, neatness of dress, deferential treatment to superiors and a shot of rum every night. People getting crushed in watertight doors was not part of his plan. It defied all his ideas of how a ship ought to be run.

He was also uncomfortable about allowing a woman aboard to investigate the affair, though he had to confess he was running low on alternative options at that moment in time and with the shipping company executives breathing down his neck he needed to do something other than wait for the police to get on with things. He watched the young woman who approached his gangplank with uncertainty. She looked a little too young for this business and definitely she was too female. Women should not be dealing with people being crushed to death, it was just not right. If someone could have suggested a reliable male private detective for him to hire, he certainly would have done so.

Despite his reservations, he put a brave face on things.

"You must be Miss Fitzgerald?"

He gave the young lady a stately bow, doffing his cap.

"I have explained the situation to Miss Fitzgerald," Lieutenant Harper said.

Captain Blowers winced a little at this news. To his mind, explaining to a woman that a man had had his life squashed out of him by a heavy metal door would surely result in hysterics and smelling salts. He admired Harper for his bravery.

"I am very sorry to have brought this to you," he apologised profusely. "It is not the sort of thing a lady ought to hear about."

"Whyever not?" Clara asked him calmly.

"Well, it is unseemly," Blowers answered, feeling wrong-footed.

"Sudden death generally is," Clara replied. "There are few nice ways for a young person to unexpectedly die. Typically, they perish in ghastly accidents, or from some savage sickness, or at the hands of another. Being crushed to death is just one of the ways a man can meet his peril suddenly."

Clara had one eye on the captain, who was looking more shocked by the moment at her talk, and one eye on the liner, which was very smart, very smart indeed. Clara's overall impression was of a large landscape of white metal and wood, all glistening in the afternoon sunshine.

"I suppose… when you put it that way…" Blowers was finding the situation tumbling out of his grasp.

"I was a nurse during the war," Clara informed him. "People forget that in times of crisis the ones who tend to pick up the pieces are women. Nurses see some terrible things. Things even some men cannot handle. You have to be silently strong and do your best."

"Oh," Blowers said, realising she had a point.

"One of the first to the scene I believe was the night

nurse," Clara added.

Blowers was not a stupid man and understood her point.

"Yes, of course," he said. "Sometimes, one forgets that a nurse is also a lady."

Blowers had the decency to look sheepish at this confession. Clara smiled at his honesty.

"I think we shall work well together, Captain Blowers, we are both professionals who take pride in our work and try to do our very best whenever we can."

Captain Blowers returned the smile, the ice broken.

"Where would you like to begin, Miss Fitzgerald?" Blowers asked.

"I would like to meet the victim," Clara said. "Getting to know the victim can help to shine a light on who might have wished them harmed. It also seems only polite when investigating a death to first pay one's respects to the deceased."

Blowers understood all this, found a certain logic in it. He was beginning to like Miss Fitzgerald. She thought a lot like him.

"We shall have to go down to the ship's stores for that," he said. "We have placed Mr Matlock in one of the large refrigeration units we have aboard for fresh food. Normally it contains meat, but with our voyage near its end, our fridges are virtually empty."

He did not add that had Matlock died earlier in the voyage the situation would have been a lot more awkward.

"We would normally bury a deceased crewman at sea," Blowers continued as he led the way to a set of stairs leading down into the belly of the ship. "We do get occasional deaths from natural causes, or accidents. We have a large crew after all, and people get sick and perish."

Clara did not need the explanation, she understood that when at sea certain practicalities had to be observed. Transporting dead bodies was not a luxury they could afford unless the deceased happened to be a passenger.

"Because of the circumstances of Matlock's death, we

have been advised to retain his body in a suitable location until such a time as a decision is made regarding how he came to his fate."

They were heading deeper and deeper into the ship. Clara noticed how the sound was changing, from the steady slosh of the waves on the upper levels to the quiet peacefulness of the passengers' quarters, and now to the grinding, clanking functional part of the ship.

"You must have had your concerns about the death of Matlock right from the start?" Clara asked Blowers. "Otherwise, you would not have telegraphed to shore concerning it."

Blowers gave a soft sigh, partly regretting his conscience over the affair, yet also certain he had made the right decision.

"The circumstances troubled me," Blowers admitted. "An able man should not have ended up crushed in such a fashion. It ought to be impossible. The watertight doors close slowly for a reason."

"Which makes a person begin to consider very unhappy thoughts," Clara concluded for him.

Blowers gave her a knowing look.

"I am not suggesting anything truly sinister," he hastened to add. "Perhaps Mr Matlock fell asleep?"

"In the very brief time it took for the door to close?" Clara said.

"I admit, that does seem unlikely. Another possibility is he somehow stumbled and knocked himself out on the doorframe, thus he was too dazed to get out of the way."

Captain Blowers' hopes for an innocent explanation were obvious. Clara did not push harder to dissuade him of that possibility. She was open-minded about the matter, and, at this stage, it seemed far more likely Matlock had succumbed to a fluke accident than anything else. The simple question was, how did it happen?

They had entered a corridor where a low hum spoke of the refrigeration units operating nearby. Refrigeration was a relatively new technology, having been around just over forty years. It had started as a means of preserving meat being transported from New Zealand to Britain and its commercial success had led to an expansion of the technology. It required large, industrial units to serve the purpose of channelling heat away from a specific location, usually a large walk-in compartment, like a huge cupboard. There were many systems in operation, all with their downsides as well as advantages. The King Edward had one of the newer models, being refitted just after the war. The units normally stored large quantities of fresh meat and vegetables, along with other necessities such as milk and butter.

When Blowers opened the door of refrigeration unit number three, Clara was greeted by a great waft of cold air, that cast its icy fingers over her and made her shiver. When she recovered from the surprise, she looked into the fridge and saw a table had been set in the middle and lying upon it was a covered corpse.

Blowers led the way inside, shivering himself at the cold in the room. He moved aside a case of fresh strawberries and a large cast iron container that sloshed as it moved, suggesting it contained fluid of some sort. Blowers took the edges of the thin blanket that covered Matlock's mortal remains and nearly asked Clara if she was ready to look upon him, then he recalled their earlier conversation and decided he was best to simply get on with things.

He drew back the blanket to Matlock's neck and revealed the youth lying in repose. Matlock looked as though he was sleeping. His lips were gently parted, and his closed eyelids looked as if at any moment they would spring open. The bluish tint to his face revealed his true nature, but the icy conditions of the fridge were preventing decomposition and caused him to seem more alive than dead. There were no obvious signs of trauma to his body.

Clara had imagined he would be mangled, his head unpleasantly squashed, bones broken, or something along those lines. Instead, he seemed virtually untouched. At a glance, you would not know he had been crushed to death.

"The damage was more to the torso area," Blowers explained, correctly interpreting Clara's frown. "Our doctor performed a post-mortem. He is allowed to do that as we are at sea and not always able to get help from ashore. He found the lungs had been compressed and several ribs were broken. Other organs showed signs of being placed under pressure, but he tells me it was the crushing of the lungs that finished off Matlock."

"He suffocated," Clara nodded. "The weight of the door prevented him taking in a single breath. How swiftly would he have become unconscious?"

"You will have to discuss such technicalities with the ship's doctor," Blowers answered. "I believe he has written up a report."

They both stared at the face of Matlock, who looked very young and innocent in death.

"How old was he?" Clara asked.

"Seventeen. He was one of our newest crew members. Replaced a fellow who decided to stay ashore and get married."

"And he was an engineer?"

"An apprentice engineer, if you like," Blowers explained. "He was learning the ropes and, of course, had all the menial and dull jobs to attend to as a consequence. One of his duties was to go around the engines and make sure all the parts were oiled. He would have been doing that when he was crushed."

Clara studied Matlock a while longer. Sometimes, when you saw a deceased person, you almost felt as if you connected with them, like they were trying to give you a hint beyond the grave. She did not feel that with Matlock. He was an empty shell; his soul had flitted away leaving behind something that could easily have been considered a statue in marble.

"Thank you, Captain Blowers," Clara said. "I have seen enough."

The blanket was replaced over Matlock's face, and they left the giant refrigerator to join Lieutenant Harper stood in the corridor.

"What are your first thoughts?" Blowers asked, trying to mask his desperation as he closed the fridge door behind them.

Clara considered his question for a second. She did not want to give him false hope.

"My first thought is that Matlock had a terrible accident. At this moment in time, nothing you have shown me suggests someone harmed him intentionally."

Blowers gave a sigh of relief, all too obvious he had been desperate to hear such an answer. Clara raised her hand to pause him.

"However, the police question such an observation and it would be remiss of me to ignore that. I am therefore unwilling to give a conclusive answer until I have seen more. This business with the door has clearly caused a lot of concern for people. I need to discover how Matlock could have ended up in such a position before I can say honestly whether his death was purely accidental."

"Of course, I appreciate your professionalism," Blowers nodded. "I see now that the recommendation to hire you was a wise one, Miss Fitzgerald. You seem very sensible, which is reassuring."

Clara was gladdened by his faith in her, even if it had not come naturally.

"Where would you like to go next?" Blowers asked.

"I want to see this door that has caused such anxiety for you all," Clara replied at once.

Blowers showed her the way, heading down another corridor, down more stairs, deeper and deeper. The noise was getting loud; thudding, thumping, banging, and clattering all filling the air with a heavy cacophony of sound. It was almost overwhelming and made you feel as if you could not think straight. The corridors were stuffy down here and there was a stink of oil and other chemicals that gave Clara a headache and made her feel sick. The closer they neared to the engine rooms, the worse the heat and noise grew. Blowers was sweating in his uniform and discreetly took a handkerchief from his pocket to wipe his forehead.

They finally paused before a steel door that looked very much like the previous dozen steel doors they had walked through. Blowers indicated the number painted onto it.

"Watertight door number nine," he said.

The door looked innocuous, as if it had never killed anyone, ever.

"How was Matlock positioned in the door when he was found?" Clara asked.

It was Harper's turn to speak. He had been silent until now, but at last he had a reason to speak.

"Matlock was stood upright here, where the edge of the door closes and sits snug against this outer panel," Harper placed himself in the spot where he had seen Matlock.

"Upright?"

"Yes. He was also stood sideways, so the door had pressed into his right arm and shoulder first. It was a very peculiar thing to see."

Clara contemplated the doorway a while. What was significant about Matlock being upright when he was crushed? Was there any significance? She tried to visualise how it had looked when Harper arrived, not that it gave her any greater understand of what had occurred.

"Has anything like this happened before?" Clara asked.

"Never," Blowers said firmly. "The slow closing, as I keep saying, is a feature to prevent such things. The only time a man might be hurt is if he had his hand or foot in the doorway for some reason. But no one would simply stand there and be crushed."

Clara understood why he found the matter so preposterous, but someone had stood in that doorway and paid the price. Why had Matlock gone so quietly to his death?

"The door does not tell us much," Harper said at last. "It just asks more questions."

Clara placed her hand on the heavy steel door, feeling its rigidity and its strength. She did not like to think what it would be like to be trapped between it and the doorway.

"Where now, Miss Fitzgerald?" Blowers asked.

Clara roused from her thoughts.

"I think I better speak to the ship's doctor next."

Chapter Five

Jim Reed was furious. He had turned a strange shade of purple and there was a distinct possibility of metaphorical steam coming out of his ears. He glared around the room at his teammates and then at his rivals.

"Someone say something!" he demanded though it was not obvious what anyone could say at this point to improve the situation.

"Seems to me," Captain Welles of the Brighton Badgers said steadily, "that this missing bag is further proof of cheating."

"What?" Reed declared; his words nearly spat across the room. "How can you say that?"

"Someone did not want us looking at your mitt," Welles persisted bluntly, he was not a man known for his tact. "That suggests a guilty conscience over something. If we saw that mitt, maybe we would discover how you cheated us."

"Hold on," Mr Hardcastle tried to intercede, "we mustn't just spout accusations."

"If we want to play that game," Jim Reed barked, "how about we discuss how the bag went missing after it had been proved the ball was sound. Surely that indicates someone from the Badgers hid it up to prevent us proving our innocence!"

Reed's teammates agreed with him, cheering their support.

"Preposterous!" Welles countered. "We have all been here, the whole time!"

"So have we!" Reed retorted.

"Enough!" Mr Hardcastle held up his hands like he was trying to push the two arguing teams apart. "I am sure it is just a case of the bag being somewhere it was not expected to be. If we all look for it, we are bound to find it."

"I don't want a Badger touching my bag or my mitt," Reed snapped.

"Then everyone can wait in here while I go with the umpires to look for the bag," Hardcastle told them. "You surely do not doubt the honesty of the umpires or myself?"

It was a loaded question, Hardcastle daring anyone to argue. There was a satisfying silence.

"Right, now, behave like gentlemen while I am gone, understood?"

He cast a fierce gaze at both teams then departed with the umpires. An awkward gulf surfaced in the room between the two teams. Both teams were trying to dominate their side of the room and yet also squeeze themselves as far away from the opposition as possible, leaving the centre of the room as an eerie No-Man's-Land across which they cast scowls at one another.

"I am so very sorry," Annie said quietly to the Badgers. "I should not have opened my mouth."

"You spoke from the heart, Annie, you did not do this maliciously," Tommy consoled her.

No one else offered a comforting word and Annie had the impression they did blame her for ruining a perfectly good cricket match, even if the Badgers had been losing it.

"You didn't deserve to be knocked out of the game, old boy," Welles told Tommy. "You were playing as good as I have ever seen. That ball should have flown for miles."

They all paused as his words sunk in, their minds

flicking back to that fateful run when the cricket ball that had seemed to be soaring into the heavens suddenly thudded into Reed's mitt. Welles frowned.

"Let's be honest fellows, how many of us were thinking at that moment there was something odd about the game?"

Welles' teammates made murmurs of agreement.

"Nothing we can do about it, if that mitt is truly missing," Tommy sighed. "The ball was of no use to us."

"Own up fellows, just so I know," Welles turned to his men. "I shan't tell a soul, but speak it now so we are all on the same page, did any of your move that bag?"

There was silence, though the men glanced at one another to see if anyone was going to speak.

"On our word of honour as cricketers, if anyone confesses to moving that bag, we shall not reveal him, agreed?" Welles pressed them.

The men muttered their agreement.

"Now, did any one of you move that bag?"

There was the same response, silent denial.

"Well, that deals with that," Welles said solemnly, satisfied by their response. "The Hove team did it."

Annie was looking across the room at the Hove players who were huddled in a similar fashion to the Badgers and probably discussing the same situation.

"They will deny it, of course," Welles murmured. "Obvious, isn't it, they are hiding something."

"But the ball was sound," one of the players reminded him. "How could the ball be sound and they still cheat?"

No one had an answer for him.

Outside the room they could hear the umpires and Mr Hardcastle moving through the clubhouse, searching everywhere by the sounds of it. Annie wondered how long it would take before they realised that if the bag was not in the changing rooms, it must have been moved for a very deliberate reason.

Her eyes found Reed in the Hove huddle. He looked angry and worried, but that was to be expected when a valuable item of his had been misplaced. The mitt was bespoke and had no doubt cost a pretty penny or two.

Annie felt a pang of guilt seep into her soul. Jim Reed had been desperate to get back to the sport he loved and had gone the extra mile to achieve just that, getting a mitt designed to replace his missing hand. He had already admitted the new mitt was uncomfortable to wear, but he persisted with it because it enabled him to continue playing. Was that all so different from Tommy and his legs?

When Tommy came back from the war he was in a wheelchair. His legs refused to work, but no one could say why. It turned out to be a mental block – in essence, Tommy had forgotten how to use his legs. It had taken time to convince him of this, and even longer to help him overcome his own shame that he was in some way faking his illness.

Ultimately, they had found a way to get Tommy walking again. It had taken over a year for him to develop the strength to enable him to consider returning to cricket. Annie was proud of him, more than she could put into words. Only a slight limp now marked out Tommy's injuries, though the memories of what happened to him would likely never truly fade.

Comparing Tommy to Reed made Annie feel even worse and her guilt increased. She had been so rude and volatile in her accusations. She had stormed onto the cricket pitch and made such a performance, humiliating Reed, and his teammates, and for what? The missing mitt was curious, but hardly conclusive proof of anything.

Even if they had been cheating, surely there would have been a more tactful way of approaching the matter than making such a dramatic declaration. Annie saw herself in a new light and she was not pleased. She had thought herself better than that.

She took a deep breath and then walked across the middle of the room, towards the Hove team.

"Annie?" Tommy called after her in surprise, but Annie was not to be deterred.

She had spurned an unlucky man with her accusations, and he did deserve an apology.

Jim Reed looked up first as she approached, his teammates following suit. To a man they bore a scowl on their faces. Annie did not blame them.

"I owe you an apology Mr Reed," Annie said calmly. "I reacted inappropriately to my concerns. I could have raised them in a more diplomatic fashion. As it is, it appears I was incorrect in my suspicions. I hope you will accept my apology for causing this situation for you."

Annie waited patiently for Reed to politely respond, fully anticipating he would accept her apology, which was genuinely made. Reed had narrowed his eyes. There was a bitterness in them that burned deep. He took a deep breath and then sneered at her.

"No. I don't accept," he said. "You are cruel and vindictive. I saw that in your face when you marched onto the pitch. Your team was losing, and you did the worst thing you could think of to prevent that."

"I never meant this maliciously!" Annie said, flustered by his response.

"You did," Reed retorted. "I know your type. Can't bear to lose, or see your man beaten. Wasn't it when I caught the ball that knocked Tommy out of the match that you made up your mind I was cheating?"

As he said this, Annie knew it was true. That had been the moment she had convinced herself the Hove team were somehow cheating.

"That was not quite how it occurred," she said, the denial sticking in her throat.

"When this is all over, we are going to support an action to have you banned from local cricket matches," Reed persisted vindictively. "Just to prove to others you cannot go around stopping someone winning a cricket match just because they are beating your team."

"Hang on there!" Tommy was marching over. He and the Badgers had been keeping a close watch on things. "Annie only did what she felt was right. If you had been cheating, this would be another story."

"But we weren't, were we?" Reed retaliated. "We were just better than you."

"Watch your tongue!" Welles was backing up Tommy and Annie now, the rest of the Badgers close behind. "You had a bit of luck, that is all."

"Luck?" Hove's captain laughed. "If that's how you want to call being better than you lame ducks!"

His comment seemed deliberately aimed at Tommy and Annie's temper rose up like a snake inside her. She was no longer interested in playing peacemaker. Her anger was back and this time she had good reason to be furious.

"Who are you calling lame?" she demanded. "You can say what you wish about me, but this has nothing to do with Tommy and the Badgers, so mind your manners!"

"Can't bear losing, that is all it is!" Reed cackled at them; it was like a taunt. "Can't bear losing!"

"We are better losers than you!" Welles reacted. "Last time we played you, when you lost, your batsman smashed his cricket bat in two!"

"Don't speak ill of poor Fred!" the Hove captain snapped. "He took the sport seriously and he died at the Somme you know!"

Voices were now starting to be raised and everyone was offering their opinion on the matter. Mostly, the noise was so much that no one could hear anyone else, and the insults and accusations went unheard in the commotion, which was just as well as the two teams had reached a stage when they were shouting some rather nasty things at each other. Things that if they had been heard would have stung deep and made an even bigger rift between the two sides.

It was into this maelstrom of confusion that Mr Hardcastle found himself walking. He took only a moment to grasp the situation and then, in a voice like thunder, shouted across the room.

"What did I say about behaving yourselves?"

The reaction from the players was rather like something from the schoolyard. The Badgers went scuttling back to their own side of the room, trying to pretend they had been doing nothing, or if they had been doing anything it was only because the Hove Cricket Bats had started it.

The Hove players ducked their heads and tried to look hard-done-by. If anyone asked, they would insist the other team had started it. Hardcastle stared about him, frustrated at their nonsense.

"All you had to do was ignore one another," Hardcastle told them. "That was all you had to do."

"She started it!" Reed pointed a petulant finger at Annie. "She started it when she tried to apologise to me!"

As the words spluttered from his mouth, he found himself listening to them again. They had made sense in his head but now they were spoken aloud he found how illogical they were, and how they made the Hove team the bad guys in this scenario. He dropped his finger hastily and pretended he had not said anything at all.

Hardcastle waited until silence had fallen, scowling at both teams, then he brought his arm from behind his back, revealing a satchel type bag which he gently laid on the floor.

"My bag!" Reed cried out, rushing towards it, and opening it.

He pulled out a clean pullover and his ordinary shoes, dumping them on the floor before looking at Hardcastle in alarm.

"Where is my mitt?"

"A good question, Mr Reed," Hardcastle sighed. "We found the bag in a stall in the ladies' bathroom, a place I am rather certain you did not put it."

Reed ran this through his mind, shock, and confusion mingling, before a new thought struck him, and his face hardened.

"She must have put it in there!" he pointed at Annie.

Tommy was ready to retort but Hardcastle was not going to let things boil over yet again.

"Why would Mrs Fitzgerald do such a thing?" he said

to Reed calmly. "When did she even have the time?"

Reed had no answer. He gaped at them, trying to think of a good reason and failing.

"I do not know how your bag came to be in the ladies' restrooms," Hardcastle continued. "I also do not know where your mitt is. We have searched the entire clubhouse and not found it. My next thought is that it might have been hidden somewhere outside. The cricket club site is large, and I think it would be more prudent if we all participated in a search for the mitt, rather than just the two umpires and myself."

He did not add – especially as you lot cannot be in the same room together without starting an argument.

"How can we do that fairly?" Welles demanded. "If we find the mitt, they will start accusing us of tampering with it, and if they find it, we shall wonder if they have done anything to it to prevent their cheating being discovered."

He said this with such venom in his words that it nearly started a feud all over again. Hardcastle hushed the raised voices swiftly.

"I have already thought of that, and I believe I have a solution. Each member of each team will partner with a member of the opposite team for the search. Therefore, you will all be able to watch each other and whoever finds the mitt cannot be accused of tampering with it."

Hardcastle waited for further argument, he received none.

"Good," he said. "At least that is one thing you can agree upon."

Chapter Six

The sick bay aboard the King Edward was sizeable. It had to be, due to the number of passengers and crew. There was a section purely for passengers and this had several private bays for anyone who might need to stay a while. The crew section was more cramped and separated from the passenger section by a wall.

There was also a consulting room, a night nurse station, a drug store, and an office for the doctor, who was named, rather appropriately, Christopher Gulliver. He was only a handful of years older than Clara and he liked to joke that his parents had always expected him to be of a seafaring persuasion. They had been somewhat disappointed when he pursued a medical career but had perked right back up when his first position was aboard a luxury liner.

He greeted Clara affably. You had to be a people-person when working aboard such a ship.

"Dr Gulliver," he introduced himself. "What seems to be the matter? Seasickness?"

Captain Blowers interceded to correct the misapprehension.

"This is Miss Clara Fitzgerald. She is not a passenger. She is a private detective come to help us with our situation regarding Mr Matlock."

The doctor lost his smile and became solemn.

"Poor Alf," he shook his head. "That was a terrible way to go."

"I wanted to ask you a few questions, if I may?" Clara said to him.

Gulliver shrugged.

"I doubt I can tell you much. The poor man was dead when he arrived here. I am allowed to conduct post-mortems while at sea, as this enables us to…. to…" the doctor frowned as he tried to think of the best way to finish his sentence.

Once again, Captain Blowers came to his aid.

"What the doctor means is that it is necessary to bury those among the crew who might perish while on a voyage swiftly. Buried at sea, as they say. Of course, it is important we know how they died before such a thing occurs. For our records."

Clara felt there ought to be more to say about that, something along the lines of 'wasn't it for the sake of the dead they learned out how they died, not just records?' but she fancied she would not get the response she might hope for from the men. They would just be confused by her statement. They were practical souls, living very practical lives. Such was the nature of seafaring.

"You conducted a post-mortem on Alf Matlock?" Clara said instead to the doctor.

"I did," he agreed. "He was in very good health, all told."

"Aside from being crushed?"

"Well, yes," Dr Gulliver looked uncertain. "It was all rather grim inside him. You looked at his face and aside from a bit of a blue tint he looked fine, but inside ribs were smashed and organs squashed. The nurse thought he was still alive when they pulled him from the door, but I fear that was wishful thinking. In any case, a man is not going to survive his insides being mangled like that."

Dr Gulliver's face implied he had seen things that were going to keep him awake at night, and that he had not signed on to being a ship's doctor for such events. He was more used to dealing with passengers complaining of indigestion, seasickness and upset stomachs.

"I don't suppose you can say how long he was in the door by the state of his… um, internals?" Clara asked.

"I don't know if anyone could," Gulliver replied, thinking her question slightly ridiculous.

Clara had to ask it; you never knew…

"Alf was a hardworking soul, and I don't like the rumours some people have been spreading," Gulliver suddenly added, breaking into her thoughts.

Captain Blowers gave him a sharp look. It was not clear if this was to warn him to be quiet or because it was the first he had heard of any rumours, and he was concerned.

"What rumours?" Clara asked.

"Well, some are saying he was messing around with the door, trying to wedge it open to save himself the time of opening and shutting it as he travelled around the ship, and it was while he was doing that it shut on him and caught him out. That is unfair, you know. Alf was not one to cut corners."

"Dr Gulliver is correct," Captain Blowers agreed, his expression lightening up. "Mr Matlock was reliable and not the sort to do something so foolish."

"Others would," Lieutenant Harper said from behind them. He was still hanging around in the background, even if he rarely spoke. "Probably some of the others have done it in the past. But not Mr Matlock, he had a sensible head on his shoulders."

"That being said," Blowers said thoughtfully, "an unfortunate accident would make our lives a lot easier, if that was the case. I mean, just a bit of carelessness, happens all the time and Matlock was unlucky."

"Captain, you cannot seriously be considering turning this into some mishap of Alf's own creation?" Gulliver asked, managing to sound polite and deferential despite wanting to explode at the captain for such a suggestion. "We cannot hide the truth."

"What other truth could there be?" Blowers said with impeccable logic. "If it was not a sad accident, the other possibility seems too incredible to even voice."

"And yet the police are not prepared to ignore such a possibility," Clara reminded him. "And you have brought me here for the very reason that this might be something more than a tragic mistake."

"No, Miss Fitzgerald, you are here to prove it was an accident," Captain Blowers said firmly. "That is what I need, not any wild speculation. I need to get my ship moving."

Gulliver did not speak, but the set of his jaw and the tight, pale line of his lips spoke volumes. Captain Blowers wanted to move things along, get Clara away from the doctor.

"Who else do you need to speak to?" he asked. "Perhaps the man who found Matlock?"

Clara glanced briefly at Dr Gulliver, meeting his eyes, and hoping he understood she was on his side and open-minded. She would not be forced into declaring something an accident when she was not convinced that to be the case.

"I shall hope to see you again, Miss Fitzgerald," the doctor said to her. "If you need to ask me anything else, do not hesitate to seek me out. I shall always be willing to talk."

Captain Blowers hustled Clara out of the sick bay, casting a fierce glare at his doctor.

"Now, you will want to speak to…"

"Captain Blowers," Clara interrupted him firmly. "I shall not be pushed into any assumptions. I shall make up my own mind about this situation, whether it pleases you or not."

Blowers paused, spun, and looked at her.

"Miss Fitzgerald, I am not going to ask you to compromise your integrity, but you must appreciate my situation. I am stuck here until this matter is resolved. I have angry passengers who are missing trains and important meetings. I have an irate shipping company sending me telegraphs constantly, demanding to know why I have not yet moved on, and I have the police making my life difficult by dragging their feet. What else can I say to you to help you understand my position?"

"I understand it perfectly," Clara promised him. "I do not envy your position, and I think it highly vulgar of the shipping company to place such pressures upon you, but I cannot change my methods or ignore my instincts. I shall examine this case and come up with my own conclusion, based on the evidence I find. I hope you can appreciate my situation too?"

Captain Blowers did not want to agree, but he had to nod his head.

"Yes, I do see that."

"If it is any consolation, at this moment in time I see no reason to suppose this was anything but a very peculiar accident," Clara added. "We may never know exactly how Matlock ended up in that door, but if we can at least rule out foul play, you shall be able to get on with your work."

Captain Blowers was appeased, in fact he brightened up considerably and Clara rather fancied he thought she was subtly saying she already considered this an accident. Clara had not made any decisions on what this was or wasn't. She was just taking things step by step.

"Let me introduce you to Mr Barnes and I am sure he will be able to fill in the final pieces of this puzzle," Blowers said optimistically.

They had to head back down into the bowels of the ship to find Barnes. Clara did not like the endless corridors which seemed heavy with the heat of the engines and claustrophobic. The smell of oil and grease was beginning to make her nauseous again and was distracting her from the matter at hand.

Mr Barnes was an oiler, a person who kept everything oiled and running smoothly. It seemed strange to have a man dedicated to such a job, until you realised how vast the ship was, how many cogs, gears and chains needed oiling, and how often the task had to be completed. It was an endless affair and Barnes was kept suitably busy.

"Barnes, this is Miss Fitzgerald who is looking into Matlock's unfortunate accident," Captain Blowers said as they approached a man in greasy overalls, with a smut-smeared face and a large oil can in his hand. He was dripping with sweat and turned to look at them in a dull fashion, too hot and tired to really appreciate what they had said. He was also still suffering from the shock of finding a fellow worker wedged in a door, the very breath squeezed from his body.

"Hello Mr Barnes," Clara said, trying to draw his attention to her. "Could I ask you about how you came to find Alf Matlock in the door?"

Barnes swallowed dryly.

"It was horrid."

"I can imagine," Clara said sympathetically. "During the war I was a volunteer nurse and I saw some sights, including a man and child who were crushed by a runaway horse and cart. We tried to save them but could not."

Barnes did not seem to register her empathy. He wiped sweat from his eyes.

"Poor Alf. I always hated that door. Its unlucky, that one."

"Unlucky?" Clara asked.

Captain Blowers hastily cleared his throat.

"Prior to our last refit, that particular door was numbered thirteen. When the ship was reordered it was renumbered as nine, but some people cannot forget its previous designation."

"That door is bad luck," Barnes insisted. "It always sticks when you are trying to open it. It stuck that night when I was pulling poor Alf out. It was like it did not want to let him go."

"Some seafaring men can be highly superstitious," Blowers added, as if he would never even consider a superstition, let alone be influenced by it.

"What time did you find him?" Clara turned her attention back to Barnes. She was rather like Blowers and took superstitions with a good pinch of salt. However, she would never fail to consider how they might influence a person who did believe in them. To do so would be careless.

"I was on my early shift. I usually reach door nine around three in the morning," Barnes explained. "I don't wear a watch, but I know how long it takes me to do my rounds."

Clara did not question this. Many people did not wear watches and relied on an innate sense of time developed by their internal rhythms.

"What did you see as you came across Matlock?" Clara asked.

"At first, I could not quite say what I was seeing," Barnes shrugged. "It was like his head was sticking out of the doorway. I couldn't make sense of it all for a moment. Then I realised he was stuck, and I called his name. I swear his eyes fluttered in reaction. I pushed that big door, but it did not want to open. I quickly sent a message to the bridge, to let them know I needed help, then I returned to Matlock. He was limp and cold. I told him I was going to run for the night nurse, he did not respond. I thought he was gone already and then Lieutenant Harper appeared with Miss Nettles."

"When had you last seen Matlock?"

Barnes did not seem to know how to answer.

"I saw him earlier. He was in the tearoom with me as we started our shifts. At least, I think he was. Sometimes I wonder if I am really remembering that night, or if I am remembering some other night and muddling the two. I am really not sure."

Barnes hung his head, looking miserable.

"Never mind," Clara said gently. "You were not to know to pay especial attention to that night, so why should you remember?"

Barnes gave a slight nod of his head, as if he understood.

"I have seen some accidents on this ship, and on the others I have worked on, but that was a first. Him crushed in the door like that. It still seems as if it cannot be real. I keep expecting Alf to walk around the corner and give me a smile."

There seemed little else they could get from Barnes at that moment in time. Clara thanked him for the assistance and gladly started back for the upper decks. The belly of the ship had nearly overwhelmed her, and she was glad to reach the ladder that took her up on deck and into the fresh sea air. She took long gulps to restored herself.

"Barnes is not the brightest of buttons," Captain Blowers said, a pace behind her as she emerged on deck. "But he is an honest fellow. He has worked on this liner the last twelve years. He was even on her during the war. Men like Barnes are invaluable, they mean a ship like this can continue to function."

"And was Alf Matlock the same? Would he have been considered a reliable and honest worker who was highly valued had he lived?"

Captain Blowers considered the question because it did need consideration. The temptation was to simply say yes at once because it was the gracious thing to do. But was it the right answer?

"I had no bother with Matlock," Blowers replied. "He had not been here long, and he was still proving himself, but I cannot fault him. Not in the short time I had known him. He worked hard and he was keen to learn."

Clara nodded at this answer, not sure what it really told her, but storing the answer away, nonetheless.

Lieutenant Harper was looking out across the ocean. He turned back to his captain now with an unhappy look on his face.

"Captain, it appears the police are heading towards us."

Blowers wanted to swear, but there was a lady present, the best he could do was say,

"Oh bother!"

Though the inflection he managed on the words conveyed exactly what he was truly thinking.

Chapter Seven

Tommy truly felt he had drawn the short straw by being paired with Jim Reed. It wasn't that he disliked the bowler in general, but in that precise moment of time they were opposing forces and Tommy was holding a grudge over Jim's behaviour towards Annie. In response, Jim was holding a grudge over Annie being the one to accuse him of cheating and, in extension, considered Tommy to also be responsible. The fact that Mr Hardcastle had paired them together seemed to Tommy to be an act of pettiness or perhaps a means of keeping those who had the most to lose or gain over this affair together where they could watch each other.

They were certainly doing that, spending more time glancing in each other's direction than paying attention to their search of the cricket club grounds.

"I never thought you would do a thing like this, Tommy," Reed sniffed as they made a half-hearted effort to search around a large shrub with pink flowers. "Accusing me of cheating. I never thought you would be so disloyal."

"Disloyal?" Tommy said sharply.

"To a fellow cricketer and sportsman. We should stick

together and defend one another."

"For a start, I did not accuse you," Tommy said, though he admitted to himself that nearly every man on his team had wondered about Reed's sudden skill for catching balls that should have certainly been well out of reach. "And for another, I am not and never was, blindly loyal. If I think someone is not playing fair, I shall say so."

"You think I was not playing fair?" Reed latched onto the words.

"I have come to no conclusion on the subject," Tommy assured him. "I am merely saying I would not overlook a man cheating whether he was my opposition or my own teammate."

"You really are a stick in the mud," Reed sulked.

"You begin to sound as if you were cheating and are wanting me to ignore it," Tommy retorted.

"That is not it at all, I mean to say you should be faster to defend a fellow cricketer, especially one who has been through the war like you and has suffered as a consequence."

"If you mean I should allow you liberties for the sake of your lost hand, you are on a losing wicket," Tommy huffed. "If you mean I should respect you for fighting back after a debilitating injury that could have ended your cricketing passion, well, that is a given. I respect any man who defies the odds to do what he loves, as long as it is done fairly and in the spirit of the sport."

"You really hate my mitt!"

"Not at all, but you have to say you became a much better fielder wearing it."

It was a low blow and Tommy knew it the second the words left his mouth. He regretted his haste and should have immediately apologised, instead, some stubborn streak within him kept his mouth shut for a fraction longer than was prudent.

"Speak your mind, won't you?" Reed snapped sarcastically. "Do you know the hours of practice it has taken for me to be able to catch at all with that mitt? Or the amount of time and money it took to have it made in the first place? It is unique, I had to go to this fellow in Edinburgh to get it made, he was the only one capable of doing it. We had to consider the weight of the mitt, not just when it was sitting on my stump, but when I caught a fasting moving ball. We had to consider the shape and how it would hold the ball.

"We looked to American baseball for inspiration and the catcher's mitt. But a catcher is wearing it on a hand and can grip the ball, so it is not the same as for me. The mitt has to do most of the work for me. We went through so many designs to get it just right and even then, if I don't angle my mitt perfectly, the ball bounces off or slips away and there is nothing I can do about it, unless I can snatch at it with my good hand in time."

"It sounds like you have journeyed on a long road," Tommy replied, with genuine sympathy. He had been on a similar journey and knew the time put in behind closed doors to achieve the end result. How heart breaking and soul destroying it could be at times. How often you just wished the injury had never occurred, that you were the same man as before and everything was simple and easy.

"I know you get it Tommy," Reed conceded, tired of being angry. "That's why I can't fathom how you of all people would consider me a cheat? What would cheating achieve? It might win a game, but it would not make me as good a player as I was before the war, would it? I would rather try my hardest and fail fairly than to cheat for an artificial sense of glory."

Reed sounded so defeated, so morose, that Tommy found he believed him.

"That makes sense, Jim," he said. "It makes a lot of sense."

"I battled with myself over whether the mitt was right or not. I spent countless nights awake wondering if it was fair play. I know that, but no one else does. That is what hurts so bad. That I worried so much about whether this was fair or not, and then, after I finally resolve myself to the conclusion it is fair, I end up accused of cheating nonetheless."

"I see your point. You might as well have been cheating if you are going to be accused of it when playing fair."

"That is it, precisely," Reed gave him a weak smile. "I know it was your wife who did the accusing, and that makes things difficult for you, but I had to say my piece."

They ambled along to another section of shrubbery with a bench set before it, each a little lost in his thoughts. Tommy glanced beneath the bench and saw nothing more than the discarded stick of an ice lolly and a rolled-up tissue.

"Who would take your mitt, Jim?" he said when he righted himself.

"I don't know," Reed answered. "That upsets me most of all. Why would someone steal it?"

Tommy had not thought about the item being stolen until that moment, now he realised it was a very logical conclusion. The question was why would anyone want a mitt that was only good to be used by Reed?

"They could ransom it back to you," Tommy suggested, the notion suddenly coming to him.

Reed looked aghast.

"I cannot afford a ransom! I put all my savings into that mitt."

"The person who took it does not know that," Tommy said with deadly logic. "They might think you will do anything to get it back."

It had not seemed possible before then for Jim Reed to feel worse than he already did, but it turned out it was possible. He suddenly lost all heart for the search and sat down heavily on the bench.

"I'm fed up, Tommy. I just want to go home, take a bath and pretend this day never occurred."

Tommy watched him for a moment, trying to think the best way to approach this problem, then he sat down beside him and leaned his elbows on his knees.

"It has not been the day any of us wanted."

"You can say that again. The only thing that it has going for it is the sun is shining, but even that feels tainted now," Reed glanced skywards at the offending glowing orb. "If the mitt is gone, that is me done. I cannot afford another, and I am not sure I could put in the effort a second time."

Reed studied the stump where his right-hand ought to have been. It had been blow off at the wrist and had healed well enough. He had lost a lot of things when he lost that hand – his ability to write, his talent for the piano, but it was the loss of cricket that had really hurt the most. The mitt had given him hope, made him feel normal for a while, now it was gone too.

"We shall find it," Tommy said with more confidence than he felt.

Reed shook his head at him.

"It makes no sense," he sighed. "I wish I hadn't taken it off, but it hurts like hell after a while."

He showed Tommy the marks on his wrist and arm where the straps that held the mitt in place had rubbed at his flesh and left sore friction burns. Seeing them, Tommy felt even more strongly that Jim was telling the truth. He would not go through such suffering if he did not really want to play cricket for the love of the sport. He could have found an easier way to cheat, if that was his game, certainly one that did not cause him such hurt.

He was going to say something, when his attention along with Reed's was drawn to a commotion over by the goldfish pond at the edge of the clubhouse. This was for ornamentation, some notion of a past chairman who thought having a pond of hungry fish outside the club windows would somehow add sophistication to the grounds. There had been talk recently of filling it in and returning it to grass to provide extra seating space for spectators. Nothing had yet been done about it and the pond with its collection of gold, orange and silvery white fish remained a feature (and a potential hazard to those watching the match and not their step). Now several of the players from both teams had converged by the edge of the pond and Hardcastle was approaching fast too.

"I have this bad feeling," Reed said quietly.

Then he got to his feet and hurried in the direction of the pond. Tommy followed, his mind rushing through a range of possibilities, including the likelihood of a body suddenly appearing in the pond. That was an outside chance, what with all the players and umpires being accounted for, but when you spent a lot of time with Clara, you began to expect the unexpected.

Fortunately, it was not a floating corpse that had drawn the attention of the search party, it was the discovery of a bag at the bottom of the pond, almost completely hidden by the weed and the shadows of the pool. A lucky glance had brought it to the attention of a Brighton Badger, who had then begun fumbling in the water, attracting over everyone else.

The pond was not very deep, but the bag had been flung into the middle and after watching people fruitlessly trying to reach for it by hand, Hardcastle made the decision to find a pole, or some similar object better suited to the task. As it happened, there was a long pole with a hook on the end stored inside the clubhouse for reaching up to change the number tiles on the scoreboard. It was fetched and with a little further effort, the bag was safely retrieved.

It was sitting soggily on the clubhouse patio when Reed and Tommy came over. Annie was hovering in the doorway of the clubhouse, preferring to keep her distance for the time being. Hardcastle was crouched by the bag which was oozing water onto the slabs of the patio. Reed stopped beside him, his face a picture of horror.

It was a leather duffel bag with buckles holding it closed.

"What's inside it?" Reed whimpered, then he became decisive. "Let me look at it."

He knelt down and fumbled with the buckles, which resisted him at first, the leather swelled with water and making it difficult to unhook anything. It was not helped by Reed having to work the buckles with his left hand alone. He was normally quite good at buckles one-handed, having had plenty of practice, but the water and his urgency was causing him to fumble.

Hardcastle eventually interceded and the flap of the bag was pulled back revealing a large, sodden leather mitt.

It was soaked through, the leather dark with water and some of its shape lost. Reed whimpered at the sight. Hardcastle removed the glove and placed it on the patio, it made an odd noise as it hit the hard surface, something that did not simply sound like waterlogged leather.

Tommy frowned and saw a matching expression on Hardcastle's face. The chairman took a closer look at the glove.

"This stitching looks loose," he said, touching an area in the palm of the mitt where a couple of strands of waxed thread were standing proud.

"Shouldn't be," Reed said miserably. "Has it been ruined by the water?"

He sounded utterly despondent. Tommy crouched down beside him, trying to show some support. He was certain Reed had not dumped his beloved mitt in the pond, which meant someone else had done it.

"Actually, it appears that someone was attempting to cut these threads," Hardcastle added. Without asking permission he pulled at the threads, causing the seam they held to open up further.

"What are you doing?" Reed asked, appalled. But his protest died in his throat when he saw something poking out of the seam. Something solid, dark black and heavy.

Hardcastle pulled at the object, which looked like a chunky circular coin, though considerably larger and with a hole through the middle. The seam was not loose enough to release it and the stitches refused to budge further. Hardcastle produced an old pocketknife from his jacket and popped out the blade. As he went to cut the stitches further the blade seemed to yank out of his hand a little and attached itself to the circular object with an audible thunk.

Hardcastle pulled at his pocketknife, which resisted for a moment, then reluctantly came away from the object. Thoughtfully he put it close again and once more it was sucked against the circle.

"Quite plainly it is a magnet, a strong one," Hardcastle said, mainly to Tommy who seemed the right person to confide in, but his voice was loud enough that others heard.

"A magnet?" Tommy said, trying not to leap to a singular conclusion.

He did not need to; behind him his teammates were catching onto the idea and with a triumphant cry Captain Welles spoke what everyone was thinking.

"That is proof Reed cheated! Proper proof!"

Chapter Eight

Inspector Park-Coombs was not renowned for his sea legs. He wobbled back and forth as the fishing boat they had acquired to take him out to the King Edward seemed to roll incessantly in the froth of the sea. At least he didn't feel nauseous, that was the last thing a police inspector needed on an investigation on the ocean – a sudden development of seasickness.

The inspector was a reliable figure in Brighton, one of the better sorts of policemen because he actually listened to people and generally did not jump to conclusions, though on occasion he had been known to get carried away and suddenly leap to surprising assumptions. He usually corrected himself once he had time to think them over, and if he did not, there was always Clara.

His working relationship with Clara had started awkwardly but had become a friendship over the years. He knew she was a good detective, and she was very tolerant of his methods of policing. He had never asked her if she thought he was a good inspector, or rather, a good investigator, but he liked to think the answer would be yes. In any case, he was neither alarmed nor surprised to see her standing on the deck of the King Edward. She even offered him a wave, which he returned and, as a result, nearly fell into the ocean.

He reached the liner without mishap and clambered onboard.

"Captain Blowers. Lieutenant Harper. Clara."

Inspector Park-Coombs gave them each a respective nod.

"Inspector, we were not expecting you again so soon," Blowers said, barely hiding the anxiety in his tone at the sight of the policeman.

"This matter needs to be wrapped up promptly," Park-Coombs said authoritatively. "Or so my Chief Constable tells me. I think your employers have been on the telephone to him."

"That seems likely, we have some very important passengers aboard who are eager to reach Dover," Blowers agreed. "Perhaps you have reached a conclusion on this matter?"

"Not as yet," Park-Coombs flattened his optimism with a single stroke. His attention wandered to Clara. "Are you here by chance or request?"

"By the request of Captain Blowers," Clara answered, glimpsing the good captain grimace out of the corner of her eye at the statement. "I am to provide an independent voice on this matter."

"And to solve things speedily if the police drag their feet?" Park-Coombs asked bluntly.

Clara smiled at him.

"As ever we are a perfect counterpoint to one another. Together, we shall have this matter dealt with without delay."

Park-Coombs gave her a knowing look, wanting to say something sarcastic about being perfect counterpoints, but deciding it was unprofessional in front of the captain and lieutenant.

"I came back to take another look at that door," Park-Coombs said instead, his attention back on Blowers.

"The door?" Blowers said as if this was the first he had

heard of such a contraption on his ship. He took a deep breath and composed himself, before reminding himself that he was a captain and a good one at that and he needed to take charge. "Of course, Inspector, come this way."

Clara followed as she was curious to hear more of the inspector's thoughts on the case. She fell into step beside Park-Coombs as the captain and lieutenant led the way down below once more.

"You think it was murder too?" the inspector asked her as they reached the first set of steps.

Clara had to slip behind him as they descended, the walkway being too narrow for her to stay abreast.

"I have not reached a firm conclusion, but I am struggling to see how it was an accident."

"This has foul play written all over it," Park-Coombs said staunchly. "I told the Chief Constable as much. He is getting a lot of pressure put on him by some of the influential people who are involved in the shipping company behind this liner. Some of the shareholders are significant people. He would be quite glad if I stated this was an accident."

"What did you tell him?" Clara asked.

"I informed him that I would make my decision based on the evidence available and would not be swayed by anyone influential who was growing tetchy about the delay."

"You really said that to the Chief Constable?" Clara said, impressed.

Park-Coombs cleared his throat awkwardly.

"Not exactly. I told the Chief Constable I would do my best to wrap this matter up efficiently, but I was thinking all the rest and I am sure my tone implied it."

"Of course," Clara said amused.

Park-Coombs tried not to take it to heart.

They had reached the depths again where door number nine stood and protected its little section of corridor from being flooded. The smell of fumes was cloying at Clara again and Park-Coombs was not a good deal better. He was going to keep this examination of the door as brief as possible.

"This is the precise door?" he said, for no reason other than to distract himself from the dense air and the surge of nausea it was trying to induce in him.

"The precise door," Captain Blowers said in a mildly surly tone. "Would you care for me to show you how it works?"

"It's a door, isn't it?" Park-Coombs said, thinking the captain was making fun of him. "Doors open, doors close."

"I would, personally, like to see the mechanics of the door opening and closing," Clara said politely, trying not to sound as if she was contradicting Park-Coombs. "I have never encountered such a door before. I assume they have a system for self-closing?"

"Yes," Captain Blowers answered her, and Park-Coombs felt abashed at his mistake. He had sounded unprofessional. The captain spoke directly to Clara. "These doors must always remain shut when we are at sea, so that in the event of flooding, they would prevent the entire below decks being swamped. There are many of these doors and each will gently close itself when not being held open, they can then be sealed to create a watertight barrier."

Captain Blowers took hold of a wheel set in the middle of the door and turned it vigorously, causing metallic sounds to echo about the corridor. It required a good deal of strength to turn the wheel and it impressed on Park-Coombs and Clara just how heavy and solid the door was. It made the thought of being crushed by it all the more real and disturbing.

Blowers pushed the door, it opened away from them revealing that it was considerably wider than the opening it covered, enabling it to provide a sound seal when shut. Blowers pushed the door to its widest point.

"The door is designed to close relatively slowly, for the express purpose of preventing someone being caught in it, but also to ensure it is never left accidentally open."

Blowers stepped back from the door, and it began its gentle pivot back into place. It moved with surprising grace and made only a soft thud as it reached the frame.

"Can you do that again so I can time it?" Clara asked.

Blowers repeated the procedure, and the door went through its slow motion once more.

"Twelve seconds," Clara announced.

"More than enough time for someone to step through that gap," Park-Coombs said thoughtfully. "It is not as though Matlock had some reason to be just standing there or was ignorant that the door would shut itself."

Clara stepped forward and pushed at the door, testing its weight. It was heavy, but not so much so that she could not hold its weight back easily.

"If Matlock did dawdle in this doorway, when he saw the door closing, he could have put out his hands to stop it and push it back open," she said.

"You will find when the door is in motion its momentum is rather unstoppable," Blowers interjected. "I would not care to demonstrate it, for that reason."

Clara stepped out of the way of the door and allowed it to close again.

"It is not as though Matlock was oblivious to how the door operated," Blowers added.

The door seemed ominous by the mere fact of its ordinary industrial nature. It did its job without thought or feeling, and defiant of anyone being in its way. There was something sinister about its unstoppable manner.

"Does this tell you anything?" Blowers asked Clara, his voice filled with hope.

Clara was thoughtful. What the door told her was that Alf Matlock should not have been able to get crushed in it by accident.

"Overcome by fumes!" Park-Coombs suddenly declared.

He startled Blowers who looked at him thinking this was an announcement concerning the inspector's wellbeing.

"That could be how it happened," the inspector added.

"Matlock was going through the door when he was overcome by fumes and passed out, or at least was so dazed he could not react to the door closing on him."

Blowers liked the idea, because it would turn the incident safely into an accident, but he saw an immediate issue with the explanation.

"What fumes?"

"Doesn't this place get heavy with fumes?" Park-Coombs said. "I can smell all sorts in the air."

"You can certainly smell the oil and grease of the engine," Blowers agreed. "But we do employ a ventilation system to prevent crewmen from being overcome. This is about the worst it will ever get down here."

"Unless there is a fault in the system?" Lieutenant Harper suggested to his captain. "An intermittent fault that caused the ventilation to fail in this section and so the fumes built up and Matlock walked into them and was knocked out!"

Blowers looked at his lieutenant with joy in his eyes.

"Oh yes! That could be it! Well done Harper! We just need to locate the fault and we shall have our solution!"

Clara, not wanting to be the wet blanket that damped their enthusiasm, but knowing someone had to be, butted in.

"Has anyone else mentioned fumes in this area being a problem?"

Blowers looked at her, it was more of a scowl as he saw his idea flying out the window.

"If it is an intermittent fault, then it may not have occurred again as yet," Harper said firmly, restoring his captain's hopes.

"We shall look into the matter, and we are bound to find that was exactly how it happened," Blowers said cheerfully. "What a good idea Inspector, and to think I was quite certain you would be unable to find the solution to this affair."

Park-Coombs initially preened at the praise, then his mind processed the caveat Blowers had added to it and he frowned instead.

"Do you mind if I continue to poke around while you locate your fumes?" Clara asked lightly, avoiding making her disbelief obvious.

Blowers almost hesitated. To allow Clara to continue 'poking around' would surely imply that he was not utterly convinced about his fumes theory, and there was something inside the captain that felt certain if he allowed any doubt into his mind, then the fumes theory would be destroy. Which was irrational, because if Matlock had been dazed by fumes, they would find the proof. Then again, if they did fail to find this fumes leak that he was banking all his hopes upon, it would be prudent to have allowed Clara to continue to investigate rather than lose time. Not that he thought for a moment he was wrong – after all, the inspector had come up with the idea, not him, and so it must be right!

"Yes, carry on Miss Fitzgerald," he said in a dismissive fashion, rather like telling a child to run along and play.

Clara was not offended. She was certain, soon enough, that Blowers would come back to her, cap in hand, and ask for her help again.

"I would like to speak to some more of the men who worked with Matlock," she added.

"They will be dotted about the ship," Blowers replied dismissively. "There is a break room where they can keep their work things and take their breaks, perhaps if you were to loiter there you would catch some of them for a moment?"

Clara felt her first pang of annoyance. Not so long-ago Blowers had been fawning over her, desperate for her aid, now he had lost all interest. Fortunately, Lieutenant Harper interceded on her behalf.

"I shall show you to the break room," he said to her. "It is this way."

Park-Coombs watched as Clara left, torn between waiting there and having his theory proved right, or following her and finding out more concerning the other crewmen. His mind was made up by a fresh wave of scent from the engines that made him want to retch. Someone must have opened a door or something.

"I shall go with Clara," he told Blowers. "Best keep an eye on her."

"Of course," Blowers replied, though he was not really listening. He was already trying to think how they would find the elusive leak.

Park-Coombs hurried after Clara and caught up with her at a junction in the corridors. She gave him a slight scowl.

"Are you not waiting to locate the ventilation problem?"

"I thought I would be of more use with you. This matter is not over just yet."

Clara shrugged but did not argue.

"Not so long ago you were convinced this was murder," she whispered to Park-Coombs as they walked along, trying not to let Harper overhear. "What changed your mind?"

"Before I could not see how anyone could have died accidentally in that door, but now I do," Park-Coombs replied. "It is called being open-minded."

Clara nearly spluttered at him for using that against her. She choked down on her outrage.

"Very well, I am glad you are discovering how to be open-minded, but does that not also mean that until this matter is resolved one way or another, we must not dismiss other options."

Park-Coombs was not sure that was what he meant at all. He had just wanted Clara to admit that for once he had been the one with the correct idea instead of her.

"Fumes are funny things," he said, changing the direction of their conversation. "Can catch you out unawares. My granny once forgot to turn her gas off and nearly finished herself off. I have been to a few cases where someone has snuffed it due to gas. And there was this case on a farm where someone fell into an old slurry tank and the fumes suffocated them. What a way to go."

Clara was not appeased, but she decided to say nothing.

"You know, it would not hurt for me to be right once in a while," Park-Coombs said.

The look Clara gave him was all the response he needed, and he said no more.

Chapter Nine

Tommy happened to be looking at Reed when the mitt was exposed for containing a magnet. He saw his shock, fast followed by horror and then a terrible mix of shame and disgust.

"Wait, wait," said Captain Rhodes of the Hove Cricket Bats. "How does this prove anything? A magnet on its own is not a secret weapon for winning cricket."

"It is if the cricket ball has a piece of metal in it," Captain Welles of the Badgers piped up.

"The cricket ball was empty," Captain Rhodes pointed out with sound logic.

There was a pause, before Harvey Lane, the Badgers best fielder spoke up.

"If the mitt went missing, who is to say that ball we found on the pitch was the actual one used in the game?"

No one said a word. The implication hung heavily over them. It made good sense, of course it did. They had abandoned the ball when they all went inside and then had sent the umpire back out to find it. Anyone could have picked it up the suspect ball and swapped it for a ball that had not been tampered with.

"We should search that pond a little more," someone

said quietly, almost ashamed to make the suggestion.

Suddenly, people were not so righteous in their indignation, instead they were feeling saddened that one of their own had stooped to such a thing and placed a taint over the glorious game of cricket. Tommy found his eyes straying to Reed once more who was hanging his head. Was it guilt he felt now, or devastation that his antics had been discovered? Tommy tried to get a sense for what he was feeling, he found it impossible.

They were still discussing investigating the pond further. It was finally agreed they would locate the groundsman – who had waders for when he needed to get into the pond to do repairs or clean the bottom – and ask him to conduct a thorough search of the pool. Everyone was avoiding looking at Reed, rather pretending he did not exist in that moment. No one wanted to acknowledge him and what he was suspected of doing.

There seemed to be a puddle of loneliness opening up around Reed, as if everyone had taken a step away from him without anyone noticing. Tommy felt that expanding circle as a lead weight in his chest. They were distancing themselves from Reed, and was that not logical when he had done something so awful? He had rigged his mitt to cheat and there was nothing you could say about that.

Tommy ought to be angry. He ought to want to distance himself too. Strangely, he did not, he felt the opposite, he felt sorry for Reed.

After another moment of watching his rival bowler being isolated by both his own teammates and his opposing players, he made a decision. He walked up to Reed and patted his shoulder, just a small act of solidarity, but one Tommy felt compelled to make.

Reed looked up at him cautiously at first, then with relief. Tommy had never seen a man looking so defeated as Reed did in that moment.

"I didn't do it Tommy," he said in a whisper. "I would swear that on a Bible. I never rigged the mitt."

Tommy found it hard to believe that, yet at the same

time he was not ready to dismiss Reed's protests of innocence so lightly. It was only fair to hear him out.

"Did you notice anything wrong with the mitt today?" he asked.

The gratitude in Reed's eyes that Tommy was prepared to give him the benefit of the doubt was choking. It made Tommy question himself further – Reed was either a very good actor, or he really had no notion of the magnet in his mitt.

"It felt heavier," Reed said, but it was the sort of thing that was obvious to say and meant nothing. "I thought I was just feeling the nerves of the game when I noticed that, you know how it is, everything feels different just before a match. Things you normally would not pay attention to suddenly snap into focus and seem odd. I wrote off the sensation as something like that. The mitt is heavy anyway, so it was not as though it was a really noticeable difference."

"Who has access to the mitt?" Tommy asked next.

Reed's eyes widened as he tried to think of who could have come into contact with the mitt. His mind had gone blank.

"I take it home with me, after a match or practice," he said. "It remains in the changing rooms when I am not using it during a game."

"Then, it is possible for someone to have access to it," Tommy said thoughtfully. "Someone other than you."

"Tommy, can I make an observation that perhaps is rather obvious to me but no one else seems to have considered it?"

Tommy nodded his head in agreement. Reed held up his arm with the missing appendage.

"I was right-handed before I lost my hand. Adapting to using my left hand for tasks has been difficult. I can just about write, but it isn't pretty. To suppose I could sew up that mitt after inserting a magnet with such care no one was likely to notice the alteration seems preposterous to me. I couldn't have done it for that purely practical reason."

He put down his arms.

"Of course, that is just my word on the matter, people may not believe me."

Tommy was thinking hard about what Reed had said. He had known other men who had lost their dominant hands, even whole arms, and the struggle it was for them to learn to use the other hand. Some never adjusted. Sewing required a certain finesse, if you wanted to do it well, and the mitt was made of leather, which required a degree of force to get a needle through. He was starting to think Reed had a point.

"If you did not do this, then we are supposing it was one of your teammates?" he said quietly.

Reed looked solemn, that was not a thought he wanted to consider.

"I don't know," he admitted. "I am having trouble taking this all in. I have always played fair Tommy, always. It is not in my nature to cheat. I feel sick about all this."

Tommy patted his shoulder again. Now he did believe him.

The groundsman had arrived, wearing his tall rubber waders. He squeaked as he walked in them. He had been briefed by one of the umpires as to what he was needed to do, and he had a small net in one hand and a rake to aid him. He eyed up the cricketers with a look that could be best described as disapproval. Reed caught it and folded deeper into himself. He moved away to be alone, finding a spot on a wooden bench that sat against the wall of the clubhouse.

The groundsman carefully stepped into the pond, disturbing the fish who hurried to one side away from him. He started to carefully fudge among the plants in the pond looking for a ball.

"Bad business," Captain Welles had come alongside Tommy. "Can't see the Hove Cricket Bats recovering from this any time soon. They may have to disband the entire team."

"That is rather drastic," Tommy said, feeling sorry for

his rivals.

"Has to be done, to make an example. We cannot mess around, not when the honour of the game is at stake. At the very least, Reed will have to be banned and shall never be able to set foot on a cricket pitch again."

Tommy would have agreed, had he believed Reed had been cheating. Instead, he was worried an innocent man was going to lose something very precious to him, something he had fought hard to find a way back to. He could not explain why or how Reed had been framed, in fact is seemed preposterous, yet at the same time he found himself suddenly believing that very strongly.

Perhaps just as strongly as Annie had believed there was cheating in the first place.

"Still, at least we know it was not your poor batting today that cost us," Captain Welles said cheerfully.

Tommy took a moment to register the words.

"I beg your pardon?"

"Well, normally I expect you to send the balls flying too high for any man to catch," the captain answered, not noticing the way Tommy had stiffened. "Today you were shockingly low with all your hits. Not your best form, old man. Still, you would have been just fine if folks were not cheating."

Tommy made a strangled laughing noise in the back of his throat.

"You honestly think I was off form today?"

"Nothing to be ashamed of, we all have bad days. As I say, at least it was not that that cost us the game. I mean, when you were called out, I was really surprised. Not like Tommy, I thought to myself. Reliable is Tommy. Still, can't beat a rigged mitt, can you?"

His good humour over the matter did not improve Tommy's mood. He was trying to think if his batting had really been off par that day, but he would have sworn he was doing exactly as he always did. Then it slowly dawned on him; had the rigged mitt not been found, he was going to be the one singled out and blamed for the loss of the match. That was what his captain was saying, effectively.

"Funny how you win as a team, but lose as an individual," Tommy sniped.

"Hm, what?" his captain asked, his attention had wandered.

Tommy did not have the energy to say more. He moved away, not even excusing himself and headed for Annie. His face bore a scowl as he approached her, and she frowned back in concern.

"Tommy, what's the matter?"

Tommy did not want to explain.

"Reed is denying he rigged his mitt," he said instead, which Annie assumed was the reason for his expression.

"Bad losers will deny everything even when it becomes impossible to do so," she declared stoutly.

"I believe him, Annie."

Annie looked at her husband in surprise.

"Really?"

"I have been talking to him and there are things he said that make me question whether he would do such a thing. He also made a very good point that he cannot sew with his left hand, certainly nothing as carefully done as that mitt was."

Annie paused to contemplate this.

"That is a very good point, but that merely implies someone else was involved. Reed could still have known the mitt was rigged."

"True," Tommy had to agree with that. "I just don't think he did, that's all. He seems to me to be a person who would not do a thing like that, it would go against the grain."

"We can never truly know someone," Annie said. "And you really only know Reed a little."

"I have this gut feeling Annie, I can't explain it."

Annie nodded at him, but he knew she did not believe him. Who could blame her when the evidence before them was so damning? If Reed could not sew, all it meant was he had an accomplice, not that he was oblivious to the cheating.

He wanted to explain the feeling within him that was blaring out like a siren that Reed was a victim here, just like the Badgers, but he knew he could not. If he thought Reed was innocent, he was just going to have to prove it.

The groundsman gave a cry at that moment and raised his net with something round inside. You could suppose it was an apple or orange at a distance, the way it hung in the net. Of course, it was a cricket ball, but was it the cricket ball? Over the recent months of practice and play, could not the odd ball have fallen into the pond and been forgotten?

The cricketers pushed forward to see if this ball was the conclusive proof of Reed's cheating. The unfortunate bowler remained seated on the bench, unable to bear coming forward to see what they had found.

The groundsman gave the ball to Hardcastle who once more produced his pocketknife and began the process of cutting the ball open. The leather was swollen from the water, and the stitches resisted his blade at first, then they sprang apart, and the tight stuffing was revealed. Hardcastle cut through the cotton layers and revealed what at first appeared to be just an ordinary cork core. There was a collective sigh - partly of relief, partly of disappointment.

Hardcastle studied the cork thoughtfully, turning it this way and that, then he ran his finger carefully along its edge.

"There is a seam," he said and with care he took his knife to it and cut smoothly. The seam revealed that the core had been split in half, and when he twisted and wrenched the sides apart, rather like the act of separating the halves of an apricot from its stone, he revealed a ball of metal in the centre.

Someone had halved the cork core, hollowed it out and inserted a lump of metal, before very neatly gluing it together and creating the cricket ball around it. The elaborateness of the fraud, the care taken was remarkable and elicited a hint of admiration in Hardcastle. Sophisticated cheating like this did not occur every day and certainly not in local team cricket.

After they had all taken a good look at the ball and its accusing innards, they found themselves looking towards Reed stationed on his lonely bench. He had lifted his head and met their gazes sorrowfully.

"Is it true?" he asked, which was not the question you expected from someone who knew they had been cheating.

"The cricket ball was tampered with," Hardcastle said. "Your glove was tampered with. The evidence before us is stark and it seems to me there can be only one outcome, a lifelong ban from playing cricket Mr Reed or being involved in the game at all."

Reed's face contorted into a look of absolute despair. His world had fallen apart. Tommy couldn't bear it. It was insane, for the evidence was obvious and impossible to deny, but the more he looked at it, the more he was convinced Reed had not set out to cheat.

"Mr Hardcastle, I don't think we should jump to conclusions," he found himself saying.

Hardcastle stared at him in astonishment.

"I beg your pardon Mr Fitzgerald?"

"There are things about this that do not make sense," Tommy insisted. "For a start, Mr Reed does not have the dexterity to undertake the task you accuse him of."

Hardcastle still looked astonished.

"We need to ask a few more questions, that is all," Tommy explained. "Just so we know for sure, before we ban a man from the sport he lives for."

Chapter Ten

The break room aboard the King Edward was probably an afterthought on the part of the designers. It was a box-like space wedged between the coal storage and a cargo hold. The room had a table, a row of wooden benches and a handful of lockers where men could store belongings. Everything was fixed either to the floor or walls to prevent it shifting in heavy seas. Clara did not like the internal space which felt more claustrophobic than anywhere else on the ship she had seen so far. She was going to be glad to get back out in the open air again once this was over.

There were a couple of men in the room, smoking and talking in low voices. They looked tired and not really interested in the arrival of Clara and Park-Coombs. They barely looked up when Lieutenant Harper approached them.

"This is Inspector Park-Coombs and Miss Fitzgerald," Harper informed them. "They want to talk to everyone who worked with Alf Matlock."

The men looked grim at the mention of the name, but they made no other response.

"If you remain here a while, you ought to be able to speak to everyone who knew Mr Matlock," Harper said to

Clara and the inspector as he departed to attend to his other duties.

Clara's attention turned to the men sitting on the benches; they were endeavouring to ignore her. She did not consider that suspicious. She supposed they only had a short time for their break and just wanted to sit for a while and rest, not talk about a nasty accident.

"Hello," Clara said, stepping forward.

Park-Coombs was taking a back seat in the investigation, having settled nicely on the idea of Matlock being overcome by fumes at the time he died. He was growing into the idea in a cosy fashion, developing it as he went along and becoming and more certain he was correct with each moment. All they had to do was find how the leakage of fumes occurred and voila! As the French would say.

"Terrible thing that happened to Mr Matlock," Clara said to the men to try to alert some response from them. "Did you know him well?"

"We work the day shift," one of the men told her. "We don't really see the night shift."

"Does that mean you did not know him?"

"Maybe to share a word or two with," the man responded.

His companion was sombre and had lost interest in his cigarette, which was burning slowly down to his fingers.

"He was new," the talkative man said. "Takes a while to get to know new people, what with there being so many crewmen on the ship."

"Were you surprised by his accident?" Clara asked, her eyes on the silent man who struck her as knowing more than he was letting on, at least that seemed to be why he was so solemn.

The talkative man shrugged.

"I don't think any accident on this ship surprises me. Things happen, mostly falls from high places. You just take it for what it is, one of them things."

He seemed bored with the conversation and Clara

doubted she would get anymore from him.

On the wall, a clock with thick hands suddenly gave a tinny ring to mark the quarter hour. The two men looked up.

"Back to work," the talkative one sighed. "I am fed up being stuck here. I want to get ashore. At this rate I shall have no time with my family before the next voyage."

"Yes, how inconsiderate of Mr Matlock," Clara remarked with a smile.

The man did not know how to take her response. He looked at her a moment, trying to decide if she was being genuine or sarcastic. He eventually gave up the effort and wandered out of the room, adjusting his work overalls as he went.

The other man had not moved other than to look at the clock. He seemed fixed in place, staring at it. Clara knew something was coming, something he wanted to say, but then he just stood up and walked off. She was disappointed.

"Good start," Park-Coombs said from the corner.

Clara cast him a look.

"It is more of a start than you think, clearly the silent man had something on his mind."

"Maybe he is tired of being stuck at sea?"

"Or maybe he has been thinking over the accident and is not convinced it was what people are saying?"

"That would be clutching at straws, Clara," Park-Coombs said firmly.

She would have argued more, but five men now arrived in the break room. They were surprised to see two unfamiliar people there and stopped their conversation at the sight of them.

"I am working on behalf of Captain Blowers," Clara said hastily. "I am looking into the death of Alf Matlock and want to talk to anyone who knew him."

The men eyed her up as if she had just informed them she was looking for volunteers to act as shark bait. She was starting to wonder why a supposedly simple accident had these men acting so shifty.

"Could you spare me a moment?" she asked.

"Look, we get fifteen minutes to take a break," one of the men spoke up. "We just want to sit, maybe grab a cup of tea or coffee, smoke and relax a while before we begin again."

He stormed past her to one of the lockers producing a kettle from it.

"My turn to make it lads, give us your mugs."

The others went to their lockers and produced battered enamel mugs which the fellow with the kettle took as he stalked off to make their tea somewhere else. The room had an unpleasant aura hanging over it now. Clara sensed she was not welcome, was it just because she was a woman wandering into male territory?

"This business with Alf," Clara said, dropping some of her formality to see if this produced a better response. "It is awful, terrible, absolutely dreadful."

"Accidents happen," one of the men muttered.

Clara was getting nowhere fast and was beginning to lose patience, especially with the inspector watching her from the side lines. He was aiming to not look smug and self-satisfied. He was failing.

"What if it wasn't an accident?" Clara threw out the suggestion to get their attention.

"What else would it be?" one of the men asked, and it seemed to Clara that he was more than just simply curious, he seemed alarmed.

"Well, it could be murder or manslaughter," Clara explained. "If someone else was there and interfered with the door or did something that prevented Alf from getting out of the way it would be different from an accident."

That caused them all to hesitate.

"Were you not curious as to how a man could be trapped in a door that closes slowly for the express reason to avoid such a thing?"

The men looked between them.

"Strange things happen," one said. "You learn not to think about it. Fluke accidents can play on your mind if you are not careful. You might never be able to get on with your work."

"But this one, was it not very odd? To the point where it was almost impossible to understand how it could have occurred?"

"Clara, do not start putting ideas into their heads," Park-Coombs rumbled from the corner. "Just to prove a point."

Clara wanted to grumble back at him, knowing he was only saying such a thing because he did not want his own idea being quashed. She kept her attention on the men before her.

"It is obvious something very strange has occurred," Clara said to them. "All I want to know is what Alf was like and if anyone might have had a grudge against him."

That brought their attention firmly back to her and with fresh looks of alarm and fear.

"Alf was a good sort," one of the men said, he wore a dusty cap which had a rip across the brim. "Hardworking. No one would have a grudge against him."

"He had only been here a short time. Not long enough for people to get to know him," another said.

This received a unified chorus of agreement from the others and Clara knew she was going to get very little from these men. At that moment, the kettle man reappeared.

"Still here?" he asked Clara, though his surly inflection implied it was not so much a question as a hefty nudge to get her to leave.

"She says people don't think Alf died by accident," one of the men told him.

The kettle man made a strange noise at the back of his throat, a sort of rattling huff of amusement that also suggested a good deal of distaste for Clara.

"What people? We all know accidents happen. It was just last year that old Charlie was crushed in that engine accident. Piston came down on him. Should not have been able to happen, but it did."

"Another crushing?" Clara said, thinking this was

starting to suggest a curious coincidence.

"Just his foot," one of the other men elaborated. "He is all right, just limps a lot."

"Strange things happen aboard a ship full of industrial machinery," the kettle man carried on. "My point is, you don't start seeing murder where it was just bad luck."

"And if it was not bad luck?" Clara said.

She was rewarded by a sharp look from the kettle man.

"Miss, I am being polite as you are a lady, and you are new to these things but let me make myself plainer. Don't poke your nose into things you do not understand. This is ship business and that is that."

He would have said more, but he was tempered by the presence of Park-Coombs. Clara would not have cared if he had said worse, at least she would have felt she was getting somewhere. People generally did not start to get agitated unless there was something they wanted to hide. However, she was also not getting anywhere at that moment in time. The men seemed determined to keep their mouths shut.

"You know, the faster I can rule out any suspicions of foul play, the faster this liner will get moving," she said, trying to appeal to their pragmatic sides.

Her words once again fell on stony ground. The kettle man had poured out five cups of tea, having produced a teapot from somewhere. The men had settled to drink and were ignoring her. Clara could see this becoming the pattern of her day and was frustrated by the thought. A quick glance at Park-Coombs revealed he was smirking, which did not improve her mood.

"Look, this is becoming tedious," she snapped at the men. "I have a job to do just like you. I am not asking you to do anything drastic, all I want is to know what Alf Matlock was like to work with and whether anyone had a disagreement with him."

"We don't want to talk about him," the kettle man informed her. "It is bad luck to talk about an accident like that when you are at sea."

"Oh, for crying out loud! This is the twentieth century,

not the time of Dickens. Bad luck does not come from speaking about something unpleasant that occurred. What does happen is the truth comes out. I suppose if you have a guilty conscience…"

"What?" the kettle man glowered at her. "There is no guilt here! None at all!"

Clara smiled at him; it was one of those smiles that says a person is not believed but the smiler is too polite to say so aloud. The kettle man was riled by the look, which was just what Clara had hoped for.

"Alf Matlock was a fool, that's all you need to know!" he snapped at Clara. "He got himself involved in a bet that has been going around the ship for a while. A man waits until the very last moment to get out of the way of one of the watertight doors. The man who can resist moving the longest wins the bet. Alf clearly waited too long and was crushed."

The kettle man's outburst had roused Park-Coombs from his thoughts.

"If that were the case," he said carefully, "would not someone else have been present to adjudicate the bet? Someone to time it, for instance? Otherwise, it would just be Alf's word at how long he waited out the door and no one would believe him."

The kettle man froze as he realised what he had said and what it had led to.

"That is not… he was probably just practicing," he said, licking his lips and looking as if he had made a grave mistake.

"No one practices a thing like that," Clara snorted. "Park-Coombs is right, if that is what Alf was doing then someone else must have been present to watch and time him. That also implies that this person ran off rather than save Alf from the door. Had they acted, he may have survived."

The terribleness of this thought hung over them all, even the kettle man had lost his fire.

"I spoke out of place," he said at last. "I don't know that

anything like that actually occurred. I was just guessing."

"Then, Alf Matlock was not involved in this bet?" Clara demanded.

The kettle man was trying to illicit help from his companions, but they were quite happy to leave him to it.

"He was, he was," the kettle man said. "Maybe not that night, but then we all just assumed…"

His voice trailed off and he looked at his fellow workers. They were all looking stunned. Clearly, they had been content to imagine Alf had died as the result of a bet gone wrong. They had not taken that scenario one step further as they should have done and realised that they were implying another person was present to witness the bet.

"He was practicing," the kettle man repeated. "Alf was the sort."

There was a murmur of agreement, but the others did not seem convinced.

"Practicing," Clara repeated the words and let them fall over them.

She might have had more of a response, but just then the clock in the break room made its tinny noise and the men were only too glad to get away and back to their work.

Once they were gone, Park-Coombs wandered over to Clara.

"This is starting to sound like murder again," he said, looking disappointed.

"It certainly is beginning to look that way," Clara replied. "Or at least manslaughter. If someone was there and did not help Alf, they effectively assisted him to his death."

"But none of these workers are going to talk to us," Park-Coombs sniffed. "I can see that."

"Someone will talk," Clara said firmly. "We just have to find the right way to entice them."

Chapter Eleven

"This is quite a challenging situation," Hardcastle rubbed at his chin thoughtfully. "I assume, Mr Reed, you deny all knowledge of this?"

Jim Reed had become fixated on the cricket ball and its terrible contents. His world seemed to have narrowed to that lump of metal and the implications it held for him. He did not at first hear Hardcastle speaking.

"Mr Reed?"

Tommy gave him a gentle nudge and Reed snapped back to reality.

"No, I would never do this," Reed insisted. "I value the game of cricket too highly to cheat. Anyone who truly knows me will agree with that."

"Yes, I shall agree with him," Captain Rhodes said. "Reed is a fair player. He is honest and reliable. This does not make sense."

Hardcastle turned the cricket ball in his hands.

"The evidence is somewhat damning," he said carefully.

There was not a lot anyone could say to that, but Tommy was going to try.

"If I may, we need to look beyond what is obvious, or

rather question what we are seeing."

Hardcastle stared at him hard, his look far from friendly.

"Mr Fitzgerald you seem to have a bee in your bonnet about all this."

"Mr Hardcastle, while there are some very damning pieces of evidence before us, all I ask is we pause and consider before reaching a conclusion. I reiterate my point that Reed could not have made the alterations to the mitt and ball, not with the level of skill required to mask the changes."

"That is true," Captain Rhodes piped up again. "Reed was never good at sewing before he lost his right hand. I remember the time he tried to make an emergency repair to his cricket trousers one summer's match and the repair split ten minutes into the game."

There were murmurs of agreement from the other players, recalling the incident. Reed was silent, the horror of the moment still sinking in.

"I doubt Reed could so much as thread a needle, let alone do the neat work on that mitt and ball," Captain Rhodes persisted. "After all, the mitt might only be seen by Reed, but the ball was handled by everyone, and bad stitching would surely have been noticed."

Hardcastle was considering this and the logic of their arguments. He had to admit it did seem unlikely the one-armed Reed could have performed such a feat that his tampering went unnoticed.

"We have to consider other things too," Tommy continued. "The suspect ball was switched and lost in the pond at some point, however, Reed was inside with us. Similarly, his bag was removed and dumped while Reed was under our gaze."

"How I see things," Hardcastle went on, "is that Mr Reed must have an accomplice. Someone who changed the ball and the mitt for him."

Reed dropped his head. He would have denied it all, but he did not seem to have the strength left in him and the words sounded weak, anyway. He felt he was doomed and there was nothing else to say.

"This does not make any sense," Annie was the one to speak now and step forward. "Let me look at that mitt and ball."

She took them from Hardcastle and examined the stitching.

"This is good work, done by someone who knew their task," she said. "This was not done by simply anyone."

"May I remind you, Mrs Fitzgerald, that it was you who alerted us to this problem," Hardcastle said.

"You are correct, and clearly I was right, but I am as keen as anyone to discover the genuine culprit and not merely pin the blame on someone. I shall stand by Mr Reed on this. It strikes me that he is as heartbroken about this affair as we are. I believe he did not know anything about this. Someone used him to rig the game."

Annie's words hung heavy in the air. There seemed something worse about the notion that someone had used Reed, had him cheat unwittingly, than just discovering Reed had been responsible. It seemed to take things to another depth of duplicity and sordidness.

"All right," Hardcastle said. "Look, let's go inside. I shall have tea and sandwiches made for us and we can discuss this properly and come to a conclusion. Reed, you need to be utterly honest with us if we are to get a handle on this matter. Understood?"

Reed nodded. They headed indoors, back to the meeting room where they all settled around the long table where cricket business of great import was usually discussed – such as did the pitch lines need repainting with white chalk just yet. Or, whether it was possible to avoid the expense of serving strawberries and cream at the next match.

Hardcastle sat at the head of the table and the two cricket teams split themselves either side, facing one another. The two umpires took positions near Hardcastle. They looked grim; their own reputations called into question by the evidence of cheating.

"Right, let's begin by establishing who supplied this cricket ball for the match," Hardcastle put the ball on the table before them. It looked a sorry thing with its innards falling out.

"You supplied them," Captain Rhodes declared. "Balls are the responsibility of the home team."

"I am aware of that, Captain Rhodes, but I would hardly supply a tampered with cricket ball that would see my team lose, would I?" Hardcastle said patiently. "That leads us to wonder where this ball came from. How did it end up with the others?"

Hardcastle suddenly snapped his fingers as an idea came to him.

"We need all the balls from the match, all of them. Go get them at once," he turned to an umpire and gave his instruction. The man left hastily to go about his task.

"Is the ball the same as the ones we usually play with?" Tommy asked.

Hardcastle picked up the ball and looked at it.

"There are not that many cricket ball makers. This appears identical to our regular ones," he offered the ball to the Brighton Badgers so they could confirm his opinion.

The ball did appear identical to the usual ones the teams played with and that made sense, as whoever had tampered with it did not want to raise any alarm by using an obviously different ball.

"Pretty much everyone touched that ball and the others during the game," Hardcastle added. "No one noticed something odd?"

"It feels a fraction heavier than a normal ball," Tommy said. "But maybe I am saying that because I know what is inside. I never noticed anything during the match."

The ball was taken from him and bounced on the floor. What remained of the cork in it seemed to still supply a springiness to the ball, but there might have been a little less height to its bounce.

The umpire returned with a handful of four cricket balls, the ones used during the match. He placed them on the table in a row, including the one Hardcastle had originally cut open.

"These are our balls?" Hardcastle asked.

"Yes, I took them from the bag they were kept in, except the one you opened which we found on the pitch," the umpire replied.

"We supplied four balls for the game, which means our fifth suspect ball was smuggled in somehow," Hardcastle declared.

Tommy was looking at the cricket balls all in a row. Something was nagging at him, but he could not place his finger on it.

"Well, that takes us back to square one, as anyone could have added in that extra ball," Hardcastle shrugged.

"But not everyone had the chance to switch it again when the accusations of cheating began," Captain Rhodes pointed out quickly. "We were all hovering around, listening to Mrs Fitzgerald."

There was a note of accusation in his tone, as if Annie had masterminded this entire thing. He did not seem to appreciate that she had been utterly right.

"No one saw anything suspicious, so that hardly helps us," Hardcastle grunted, fed up with all of this. "Reed, perhaps you can tell us about your bag with the mitt in it, at any time has it left your care?"

Reed had been a bit dazed during the whole debate on balls. He looked up at the chairman slowly.

"It is always with me," he said, though the words condemned him further.

It was his captain who interrupted sharply.

"It was not, Reed. Remember the other week you sent it to the shoemaker to have the leather buffed and that rip repaired."

Reed blinked.

"Oh, yes I did."

"It was gone a week," Captain Rhodes added. "Prime time for someone to tamper with it."

"But why would a shoemaker do something like that?"

Tommy asked the obvious. "He had no reason to interfere."

"There were other times, perhaps?" Hardcastle asked Reed.

"No," Reed shook his head firmly. "If the mitt was not with me, it was in my bag in the changing room, and that was never for long. Not long enough for someone to do this."

He flicked his good hand at the mitt, a hint of disgust in his voice. All his hard work, all his endeavours seemed to have been thrown back in his face. He no longer saw the mitt as the thing that had saved him, enabled him to carry on with the sport he loved. Now it was something that condemned him, made people question his integrity. He was beginning to hate it.

"The shoemaker would have had all the right tools for the job," Annie said, breaking the silence that had fallen. "He would have the right needles and thread for working leather and he would know how to do something like this neatly."

"We fall back to the question of why?" Hardcastle reminded her.

"We need to speak to the shoemaker who had Reed's glove," Tommy said, ignoring the chairman's statement. "We should do it right away."

He glanced at the clock in the room. Time would be tight to get to Hove before the shoemaker closed for the day, but if he was prepared to disturb the man after his shop was shut, that would not be an issue.

"I shall go and speak to him," he said. "If that is acceptable to Reed."

Reed shot his head up, and a strange look crossed his face. A mixture of relief, gratitude and yet also anger. Hardcastle was not so keen on this suggestion.

"I would rather we resolved this here and now, so people do not go away and dwell on all this," he said.

"Without all the relevant information, we cannot resolve this today," Tommy reminded him. "And we cannot make a rush decision just because we want to have this over and done with. We must be fair."

"I agree," Captain Rhodes said sharply. "Not only is my star fielder's reputation at stake, but also the reputation of my team. I cannot just forget about this and go home to my supper. I will wait up all night to find the truth if needs be."

"Surely not," Hardcastle said in alarm, thinking of his comfortable armchair and his nice dinner, all of which he would miss if this matter was delayed further.

"This is very serious," Captain Rhodes persisted. "You cannot deny us a chance to clear our names."

Reed was touched that his captain and teammates were standing behind him. It would have been easy for them to walk away and leave him to swing. Instead, they were sticking with him.

"Thank you," he said to his captain, though the man did not quite meet his eyes.

For him, it was more about his team than Reed. He did not want to have his team banned for the whole season because of this. He would sacrifice Reed if he needed to.

Hardcastle sighed to himself.

"Very well. Tommy, go to Hove and speak to the shoemaker who Reed charged with repairing the mitt. How will you get there swiftly?"

Tommy already had an idea in mind. His friend, Captain O'Harris, owned a car and would probably let him borrow it along with his driver. Getting to Hove by car should not take long.

"I shall borrow a car. I shall do my best to have information for you speedily," he reassured them all.

"In the meantime, I suppose we shall remain here and, I don't know, twiddle our thumbs," Hardcastle groaned. "This is really a mess. Where are those sandwiches and tea?"

Tommy rose from the table and headed out of the meeting room to use the telephone in the main office. Annie and Reed followed him. The latter was trying to comprehend how his life had changed so suddenly, and why

Tommy had abruptly become his best advocate.

"Tommy, I…" he hesitated, aware of Annie by his side. "This is good of you."

"I am going to find the truth," Tommy told him, wanting him to be aware that whatever that truth was, he would speak it. "We all deserve that."

"I would not ask for anything less," Reed replied. "I appreciate you giving me the benefit of the doubt. If you were not here, well, it would all be over already. I would be banned for something I did not do."

Annie was looking uncomfortable beside him – his accuser now become one of the people trying to prove him innocent. She was confused too, finding all this strangeness too much to get straight in her head.

Tommy smiled at them both.

"Every man deserves a fair trial. That is all," he said. "It still looks very bleak against you, Reed."

"I know. I am surprised you have been allowed this leeway at all. Whatever happens, I just want to say thank you."

Tommy was not sure he deserved that. His smile became a little fixed.

"It is nothing. Now, let's get to Hove."

Chapter Twelve

Clara and Park-Coombs found their way to the crew's canteen, which was not so deep in the bowels of the ship and had portholes looking onto the ocean. It was a relief to see the sky after the claustrophobia of the rooms below.

"Makes you think about those fellows who sailed in submarines during the war," Park-Coombs observed, glancing out the nearest porthole at a passing seagull.

They were sitting at a metal table, upon metal chairs, all of which were securely fixed to the floor, and were drinking out of heavy-duty ceramic mugs. The sort that could fall off a table or shelf without incurring more than a slight chip. In fact, by the looks of the mugs, they had fallen off a shelf once or twice already.

"I cannot say I ever gave it much thought," Clara replied to Park-Coombs.

"I read something about it, in a book, or maybe it was a magazine," Park-Coombs frowned at his inability to recall where he had seen the information. "In any case, it was an interview with a former submariner and the things he told made the mind boggle. No facilities to wash on a submarine, so you wore the same set of clothes the entire voyage, and if something went wrong and you could not rise to the surface after you submerged, well, you were doomed. The pressure or suffocation would get you. Honestly, I quite had nightmares after reading that."

"There are some very brave men about," Clara said thoughtfully. "Being prepared to go in such a contraption for their country."

"Brave or foolhardy? No, that is the wrong thing to say. I respect them for what they did, I just know I could not have done it. Being down in the hull of this ship today has confirmed that to me."

"I have been thinking," Clara said after a moment. "Perhaps it was all a terrible accident. Being down in those corridors after a while makes the mind boggle, and things seem different."

Clara wasn't sure how to explain herself, or how being deep in the metal workings of the liner had affected her.

"It could be he fainted in the doorway, as you said. Maybe he was exhausted."

"Or he had a fit, something no one knew about. People do."

Clara nodded. Odd things did happen, and it did not always have to be murder.

"Still leaves us with the same problem," Park-Coombs said miserably. "Proving it."

"Yes, right now we have nothing to say either way what occurred," Clara turned her mug of tea slowly around on the table before her. "Might have been an accident, might have been murder, or manslaughter. But the only person who could tell us is dead."

Park-Coombs sighed to himself.

"I could write it off as an accident you know, say I was certain about it, but it doesn't feel right to do that just for expediency's sake. Matlock had a family, and they will mourn him. They will want answers, at the very least, they will want proof he was not murdered."

With that they were straight back to the exact same problem. They could not explain how Alf had ended up crushed in a doorway.

"It is good tea, at least," Clara said, changing the subject to give them a break from worrying over the topic of Matlock's demise. "Nice and strong."

"Imagine how much tea a liner like this must have to carry on a voyage," Park-Coombs said, his mind circling around the idea. "You could not just stop and get some if you ran out. You would need to make sure you had a good supply."

The notion of running out of tea on the ocean troubled him greatly, he discovered, and put another nail in the coffin of any idea of sea voyaging he might have had.

"What do we do next?" Clara asked, because she was stumped on this matter.

The inspector was going to respond that he had no idea, but his attention diverted to a man in overalls who was wandering in their direction. He almost walked past them, as if he was just ambling along to get a cup of tea, then he hesitated and stopped by their table. He had frozen facing towards the canteen service counter, his body and face side on to them and not making eye contact. He could have just happened to pause there, just a coincidence, but then he gave the smallest of glances in their direction.

"You have been asking questions about Alf?"

"Yes," Park-Coombs and Clara said in unison because this was the first time any of the workers aboard the ship had shown an interest in their investigation.

The man sucked in his lower lip and stared at the service counter a while longer. The canteen was rather empty at this time of day, no one to overhear them or to see him talking to them. After a lengthy pause of indecision, he came to a point of no return, gave a small moan, and took the seat next to Park-Coombs.

"Roger Langley," he introduced himself. "Engineer first class. I served in the Royal Navy before I went to civilian ships."

Roger was a man in his fifties, short, stocky, the type of man who in the days of sailing ships could be imagined walking across a rocking wooden deck in a storm without any concerns of losing his footing. He seemed incredibly solid and grounded. He was also smeared with grease and dirt from his day's work. His hands were largely black, the nails ripped and torn from manual labour. He fussed at one worn thumbnail as he talked.

"The boys aren't happy you are asking all these questions about Alf," he said.

"Why?" Clara asked.

"Because we don't get paid until we get into dock and this delay is costing us. We are going to lose the next voyage too. The company will be shuffling passengers onto other liners to get them where they need to be while we sit here, stuck. We might end up sitting in dock for ages because of this, waiting for more passengers and we don't get paid for sitting in dock."

"I am sorry about that," Clara told him, and she did feel for him. He probably had a family ashore who were dependent on his money, as surely did most of the men. "What your fellows do not appreciate is the sooner they talk to us and answer our questions, the swifter we shall resolve this, and you can get on your way."

"They don't think like that," Roger said. "They are just angry and worried, and they resent all this. That is why they are not talking."

"Cutting off their noses to spite their faces," Clara observed. "Well, would not be the first time. Yet, you do not think the same?"

Roger hefted his shoulders, eyes wandering the canteen to see if anyone was watching. There was no one about, except for a carpenter and his mate at the far end. They didn't have much to do at the best of times, but you never knew when a wooden deck would suddenly crack in two during high seas. Ships still had a lot of wood in them, and someone needed to take care of it.

"I think we should take a little less time troubling about ourselves and consider Alf for a moment," Roger said. "He was a good lad. Hard working."

"We have heard that a lot," Park-Coombs rumbled.

"That does not explain how he ended up in the doorway."

"You know, if it had been any other lad, I would have said it was carelessness," Roger sucked in his lip again. "Some of them you wonder how they have survived this long. I had one lad who was coming through the watertight door and his matchbox fell from his pocket. He started to pick the spilled matches up, more worried about losing them than thinking about the door. I had to grab his arm and yank him away."

"Then, it is possible for a person to accidentally become stuck in a door?" Clara said, realising they may have their solution after all.

"Careless people," Roger replied. "Not lads like Alf. He would never have stopped to rescue his matches from the doorway, for that matter, he would not have been carrying them on him. You can't smoke during your shift. Those are the rules for safety."

"It seems to me that everyone is very confused how Alf ended up dead," Park-Coombs remarked.

"You are right there," Roger agreed. "We have discussed it among ourselves and none of us can fathom it."

"I have suggested a theory that the ventilation may have failed in the corridor where the door is and Alf was overcome by fumes," Park-Coombs added keenly, hoping to have his idea confirmed. "Captain Blowers is investigating that possibility as we speak."

"No, not fumes," Roger shook his head. "I have to go through that corridor a dozen times a day and I have never noticed anything."

"It could be an intermittent fault," Park-Coombs added.

The look Roger gave him silenced him.

"Was Alf well liked?" Clara asked the engineer, changing tack.

"I should say mostly," Roger answered her. "When you have a large crew, you can't get on with everyone, even a nice fella like Alf."

"There were disagreements?" Clara pressed.

"Minor things," Roger shook his head. "A job not done

as well as it could be. Tools being misplaced. Sometimes you just argue because you can't stand the way a man sucks his teeth anymore. When you are cooped together so long, things can get to you."

"You can think of no one who might have taken against Alf?" Clara pressed.

Roger gave her a wary look, once more his eyes surveyed the canteen.

"Murder, you mean?" he said, not looking directly at her.

"Maybe not intentionally, but yes. Perhaps someone was messing around with Alf and things went badly wrong."

Roger took a deep inhale through his nose.

"Could be a fellow held him in that doorway," he said, voicing an idea that had troubled his mind in the deep, dark hours of night. "Could be they was just threatening him, or tormenting him, but they left it too late, and he was caught up."

"That would be very serious," Park-Coombs said solemnly.

"Have you anyone in mind who would be likely to do such a thing?" Clara asked Roger.

He was staring at his fingers now, studying the lines of dirt intently.

"I can't say I do," he said, except they both sensed it was a lie.

"That's a shame. We could be getting on with things so much better if we had a little help," Clara said as lightly as she could, not wanting to alienate Roger.

"If you found it was an accident, rightly, we could go?" Roger asked instead.

Clara did not like his tone. She smiled at him, however.

"Yes, if there was proof of that, but we have found nothing so far."

Roger nodded his understanding.

"You need proof," he said, rising from the table and moving away without a backward glance.

Clara watched him depart, feeling he had wanted to say much more but had not dared. What precisely was going on aboard this ship that had everyone so afraid to speak out?

"That was curious," Park-Coombs echoed her thoughts. "Seemed almost as if he was going to tell us something then lost his nerve."

"I think there is more going on here than we have realised," Clara agreed. "Perhaps this wall of silence we are facing is more to do with people being worried about speaking out than just being frustrated with us?"

Park-Coombs tapped his fingers in a quick rhythm on the tabletop.

"How do we break through that silence?" he said.

"In that regard I am not sure," Clara admitted. "If there is something, or rather someone, they fear, how can we encourage them to come forward?"

"Place like this, you become your own world," Park-Coombs said. "You get lost in it and forget what it is outside because you never escape it. Becomes hard to see anything beyond it."

It was an accurate observation, but it did not take them further forward.

"If we could convince people that anything they told us was in confidence, then perhaps someone would come forward," Clara glanced out a porthole. "But we have already tried that, haven't we? We have not been fearsome or unapproachable."

Park-Coombs drained his mug. The dregs of tea were cold, but they went down the hatch smoothly enough.

"Another cuppa?" he asked Clara. "I am starting to think sitting here is not such a bad way to spend the afternoon."

Clara didn't understand, wondering why he suddenly was interested in loafing around. Then Park-Coombs flicked his eyes to her right, giving her a sign. She discreetly looked and saw another of the liner workers had entered the canteen and was watching them.

"Maybe, if we hang around, someone else will stop to chat," he suggested, before he took Clara's mug and went to get a refill.

Left alone, Clara looked out the window at the seagulls, who were taking a great interest in the liner and its potential to offer them food scraps. As she was watching, someone a few decks above threw out bread crusts for the birds and there was a flurry of white wings and grey backs as the gulls descended.

She was so distracted by this scene that she did not at first realise someone was behind her, until a large and oily hand landed on her shoulder. She started, and then glanced sideways into the face of a burly man who was glowering at her in an unfriendly fashion. Clara's eyes went to his hand, leaving mucky marks on the shoulder of her dress. Annie was going to be furious with her, not that it was her fault. Her gaze returned to the burly man's face.

"I shall say this once nicely," the man said in a low voice, trying not to move his lips. "It is time you got off this ship and left things well alone. No one wants people poking about in business that is nothing to do with them."

His hand tightened on her shoulder a fraction; the warning obvious.

"That is a very bad idea," she informed him.

"Maybe I did not make myself plain enough, you get off this ship now and stop asking questions," the man repeated, slightly more urgently. "Or there will be trouble."

"Is that a threat?" Clara asked.

"You can take it that way if you want," the man snorted. "I call it a friendly warning."

"Hm, what a pity," Clara pinned his eyes. "I really, really do not take kindly to friendly warnings."

Chapter Thirteen

Captain O'Harris was very accommodating about loaning Tommy his car along with his driver, Jones. He had not attended the cricket match, being somewhat overwhelmed by arrangements for an open day at his convalescence home in September. O'Harris ran a home for ex-servicemen who were suffering from the mental traumas of war. He aimed to rehabilitate them to a normal life, or at least as much as was possible. The open day was important to secure funding and convince the general populace of Brighton that his men were not psychotic lunatics liable to murder all and sundry.

After hearing what Tommy was doing, he was disappointed he had not been at the match and gladly offered his car. Jones arrived a short time later, and Annie and Tommy were soon on their way to Hove. It was a lazy afternoon, the sun shining down warmly, and Annie started to feel as if they were heading off on a day trip, rather than going to interrogate a man.

"If we had Clara's directory, we could see how many shoemakers have shops in Hove," Tommy said, nudging her from her restful state.

"I sorely regret ever saying anything about all this," she

said as she came back to the moment. "If I could have just bottled my indignation, I should now be at home preparing our supper."

Annie sank a little in her seat, thinking of Reed's face when the magnet had been found in his mitt. He had looked as stunned and shocked as everyone else. She could not imagine he had known about the trickery.

"Annie, if you had not mentioned it, it would have been bound to come out at some point later," Tommy reassured her. "I look at things this way, at least we are prepared to offer Reed the benefit of the doubt. If he had been found out by anyone else, they might not have been so generous, and he would now be permanently banned from the sport."

Annie tilted her head, almost nodding, but not really sure she agreed. Why had she interfered at all? Wouldn't it be better if this had become someone else's problem? She quietly sighed to herself.

Tommy reached out for her hand.

"You cannot regret doing the right thing," he told her. "You wouldn't be my Annie if you let something like this simply pass."

They arrived in Hove not long after three. It was busy with holidaymakers and day trippers, people wandering about looking a little lost and baffled at how sand seemed to get everywhere even when you were nowhere near the beach. It was not as busy as Brighton was this time of year, but then Brighton was heaving with strangers and sometimes it felt as if you could not breathe for the presence of so many new faces. Hove's quieter level of hustle and bustle was a welcome relief.

Reed had given Tommy the street address for the shoemaker and after a short pause to ask for directions, they found themselves outside a cobbler's shop. In the window, a three-foot model of a cobbler mending a shoe visually informed passers-by of the purpose of the premises. Unfortunately, the shoemaker closed early on Saturday afternoons.

"Who would have thought it," Annie said, glancing at

the opening times listed upon the door. "He opens late most evenings, but not on a Saturday, or a Wednesday. Well, I suppose we shall just have to go home and leave all this affair for another day."

Tommy narrowed his eyes at the door sign.

"Clara would not simply leave. Clara would knock and interrupt the shoemaker's afternoon off," he said determinedly.

Before Annie could respond, he was knocking on the door with a closed fist. He then stood back and looked upwards. There appeared to be a flat above the shop, and there was a good chance the cobbler resided there. Many small shop owners lived above their place of work, for convenience and to reduce expenditure. There was no sign of life, however, from the rooms above.

Annie was uncomfortable with such pushiness. She glanced up and down the street, fearing people were looking at them and wondering what they were doing. No one appeared to be taking any notice of their antics, but this did not console her.

Tommy knocked again, harder. The glass panel in the door rattled fiercely and Annie cringed.

"He is not home," she said, wishing to get away swiftly. "What a shame, never mind."

She was going to nudge Tommy back to the car and get gladly away from Hove, feeling deeply embarrassed about everything, but then suddenly, from above them, a sash window shot upwards, and a head peered out.

"What do you want?"

The head belonged to a middle-aged man with a thick moustache and almost completely bald scalp. He was wearing a pair of half-moon glasses, which he lifted up to see them better.

"Sorry to disturb you," Tommy said. "But we must talk at once. It is very urgent."

The cobbler did not look impressed, or likely to abandon his quiet afternoon so easily.

"What is it about?" he demanded.

Tommy did not want to shout out Reed's business in the busy street. He was starting to feel like Annie – uncomfortably aware of the number of people about who might be watching them.

"It is about the work you did for Jim Reed," Tommy said. "There is a bit of a problem."

The cobbler's attention was caught. No craftsman wants to have a problem with his work broadcast publicly in the street.

"I'll be down in a minute," he told Tommy, disappearing back inside.

A minute passed, Annie terribly aware of everyone around her, though they were blithely ignoring her. Then the cobbler's shadow appeared in his shop, and he walked towards the door. Bolts slammed back and the door was swung open. The cobbler had grown red in the face hurrying downstairs and looked angry, as much as alarmed.

"What is going on? Where is Reed? If he has a complaint, why has he not come in person?"

"Mr Reed cannot," Tommy explained. "You see, someone has tampered with his cricket mitt, and he has been accused of cheating. We are trying to find out the truth on his behalf."

The cobbler's mouth fell open and he stumbled back into his shop. He turned away, a hand rubbing over his bald head as he tried to grasp what he had just heard. Tommy and Annie followed him inside, Annie being careful to shut the door and replace the bolt so they would not be disturbed in this difficult discussion.

"What is wrong with Reed's glove?" the cobbler asked when he recovered a little.

"Someone sewed a magnet into the palm, and then they tampered with a cricket ball, putting metal inside it. The mitt would attract the ball as a result."

The cobbler turned and leaned against his counter; the colour drained from his face.

"Am I being accused of this?" he asked in a small voice.

"We are retracing the steps of the mitt, so to speak, to try to work out when it was altered," Tommy said without answering his question. "As you can appreciate, Reed is not capable of doing that sort of work himself, therefore someone either did it for him, or without his knowledge."

"And that means me?" the cobbler demanded. "I have never been accused of something like this before. It is an outrage."

"Perhaps, you were not aware of how putting a magnet in the mitt would affect the game?" Annie suggested, trying to be helpful.

The cobbler gave her a stern look.

"Do I look an imbecile? If someone told me to put a magnet in a mitt and a lump of metal in a cricket ball, I could work out what its purpose was. But let me state plainly that I did not do anything of the sort!"

The cobbler glared at them.

"Reed ought to be here to say these things, so I could put him straight!"

His temper had flared, and he looked liable to erupt further. Tommy tried to calm things.

"Perhaps you can tell us when the mitt arrived here and what work you did do to it?" he suggested.

The cobbler was not impressed, and he certainly did not want to be placated. He had never been accused of such a thing. He was an honest man with a good reputation in the community. He did not want this to be tarnished.

"I don't know what you expect me to say. Reed brought in the glove. He told me he was worried some of the stitching was coming loose. I took a good look and I saw what he meant. I told him to leave it with me for a week, so I could take my time fixing it, seeing as it was somewhat unusual."

"It was here the whole time?" Tommy asked.

"Yes, the whole time," the cobbler snapped. "In my workshop, to be precise. I worked on it in stages, seeing as it was a very specialise item and I did not want to change its fit or balance."

"And Reed then collected it?" Tommy persisted.

"Exactly," the cobbler replied. "He came, asked for the bill, paid at once and then departed. I never had any bother about this before and I have looked at his mitt a few times."

"Then, you are the person who always looks after Reed's mitt?" Tommy was careful to clarify.

"Yes. Not many cobblers could undertake such work. Some of my fellows in this town are barely capable of replacing a person's shoelaces, let along performing such delicate work."

The cobbler was duly proud of this. They were getting no further forward, as far as Tommy could see.

"Does anyone else have access to your workshop?" Annie asked.

The cobbler was distracted by her question.

"Only my wife," he said. "Are you accusing her too?"

"I was just curious if someone could have slipped in and worked on the mitt without your knowledge," Annie answered, not rising to his irate words.

The cobbler expelled air through his clenched teeth, to indicate his ire at this affair.

"You appreciate the seriousness of this all?" Tommy asked him. "The implications not just for Mr Reed, but for yourself…"

"So you are accusing me of tampering?" the cobbler snapped. "I knew it!"

"No one is accusing you," Tommy insisted. "We are just trying to work out the truth. Someone altered that mitt, and that someone is guilty of cheating at a cricket match."

"You are looking in the wrong place," the cobbler said fiercely. "And I am done with this."

"Could we just look in your workshop?" Tommy asked, somewhat desperately as he did not want to return to Brighton empty-handed.

"Whatever for?" the cobbler demanded.

Tommy honestly did not know, but he was not going to admit that.

"Just to understand where the glove was for a week.

Maybe there will be signs of an intruder in your workshop?"

"You think I would not notice?" the cobbler snorted.

"We would be remiss to come all this way and not look," Tommy said firmly.

The cobbler looked ready to kick them out but didn't. He might have been short-tempered, but he had been telling the truth about being far from stupid. He could see how bad things were for him, how rumours could start to spread about cricket match fixing, even if it was all lies. Suddenly people would be avoiding his shop and going to that fellow down Stokes Street, the one who tried to undercut his prices all the time. Half the price for half the work, that is what it was. Oh, and wouldn't he revel if gossip went about that his rival had been putting magnets in cricket mitts?

"Fine!" the cobbler said angrily, then he turned around and showed them through a doorway, across a corridor and into a workshop.

It was very neat and tidy, that was what struck Annie at first. Everything had its place and the floor had been freshly swept, scraps of leather or thread had been removed from the floorboards and disposed of. Tools were aligned carefully on a rack and a pigeonhole style set of shelves housed shoes in the process of being repaired or ready to be collected.

Annie admired the organisation, the tidiness. It sang to her soul.

"Can you see anything sinister?" the cobbler demanded, hands on hips as he glared about the room.

Tommy took a turn about the workshop, glancing at the bench where the cobbler sat and worked; his magnifying glass nearby for intricate pieces, his leather stored in an arrangement of colours, shades, and thicknesses.

Nothing jumped out at him.

"What is going on down here?"

They were interrupted by the arrival of a woman,

presumably the cobbler's wife. Annie hesitated at the sight of her, because she did not look like the right match for the small, balding cobbler. His wife was elegant and young, at least a couple of decades his junior. She was pretty too, perhaps not beautiful as such, but certainly attractive.

The cobbler turned to her, and his demeanour changed significantly, becoming beseeching and polite.

"My dear, this is no concern of yours. Merely a misunderstanding."

"This is your afternoon off Joshua," his wife replied sharply, though it was not clear precisely who her ire was aimed at.

"I know, my dear, and I shall be up right away."

His wife turned her eyes on Tommy and Annie. They were bright, fierce eyes, that seemed to blaze.

"It is uncouth to disturb a man on his afternoon off," she declared.

"It was urgent, my dear, that is all, please go back upstairs."

The cobbler herded his wife away, while she protested she had more to say to their visitors. He managed to get her to go upstairs before returning.

"My wife is protective of me," he said, slightly abashed now. "Look, if you have seen everything here, would you please leave?"

Since Tommy could see nothing in the workshop to raise alarm, he agreed to go. He trailed out of the shop with Annie. The door was slammed in place behind them with a pointedness that told them of the cobbler's feelings, then the bolts were shot into place and the chain restored.

"Glad to see the back of us," Annie sniffed, thinking just because a person was annoyed there was no call to be rude.

"I suppose we have to go back to the cricket club empty handed," Tommy was stood on the pavement looking forlorn. "I rather feel I have failed Reed."

Annie sighed.

"Look, supposing we poke around a little more?" she offered.

"Poke around where?" Tommy asked her. "We are through in this shop."

Annie met his eyes.

"If you want to know what a person is really like and if they are capable of doing something underhand, it seems to me the person you need to speak to is their rival."

Chapter Fourteen

In the short few moments during which Clara was being threatened by a man who stood partially behind her (cowardly in her opinion, attempting to avoid her seeing his face) she had perused the table before her for something useful. There was a teaspoon and some sugar cubes. Teaspoons were not an obvious offensive device, but these were of the cheap thin type that had surprisingly sharp edges to the curved end of their handle. Not as good as a fork, but when wielded with significant force, there was nothing to stop them being quite harmful. Clara picked up the spoon, bowl end in her hand and then sharply swung around with her left hand to plunge the end of the spoon handle into her assailant's hand on her right shoulder. She put as much force behind it as she could and was mildly delighted that it sunk into the man's flesh, leaving a shallow gash. Not debilitating, of course, but certainly enough to make the man jump away from her with a cry.

Over at the service counter, Park-Coombs heard the cry and turned to see what was happening. Clara was up on her feet, still armed with the spoon. She kicked the man as hard as she could on his shin before he could think about retaliating. He stumbled backwards against a table and groaned mournfully to himself, while the canteen staff and remaining customers looked on in astonishment.

Clara now leaned over the man and held the spoon very close to his eye. His attention focused onto it perfectly.

"Listen here, no one goes about threatening me, do you understand?"

Park-Coombs was wandering over with two fresh mugs of tea. He was not rushing; it was always entertaining to see Clara take down a bully. She generally surprised them with how ferocious and foolhardy she could be when faced with their intimidation.

"Take it easy on him, Clara," Park-Coombs said calmly. "I don't want to have to fill out a lot of paperwork about how he came to lose an eye to a teaspoon."

The man whimpered at this statement, then remembered he was considerably bigger than Clara. He began to make the effort to move, to push her out of the way. She kicked him sharply in the other shin for his trouble and waved the spoon closer to his eye.

"Stop making a fuss and tell me your name!"

The thug stared at her, wondering quite what was going on. He was used to intimidating people, he knew the format. Wander over, make a subtle display of strength, use some loosely threatening phrases and normally the person reacted by doing exactly as he wanted. It was rare for his targets to fight back, because he picked the sort of person who was not going to take him on. That was why he had targeted Clara and not the police inspector. He thought she would be frightened by him, and she seemed the bigger problem than the policeman who was working up to be quite happy the death of Alf Matlock had been an accident. Never had he thought she would turn on him and savage him with a teaspoon, of all things! How would he ever explain this to his mates?

"Look, miss, this has all been a big mistake."

"I should say so," Clara waggled the spoon at him. "Now you have dropped yourself in it. Before you came along, I was mulling over the possibility of Alf's death being a fluke accident, now I am sure there was something more to it. If there were not, you would not be barking at me to get off the ship."

The man whimpered, believing Clara, and regretting his interference.

"Tell me your name," Clara repeated, calmer now, but still with authority.

The thug sniffed forlornly.

"Anthony Cockle," he said. "But everyone calls me Ant, because of my height."

Something about Clara's presence made Ant start to babble.

"It's a joke, isn't it? Because I am very big and ants are so small."

"I worked that out for myself," Clara told him dismissively.

Ant started to shuffle again, and she rammed an elbow into his shoulder, pinning him with the spoon still too close to his eye for comfort.

"We are not finished here."

"My back hurts," Ant said pathetically. "It's all twisted up against this table."

"And whose fault is that?" Clara demanded of him.

Ant, who was not renowned for his intelligence, did not understand the question, but was very sure that answering 'yours, miss' was not the right answer. So he just frowned and squirmed.

"Come sit at this table," Clara told him, relenting because she was finding it uncomfortable leaning over him and there was only so long she wanted to stare into the man's eyes.

Ant was glad to lever himself up from the table and took a seat indicated by Clara meekly.

"Shuffle along," Park-Coombs told him, so Ant shuffled along the fixed chairs, freeing up a space for the inspector and forcing him to be trapped again.

"Your tea, Clara," Park-Coombs indicated a mug with his finger. "I haven't added any sugar, though you may now need it."

"I am perfectly fine," Clara informed him. "It takes rather more than our friend Ant here to shake me these days."

She took a sip of her tea with satisfaction.

"Well, Mr Cockle, who told you to come here and threaten me, or did you come up with that idea all by yourself?"

If Cockle registered the facetiousness in Clara's last remark, he did not show it. He looked cowed, like most bullies do when their victim has stood up to them.

"It was my idea," he said, though something about his face suggested that was a lie.

"Why do you want me and the inspector off the ship?" Clara asked.

Ant almost chuckled at such an obvious question, then he saw that Clara was expecting an answer.

"We need to get on, get to harbour and get our pay. Then we can go straight back out on the next voyage."

"That is it?" Clara asked him. "Seems to me there is more to this than just mere impatience."

Ant clenched his lips together, not wanting to say more. He fixed his attention on the tabletop, though that caused his gaze to wander to the teaspoon Clara had thrust at him and the blood on its end. He was uncomfortably aware of the sting in the back of his hand and his confidence faltered.

"There is more to this," Clara repeated carefully. "Someone knows what really happened to Alf and they do not want anything mentioned. They want the whole matter to be forgotten about."

"No, that is not it," Ant lied. "Not it at all."

Clara said nothing, the inspector was silent, acting as if he did not care that Ant was sitting next to him. Ant began to sweat at their lack of response. He coughed and wondered if he could ask to leave now. The silence dragged on. Clara drank her tea. At last, he could stand it no more.

"What do you want from me?"

"The truth," Clara told him simply. "That is not so

hard."

Ant's shoulders slumped.

"If anyone sees me here…"

"What will they do?" Clara asked him.

Ant huffed.

"Not much, really, probably just not talk to me anymore," he admitted. "Word running through the lower deck crew is that no one ought to speak to you two."

"Why?" asked Park-Coombs.

"We don't need the hassle," Ant answered. "We get paid per voyage and every day we are stuck at sea we are losing money. I cannot afford that loss, no one can."

"I have heard this all before," Clara said. "The irony is if people spoke to me and the inspector, then we could get this matter wrapped up swiftly and you would be on your way. It is because people are being so obstructive, we have an issue."

Ant did not respond.

"All these secrets," Clara sighed. "All this trying to avoid talking. Alf did not die alone in a fluke accident, did he?"

Ant kept his attention on his hands, trying to pretend she was not there.

"If it was an accident, well, people would talk and state as much to get this ship under way. All this silence tells me there is something you do not want to come out."

"I am losing conviction in my random fumes theory," Park-Coombs admitted. "I felt quite confident before, but now I think there was a person involved."

"I always take a threat as an indication I am poking around in the correct direction," Clara agreed.

Ant made a worried noise as he heard this.

"Who disliked Alf?" Clara asked him directly. "Who wanted to scare him a little, not kill him, but worry him?"

"I don't know," Ant said quickly. "I honestly don't."

"Then there was someone else there," Park-Coombs muttered to himself, disappointed at the realisation.

Ant whimpered again as he realised what he had

accidentally let slip.

"It is very curious," Clara said to the inspector. "What could Alf have done to warrant such attention?"

They both looked at Ant for the answer.

"Why should I know?" Ant said plaintively.

"You must know something, otherwise why did you come here to threaten me?" Clara asked him.

His mouth dropped open and made vague shapes as he tried to consider the right words to say. Nothing sprang to mind.

"Do ocean liners have brigs?" Park-Coombs said conversationally.

"I really don't know much," Ant said, starting to see how things were mounting up against him. "I shall answer as best I can, but I really am just a bystander in all this."

"Did someone send you to threaten me?" Clara asked him.

Ant did not answer at once, realising the situation he had put himself into. Then he took a shaky breath.

"No one exactly sent me. We just all discussed that maybe if you were scared off, then things would get going again."

"We?" Clara demanded.

"Several of us," Ant said vaguely. "No one in particular."

Clara glared at him, disbelieving every word.

"Look, if I was to say someone in particular mentioned the idea more than once, would you go after them?"

"Of course," Clara said.

Ant groaned.

"Shaun Gunther. He was the one going on about it the most."

This was a name new to them. Clara was intrigued.

"Did Gunther have a grudge against Alf?" she asked.

"He didn't much like him," Ant explained. "They both worked as greasers on the last voyage and there was a falling out between them, though no one ever said what it was all about."

"Did he wish Alf harm?" Clara pressed.

"No!" Ant said in alarm, but there was just that slight hesitation that let them know he was not convinced by his own words. "Not harm as such. Not real harm."

"Just the pretend sort?" Park-Coombs asked.

Ant winced.

"He wasn't there when Alf died," he insisted. "That I know for sure."

"How do you know it for sure?" Clara found his eyes and held his gaze.

"He was having a game of cards in the coal bunker," he replied.

"Was he not meant to be going about the ship doing his job?"

"He were taking a break. The engines are looked at by dozens of eyes over the course of the day. If there is a problem, someone would say something."

"Maybe Alf did not agree?" Park-Coombs postulated.

Ant shrugged.

"None of his business," he sounded surly. "None of your business."

"Which is what you were kindly trying to tell me," Clara said to him ironically.

Ant winced, recognising sarcasm when he heard it.

"Can I go now?"

"Do you have a theory about the falling out between Shaun Gunther and Alf Matlock?" Park-Coombs asked him.

"Me? No!" Ant insisted. "I stay out of those things."

He did not seem likely to give them anything else. Park-Coombs glanced at Clara, then stood up and moved away from the table. Ant was plainly relieved and slipped out himself and departed as fast as he could.

"You had finished with him?" Park-Coombs asked Clara.

She was watching the back of the disappearing man.

"I don't think he was going to say more," she answered.

Park-Coombs nodded.

"My thoughts exactly. So, it seems that maybe we do

have a murder on our hands after all?"

"We need to know more about this Gunther fellow, perhaps he is the key?"

"He had someone kill Alf for a reason we do not know." Park-Coombs nodded. "Seems to be the way we are going with this case."

Clara finished her tea.

"Where shall we begin the hunt for Gunther?"

"With the captain," Park-Coombs said firmly. "He will know where he is assigned to work today."

Park-Coombs paused.

"Look, Clara, are you all right? A man did just threaten you."

"You never need to fret about me," Clara promised him. "It takes more than a bully with his hand on my shoulder to shake me. I do hope he develops a dread of teaspoons as a result of all this."

Park-Coombs was not quite sure how to respond to that.

"It is hardly the first time someone has taken a dislike to my investigative skills," Clara reminded him. "It shall not be the last, either, but, as I always say, you know you are on the right track when people start threatening you and, for the first time, I feel my doubts that Alf was murdered slipping away. Something else happened to the poor lad, something much more sinister."

"Seems that way," Park-Coombs nodded. "I can't see him being killed over a secret game of cards, though."

"That seems unlikely," Clara concurred. "Something more serious happened. I just do not know what yet."

She rose up to follow the inspector. He glanced at her hand.

"Care to leave the spoon behind?"

Clara had not realised she had picked it up again, or that it was clutched ferociously in her hand, the skin of her knuckles white from the force. She looked at the spoon, then gave a weak laugh and tossed it onto the table.

"I forgot I had it," she shrugged off the mistake.

Park-Coombs did not believe her but preferred to give her the benefit of the doubt.

"Never seen a man threatened with a teaspoon before," he said. "Being with you is always an education."

Clara thought about this a moment.

"Is that to be taken as a compliment?" she asked.

"It was how I meant it," Park-Coombs replied. "I think."

"Then, it is a good compliment," Clara said before she too paused and then added. "I think, anyway."

Chapter Fifteen

Tommy and Annie travelled across Hove towards the next nearest cobbler's shop. They were looking for a needle in a haystack, tracking down someone who was enough of a rival to Joshua Mackintosh that they might be prepared to say something against him, something useful.

"The mitt had to have been altered at his shop," Tommy said for the third time, a frown on his face as they sat in the back of the car. "It was skilled work to alter it that way."

Annie just nodded at him sympathetically.

To locate further cobblers in Hove, Tommy had dashed into the local Post Office, which happened to be part of a larger shop that sold souvenirs and postcards to visitors. The Post Office counter was closed, but to one side was a stack of local directories. It did not take long for Tommy to flick one open and compile a list of local cobblers and their respective addresses.

He had handed these to Jones, who was a master at efficient navigation. He kept maps in the glove compartment of the car and retrieved one for Hove and charted where each of the cobblers' shops were located and the best route to travel around them.

He took them first to the shop of Mr Peebles, whose

sign above his door proclaimed he was the oldest cobbler in Hove. Not literally, for Mr Peebles was a younger man, but his father and grandfather, and great grandfather had all been cobblers and had worked out of the exact same premises. Such a long-established business ought to warrant a bit of respect in the town, supplying patrons with confidence at the ability of the man in charge. But competition was getting harder for cobblers, what with the arrival of these new chain stores that sold cheap shoes, so people did not get repairs so often, and did not get their footwear made bespoke. Mr Peebles was starting to feel a little fraught about his future prospects.

It was serendipitous that Tommy and Annie picked him as their first port of call; he also happened to be the cobbler closest to Mr Mackintosh. A little too close for comfort, Peebles would say when in a bad mood, but it was also lucky they caught him in a gloomy mood when he had just counted up the takings for the week and been filled with disappointment.

In short, they could not have planned better which cobbler to interview next and when to do it. Sometimes, in the detective business, luck was on your side.

Peebles glanced up hopefully when his shop bell rang. He glanced at the newcomers who were his first customers in half an hour and was satisfied they appeared to be of a calibre who could afford good shoes and might be prepared to spend money on repairs. He had just finished putting up a new display of men's shoes which he hoped would bring in some good takings. He eyed Tommy up with delight. He looked just the sort of man who would appreciate a nice pair of shoes. He also noted Tommy's slight limp and quickly ran through his head a range of possible alterations he could make to shoes to improve it, or at least make it less noticeable.

He fixed a smile onto his face and thought about the possibility of decent sales.

"Good afternoon!" he said enthusiastically. "Isn't it a fine afternoon? Would you be looking for men's shoes or ladies' shoes? Or both?"

"Actually, we are looking for a bit of information," Tommy said.

Peebles deflated instantly.

"Directions, is it?" he said crossly. "What particular landmark or civic building are you after? Or is it to find the nearest bus stop?"

Tommy stepped a bit closer, the man's surliness not deterring him.

"I was looking for information concerning another cobbler. Mr Joshua Mackintosh."

Peebles' eyes lit up, there was no mistaking it. At first, he thought from Tommy's tone, that something was afoot. There had been a way he said the words, as if he was going to be asking the sort of questions that would put Mackintosh in a dubious light. Then he doubted himself and started to fear that Tommy just wanted directions to his rival's shop. That happened sometimes, people seemed to think it was perfectly fine to ask about a competitor's business, as if he should be happy to tell them how to take trade away from him.

A mixture of emotions played across his face as he ran this tormented logic through his mind. Tommy did not let him suffer for long.

"Mr Mackintosh has been accused of making suspicious alterations to an item he was repairing. He denies the possibility, but we are not entirely satisfied."

Peebles' hope returned, but he was cautious still.

"Who are you?"

"Tommy Fitzgerald of the Brighton Badgers," Tommy said proudly. "This matter concerns a cricket game and the fear that Mackintosh tampered with equipment to fix the match. This is my wife, Annie, whose sharp eyes alerted us to the mischief."

Annie blushed at little at the introduction, especially when Peebles turned his gaze on her.

"A cricket match, fixed?" Peebles said. "I don't really know much about cricket. Never been my cup of tea. More of a football fellow."

Tommy did not take offence at the comment.

"How did he fix the match?" Peebles asked, trying to picture how one could alter a pair of shoes to improve a man's cricketing performance.

"One of the Hove players wears a special mitt due to the loss of his hand in the war…" Tommy began, but before he had said much Peebles' eyes had lit up.

"I know the man you mean, Mr Reed!" he declared. "He went to Edinburgh for that mitt. We discussed it at the annual cobblers' and leather workers' winter dinner. Caused offence, it did, him carting off to another country for his mitt. Seemed to suggest he did not think his local cobblers were of the quality to make it."

Peebles sniffed, remembering how hurt he had been when he had heard about the special mitt. There he was, part of the oldest established cobbling business in Hove, and Reed had not considered him fit to make a mitt for him. He would have done a fine job too, and the mitt would have been a feather in his cap. Imagine the publicity for his little shop!

Peebles admitted to himself that advertising his business was part of his troubles. His shop was tucked down a side street, in an old Tudor building with beams running across the ceiling and lopsided windows due to the timber settling. It was a place you had to know about to find, which had never been an issue in his father's or grandfather's day. Word of mouth had been sufficient to bring customers to the door, and most of them were regulars who had used the family for generations. It was a nice harmonious process.

Then Hove started to attract visitors in droves, and more and more outsiders came and settled in the town. They did not know about his shop, and they did not happen to see it as they were walking about. Instead, they spied some of the newer cobbling businesses, like Mr Mackintosh's, with their big window displays that were so gaudy and gauche. Suddenly it was not about reputation and how longstanding the business was. It was about a snazzy window display and accessibility.

People no longer took the time to find the best cobbler, they just wanted the most obvious one, the one with the most interesting window display, the one they spotted first.

"Mr Mackintosh was to do some repairs on the mitt," Tommy said, causing Peebles to pull a satisfied smile that the work from Edinburgh was already in need of attention. "While the mitt was in his care, someone placed a magnet inside it and did a very good job of masking the alteration. They also sabotaged a cricket ball. Mr Mackintosh denies it was him."

"He is a liar," Peebles said fiercely.

"That may be," Tommy said politely. "Or it may be that someone else had access to the mitt and made the alterations without his knowledge."

"I always said Reed was a fool going to him," Peebles stuck his nose up in the air, remembering how he had dismissed Mackintosh's competence as a cobbler. "He has only been in the town ten years. No real time to establish a reputation and he is not from a line of cobblers. Oh no! His father was a fireman. What does a fireman know about making shoes?"

Tommy just smiled, glad to find a man who wanted to talk, but also needing to nudge him in the right direction.

"You could imagine Mackintosh being prepared to stake his reputation as a cobbler by involving himself in match fixing?" Tommy said.

Peebles nearly immediately said 'yes,' but a small spark of conscience caused him to hesitate. He was not a man, even when pushed to his limit, who could dabble in dishonesty without feeling a pang of guilt. No matter how much he detested Mackintosh, he could not quite bring himself to accuse the man of being a cheat.

"That does seem unlikely," Peebles confessed, though he was not happy about the admission. "We were all rather surprised when Reed went to him for his repairs."

"We, being?"

"The other cobblers in Hove," Peebles shrugged. "We have all been established far longer than Mackintosh. Many of us have been at this generations, though no one has such an old lineage of fine cobbling that can match my own."

"Was there talk about why he picked Mackintosh?" Tommy asked, also now beginning to wonder why Reed had used an unknown quantity to repair his mitt when he had gone to such lengths to have it made in the first place. It would have seemed more logical for him to have gone to a long-established cobbler.

Peebles had pulled a strange face, sort of a smile mixed with a grimace. He tapped his fingers on the top of his shop counter.

"We started to wonder if it was not so much about what Mackintosh knew concerning cobbling, but about who he knew."

Tommy perked up.

"And who did he know?"

Peebles leaned a little closer, it felt better for the conspiratorial nature of things, even though it was utterly unnecessary with no one else in the shop.

"There have been rumours for a while that Mr Mackintosh's darling wife has been keeping company with another. Someone involved in the cricket club."

Tommy did not seem as surprised as Peebles had thought he would be. He was mildly disappointed.

"Who at the cricket club?"

"No one seems to know," Peebles replied. "Just that she has been seen over there, and she has no reason to be hanging about. If you knew Mrs Mackintosh, you would swiftly understand her knowledge of cricket is on a parr with the average bee's understanding of the game."

"And yet, she hangs around the cricket club," Annie nodded thoughtfully. "I wonder how clever Mrs Mackintosh is with sewing leather?"

"It stills leaves us with a big question as to who would

set her up to commit such a fraud," Tommy added. "Perhaps we should look to the team captain?"

Peebles was enjoying himself now.

"It is all really rather crass," he said. "People say Mr Mackintosh is oblivious, though it is hard to see how he could be with so many rumours flying about. But if what you say is true, and the mitt was altered in his shop, well, one would imagine that would be him finished as a cobbler in the town."

"Oh, that seems harsh!" Annie said in horror. "He may not have appreciated the implications."

Tommy thought that was farfetched. Any man of minimal intelligence could see that tampering with a mitt and putting a magnet inside it was not a usual practice, even if he did not know about the cricket ball. He did not say anything, however.

"What you are saying, Mr Peebles, is that not only was Mackintosh aware of his wife's adultery, but he saw it as an opportunity to gain work through the cricket club? Namely tending to Reed's mitt, which would have been something he could boast about and earn a little free publicity for his shop through?" Tommy clarified.

"That is precisely what I am saying," Peebles nodded happily. "There is a reason he was picked to do the work. He is competent enough but lacks the subtlety of skill that comes from being born to this business."

Peebles was really enjoying himself now. It had always stuck in his throat how Mackintosh had set himself up so nearby and done all he could to draw business away from Peebles. Now he saw how revenge would be his, and how delightful it would be. As soon as he could, he would be spreading the word about the tampered mitt, by tomorrow every other cobbler would know and be casting looks of disapproval in Mackintosh's direction. Shame on him, they would be saying, shame on him.

"We are not certain the mitt was altered by Mackintosh or while it was at his shop," Annie hastened to add, having seen the man's face. "It is just a very likely hypothesis."

"I could take a look at the mitt," Peebles said in sudden delight. "I would recognise the stitching, if it was Mackintosh's hand behind it."

He was too keen, he heard it in his voice and Tommy hesitated.

"I would be utterly unbiased," Peebles added swiftly. "Just an expert opinion."

"I think we have enough to be going on with," Tommy replied. Though really they seemed to have just more questions rather than answers. "Thank you for your time."

"Not a problem at all. I am delighted to have been able to assist," Peebles grinned. "You will come back if you need anything further and tell me the outcome? There is professional pride at stake here, you know. People might suppose that all cobblers are prone to tampering with the things in their care. It would do no end of harm."

"I am sure you will hear about the outcome soon enough," Tommy assured him, thinking that rumours were going to fly sooner rather than later. "Thank you for your time."

Tommy and Annie departed, leaving Peebles with a big smile on his face. His good mood lasted for several minutes longer, as he dwelled on seeing his enemy destroyed. Such sinister enjoyment in the misfortune of others was not becoming, but Peebles could not help it.

It was only after Tommy and Annie had been gone for some time that it slowly dawned on Peebles that while they had brought him curious news, they had completely failed to buy anything. The smile faded. Rumours did not pay the bills. They had not even looked at his display of men's shoes.

Chapter Sixteen

Captain Blowers was on the ship's bridge, watching over the calm ocean which seemed to be taunting him for his lack of movement. He was fed up with sunshine and quietly lapping waters. He was really wishing for a good storm to give him something to think about and the crew some work.

His mood did not improve at the sight of the inspector and Clara.

"No news on the leak," he said solemnly. "I have several fellows examining the possibility."

Inspector Park-Coombs pulled a grim expression too.

"I am inclining back to the assumption that Mr Matlock was the victim of foul play," he admitted.

Blowers' face fell, even a good sea storm couldn't cheer him up now.

"I don't understand, you seemed so sure about the leak. You gave me such hope."

"That was before some of your crew men decided to start threatening Clara," Park-Coombs explained. "They seem rather alarmed at her general nosiness."

Clara cast him a look, but she saw the hint of a smile on his face and knew he was trying to get a rise out of her. She turned her attention back to Blowers.

"A gentleman by the name of Anthony Cockle attempted to scare me off the ship," she explained. "He regretted his actions almost immediately. There appears to be some concern about my investigation of Alf's death, which would be odd if it was just a terrible accident."

"Cockle," Blowers hissed the name under his breath. "He is a ruffian, the sort you prefer to leave at the dockside, but he is a very good engineer. Sees solutions to problems others do not. He has had me out of a tight spot with the engines more than once. I am sorry to hear he has been threatening you."

"Captain Blowers, I have been threatened by far worse men," Clara said. "I shall not waste time worrying about Cockle. In any case, the point is he was actually useful to us, for by implying we should leave he gave us the best indication he could that something more was afoot here than just an accident."

Blowers slowly understood.

"That is not what I wanted to hear," he sighed to himself. "Did he tell you anything more?"

"That Shaun Gunther was the one who suggested Clara be threatened," Park-Coombs said. "Though he is clearly too much of a coward to do so himself."

"Gunther," Blowers closed his eyes and quietly signed to himself. "Not my favourite person aboard this ship."

"Tell us about him," Clara nudged.

"Gunther is of German extraction – you might surmise that from his surname. His grandfather came to England as a young man. Gunther is as English as they come. Served in the war against the Hun and never thought twice about it. He is tough and he is devious. I have had a few run-ins with him, mainly over him cutting corners with his work and sneaking off from his shifts."

"Apparently, he was playing cards at the time Matlock was killed," Park-Coombs said. "Handy that he has an alibi."

"He was meant to be on duty," Blowers growled under

his breath. "That is it! I shall have him fired for dereliction of duty! I have warned him before, and now I am through with him!"

"Before you cast him overboard," Clara said, her tone suitably ironic. "We need to determine if he was involved in the death of Alf Matlock. His concern about our investigations suggests to me he knows more than he should and is worried about his secrets being found out."

"Ah, but we have found him out!" Blowers said with glee. "He was playing cards when he should have been working!"

"I rather think any secret Gunther has is more serious than just shirking his work," Clara deflated his hopes gently. "It is something he feared could get him into real trouble, the sort involving the police, I think."

Blowers did not know how to respond. He thought he had known his crew, known his ship, now there seemed to be holes in that knowledge. He suddenly felt as if he was running around at the top of a mountain, with no idea of what was going on down below, and anybody who was passing him messages was also passing him false information.

"We need to speak to Gunther," Park-Coombs said.

Blowers slipped back to the present moment.

"Gunther? What time is it?" he glanced at a clock on the bridge. "He shall be in crew cabin ten, sleeping, I assume. His shift does not begin until six tonight."

"I think you ought to come with us," Clara said. "I think he needs to see his captain is not going to be made a fool of."

She did not really mean that. She was hoping that the presence of Blowers would knock some edge off Gunther and make it easier to question him. But she could see that Blowers was struggling to cope with everything that had occurred, and she wanted to throw him a line. Make him feel there was a way to regain some of his power.

"Yes," Blowers nodded his head. "Yes, I must be present. Gunther cannot be allowed to think I am a fool."

Inspector Park-Coombs patted his shoulder.

"Good man."

Blowers led the way down to the crew cabins; these were long bunk rooms housing eight men in each. There was little privacy for the majority of the crew, only the higher-level officers getting their own accommodation, but that was the nature of sea voyages. For centuries, since the first ship set sail, the crew had always bunked together and learned to sleep in company.

Disturbing Gunther meant disturbing all the other men in the crew cabin, if they were not careful. Clara preferred a quieter approach, so Captain Blowers entered the cabin alone and went to Gunther's bunk. He woke the man and told him he must come outside, that it was urgent. Gunther may have suspected something, but he did not refuse.

He stepped out into the corridor rubbing sleep from his eyes. Still stained by the grease and oil of his daily work, though he had made a token effort to wash it off. His bleary-eyed state was to their advantage. He did not immediately realised Clara and Park-Coombs were waiting for him in the corridor and by the time he did, there was not a lot he could do. Blowers had closed the door to the crew cabin and had shuffled Gunther away from it so that he not only blocked the way to the room, but also the route down the corridor. Gunther glanced behind him once, then realised he was trapped, unless he was prepared to knock down his own captain. Gunther was many things, but he was not stupid.

"Hello, Mr Gunther," Clara said cheerfully. "We have been having a nice chat with your friend Cockle. About teaspoons, indeed."

Park-Coombs almost smirked at the reference but managed to maintain his decorum. Gunther glanced between them.

"I have no idea what you are talking about."

"Really?" Clara feigned disappointment. "Cockle told us you had been badgering him to threaten me, that you wanted me off the ship."

"Cockle can say what he pleases," Gunther said haughtily. "It doesn't mean it is true."

"Is it true you were playing cards when you should have been working at the time Matlock died?" Captain Blowers growled.

As Clara had hoped, the presence of his commanding officer and the man responsible for his continued employment, had Gunther unsettled. He could bluster and lie to a policeman and a woman, but his captain was another story. If he wanted to keep his job, he had to think fast.

"Did Cockle say that? He is always trying to get me into trouble," Gunther laughed off the notion.

"Then, you were working when Matlock died?" Park-Coombs said. "Did anyone see you?"

Gunther's attention sprung back to him and the look of panic in his eyes grew. He saw the snare he was in; he just did not know the way out of it.

"I am sure someone did," he said quickly. "I am sure I spoke to Ernie White."

"White should not be working in the same part of the ship as you during his shift," Blowers said in that rumbling voice full of threat.

Gunther gulped.

"He came through for a part," he said, his eyes wide. "We just passed each other and said 'hello,' nothing more."

"He will say the same?" Clara asked Gunther.

The man now looked at her, and while he was worried about being aggressive towards the two men who were interrogating him, he felt no similar qualms towards Clara. He put as much dislike and fury into his gaze as he could. Clara did not flinch.

"You do not scare me, Mr Gunther. No stern looks shall stop me poking around for the truth. Honestly, you would be better off telling the truth and getting this all over and done with, rather than playing these games which place you in a worse light. We shall learn the truth."

Gunther blinked and maybe for a moment he hesitated, but he was not going to back down that easily. Whatever it was he was hiding, he had the arrogance to believe he could keep it that way.

"Talk to Ernie," he said, going for bravado. "Bring him here and he shall tell you just what I did."

"I would rather question him alone, without you being able to assist him towards the 'truth'," Park-Coombs replied.

Gunther was keeping up a good façade of not caring, but they all sensed he was worried.

"You do that," he said, playing out the ruse. "Ernie isn't good with the right dates, mind. He may tell you about another night by accident. Forgetful, is Ernie."

"You mean, he might forget he saw you that night?" Clara pressed.

Once again Gunther deflected all his frustration and ill-humour onto her with his gaze. Clara smiled back at him, untroubled.

"Go back to your bunk, Gunther," Blowers told the engineer. "I know where Ernie will be. We shall go speak to him."

Blowers stood back to let Gunther reach the doorway and started to move past. Gunther scowled at them all, battling with himself over what to do next.

"Maybe it wasn't Ernie," he said. "Maybe it was someone else."

Blowers turned to him; his disappointment written across his face.

"I have always had my concerns about you, Gunther, but I respected you as a man who had served valiantly in the war and earned medals. I thought that stood for something. I thought if I showed you respect, you would return the favour. I see I was wrong. If this is just about you sneaking off to play cards when you should have been working, well, I already know about it, don't I? So why don't you speak the truth instead of this nonsense? Better to be caught out playing cards than to be accused of murdering a man."

Gunther stared at them, he stared and stared. It started

to seem as if he had frozen and could not speak at all. Then he smiled.

"You have me Captain Blowers. I am very ashamed of myself. I was playing cards instead of working. I knew it could cost me my job, so I wanted no one to find out. That is all."

Clara suddenly did not believe him.

"I think we should still speak to Ernie," she said. "I am guessing he was at this card game too. Which is why you suggested him?"

Gunther froze again, not for so long this time. He cleared his throat.

"I saw Ernie that night, yes I did. That is true, but he will not mention the card game, he will not want to get into trouble, will he?"

"Who else was at the card game?" Park-Coombs asked.

"Oh, the usual fellows," Gunther said. "You want to speak to them all?"

"Yes," Park-Coombs told him.

Gunther winced and his words started to come out in a stuttering fashion.

"Well, there is Lane, and… and Mohammed, and Butler," Gunther hesitated. "If you ask them if we play cards together, well, they might say yes, then again, they might deny it. No one wants to get into trouble, do they?"

Even Blowers was looking unconvinced by Gunther's speech.

"Until this matter is resolved, I think we ought to place you in the brig," he said to Gunther.

"Wait! No! I mean, it was just a quick card game, and the ship was fine. I shall work extra shifts to compensate!"

Gunther pleaded with his captain, which was never going to work. Then he turned to Park-Coombs.

"I had nothing to do with Matlock's death. It was a terrible tragedy, an awful accident. No one could have wished that upon him. Alf was a good soul, everyone liked him."

"Everyone?" Clara asked.

Yet again, Gunther could not resist casting all his anger and hate into the look he gave her. It was fortunate Clara had broad shoulders.

"You have a brig?" Park-Coombs said, distracted for a moment.

Captain Blowers shrugged.

"I use a supply cupboard," he said. "But it sounds better calling it the brig. All ships ought to have one. Though, I must admit this is the first time I have had to put anyone in it."

Gunther was despondent.

"I have done nothing wrong. At least, not much wrong. And I shall make it up to you, I most certainly will!"

Blowers just shook his head at him.

"To the brig Gunther, before I lose my temper and have you escorted off the ship and to the police station with the inspector here."

Gunther shot a panicked look at Park-Coombs.

"That won't be necessary. I mean, how could Alf have been murdered? It makes no sense," Gunther tried to laugh. "Sometimes bad things happen. That is how I look at it."

"And sometimes, people help those bad things to happen," Clara replied back.

Gunther did not glare at her this time; he was in too much shock.

"The brig, Gunther," Blowers repeated and grabbed his arm.

"This is unfair!" Gunther said. "I should not be treated like this! I am a good worker and I have never neglected my duty."

He reconsidered this last bit.

"I have never neglected my duty in a manner that has caused a problem!"

"I do not want to hear it," Blowers told him. "I am tired of this. The sooner we have this all resolved, the better."

Park-Coombs and Clara followed him as the protesting engineer was led away.

"I didn't hurt anyone!" Gunther added, just in case. "If that stupid lad had not shut himself in a door, none of this would be happening to me!"

Chapter Seventeen

"Where next?" Jones asked politely as they returned to the car.

It was a good question.

"We have a couple of leads," Tommy said, though he was not quite sure the direction they were taking him in. "Why don't we head to the Hove Cricket Club and see if anyone is about?"

Annie looked sceptical at this suggestion, but Tommy could see no better way forward. Mr Peebles had said that Mrs Mackintosh was having an affair with someone at the cricket club, so to the cricket club they would go and see if there was anyone there willing to talk. Perhaps someone had seen Mrs Mackintosh hanging around the club, even if they did not specifically know she was having an affair.

Jones did not make comment on their new direction and, once the club was located on the map, he drove them to it without a murmur.

"I still do not see how Mrs Mackintosh allegedly having an affair with someone at the cricket club would cause her husband to rig Reed's mitt," Annie said, pulling a face that indicated how unconvinced she was by this whole scenario.

"I don't understand it just yet, either," Tommy

admitted. "But we have to look at the facts before us. The work on the mitt we are all agreed was done by someone skilled with leatherwork, and the only person we know of with that skill and who had access to the glove recently was Mr Mackintosh."

Annie was thoughtful a while.

"We have to ask ourselves, how long has the mitt been altered?"

Tommy paused, mainly because he had not thought of that before.

"You mean, supposing the mitt was altered a lot longer ago?" he said.

"Maybe it always contained a magnet," Annie said darkly.

Tommy almost laughed at the possibility – almost.

"No, that could not be. Reed was clearly distressed when the magnet was found, and Mackintosh made no mention of noticing a magnet in the mitt when he was repairing it. He could have done to take the suspicion off himself."

"He was probably only doing surface repairs. He would have no reason to poke about inside the glove," Annie countered.

"But you believed him, didn't you? When he said he had nothing to do with it?"

Annie frowned and her lower lip stuck out as she considered what she was being asked. She had been a mixed bag of emotions ever since this matter had started, swinging from anger that Reed had cheated, to sympathy that he might be a victim of someone else's deviousness. When she was near Reed, when she could see his face and his emotions, she felt bad for him, but that feeling abandoned her the longer she spent time away from him. She was beginning to wonder if Reed was just very good at pulling on people's heartstrings. After all, surely he should have spotted something was amiss with his glove? He mentioned he had noticed it was heavier but had not paid any heed. Was that true or a good way to cover his crime?

"I don't know, Tommy," she replied at last. "I can't make up my mind."

Tommy gave her that, he was struggling with the situation too. He just had this hunch in his belly that Reed was too good a sportsman to behave in such a fashion as had been suggested.

They arrived at the cricket club in silence, each spun up in their own thoughts. It looked deserted, which did not bode well for their investigations.

"I guess most of the club members were at the match in Brighton," Tommy said glumly. "We know where the team is, after all."

He gazed through the open gates of the cricket club, and the modern building just beyond them. It had that empty air that buildings could possess when there was no one about. He was considering asking Jones to drive them back to Brighton, to regroup with the cricketers and try to decide their next move. Then Annie touched his arm.

"Listen!"

Tommy listened. The car window was open to allow in some air and take the edge off the heat of the day. Through it they could hear a mechanical whirring sound, the sound so often associated with summer, the rhythmic purr of a lawnmower.

"That sounds like a petrol mower," Annie said keenly. "You know, I have seen them use one at the park to cut the grass."

"The Brighton Cricket Club has one. Much easier for mowing the pitch and there is a roller attachment at the back which flattens the grass into neat stripes," Tommy added, then he realised what she was saying. "The groundskeeper is about!"

"It would explain why the gates are open," Annie added. "I doubt they just leave them that way all the time. Anyone could walk in."

"And groundskeepers are very good at noticing people about their territory. It is part of the job. They always have their eyes peeled for someone who could cause trouble."

Tommy was already clambering out of the car, new enthusiasm driving him on. Annie was smiling to herself as she followed. Jones watched them go, then produced a small, well-thumbed paperback from the glove compartment and settled down to read.

The groundskeeper was working on the pitch, as they had hoped. He was propelling an Atco motorised lawnmower back and forth, taking the grass down to a perfect, even length. It was the sort of work you could lose yourself in and become lost in your thoughts. Good thinking time was mowing. He was so absorbed, and the noise of the motor was such a clatter, that he did not realise there were two strangers walking across his grass until a gentleman in cricket whites began waving his arm at him and bellowing for him to stop.

The groundskeeper tried to process this sight, failed to comprehend why a man dressed for a game of cricket was suddenly on his pitch, when no matches were scheduled, and then came to a halt with the mower clunking and whirring away happily to itself.

The gentleman ran over to him.

"Can you turn it off?"

The groundskeeper frowned at the words, which reached him only in part as they competed with the mower and the groundskeeper's normal deafness.

"I can't hear you, not with the mower running!" he replied.

"Can you turn the mower off?"

"If you want to talk to me, I'll have to turn the mower off!"

"Yes, if you could?"

"What?"

"I said…"

The groundskeeper held up his hand to silence Tommy and then performed the necessary procedures to turn the mower off. The peace that descended after the machine's endless clattering was all the more satisfying for coming off the back of such noise.

"Thank you," Tommy said. "I apologise for the disturbance, but I had hoped to speak with you a moment."

"There is no match here today," the groundskeeper told him. "There is a match next weekend. You are a whole week too early."

"No, you misunderstand, I am with the Brighton Badgers."

"They are not playing here until the end of the month," the groundskeeper said. "You ought to be in Brighton. That is where they are playing today. It's where our team is playing. I dare say you have missed the whole thing."

"That is not what I meant," Tommy said, trying to think how he could explain swiftly and without giving too much away concerning the alleged cheating. "I have come from the Brighton Cricket Club. There has been a problem with the match. Someone tampered with the cricket balls."

It was enough information to get the groundskeeper's attention without revealing that Reed had been accused of cheating.

"Well now that is terrible," the groundskeeper said, taking off his hat and flapping it near his face to take the edge off the heat. "Who would do such a thing?"

"The suspicion is that it was someone outside of the club," Tommy said, knowing that speaking out against the Hove Cricket Bats would likely cause the groundskeeper to clam up. "I was sent here to try to figure things out. It has quite disrupted the match."

"I can imagine," the groundskeeper said. "But why are you talking to me?"

"I was rather hoping you might have seen someone about the club whose presence was unexplained, or at least curious," Tommy said, not wanting to lead the groundskeeper if he could help it.

The groundskeeper kept wafting his hat.

"Lots of people come here. There are the players and their families and friends for a start. We have a supporters' group that raises funds for the club, they meet here every other Wednesday."

Tommy was going to have to help him along.

"I was thinking of perhaps a lady who might have visited, who did not have a specific interest in cricket, yet was often around."

The groundskeeper paused with his lips forming a circle on the unspoken 'oh' he had meant to say. He scratched at this head.

"Well, ladies, is it?" he fumbled around the topic. "Now, we have the wives of the players, naturally. And there are some ladies who enjoy the game and help out at events and matches. They make sandwiches and tea."

"What about Mrs Mackintosh?" Tommy said, deciding he was going to have to be blunt.

"Mrs Mackintosh?" the groundskeeper's eyes flicked back and forth, which was enough to tell Tommy he was onto something.

"Mrs Mackintosh the wife of Mackintosh the cobbler," he continued. "I have been told she comes to the club, though her interest in cricket is minimal."

"Rumours, is it?" the groundskeeper said, trying to deflect their attention. "I don't really listen to gossip."

"But you keep your eyes open," Tommy said. "You are responsible for these grounds, and you keep an eye out for whoever comes onto them. You would have seen her about."

The groundskeeper scratched his head again, tried to think of something to say to distract them and then made out as if he had only just noticed Annie.

"Ah, my apologies miss for my manners. Didn't see you there."

The groundskeeper was going to make a fuss around Annie to avoid answering Tommy's question. Annie was not going to have that.

"Mrs Mackintosh may have been involved in the tampering of the cricket balls," Annie told him firmly. "I ought to add, that because the tampering turned the game in the Hove Cricket Bats favour, the whole team has come under suspicion and if we do not find the real culprit it could sully their reputation."

"Sully?" the groundskeeper said in horror. "Heaven help us! Who would do such a thing to the Cricket Bats?"

"They did it to aid them," Tommy reminded him. "Only because the cheating was found out has it left them in this position. We are trying to help them."

"But you are a Brighton Badger," the groundskeeper spluttered.

"That does not mean I wish to see my rivals destroyed in such a fashion. I believe in fair play, on and off the pitch. I want to unravel the truth of this, find the culprit and exonerate the innocent."

"That is a fancy big word," the groundskeeper looked worried.

"It means I do not want to see those who are innocent tarnished by this reprehensible action. I do not want to see the Hove Cricket Bats in trouble because one person decided to cheat."

"That is very decent of you," the groundskeeper nodded, still trying to comprehend all that was happening.

"That is why I want to know if you have seen Mrs Mackintosh around here," Tommy persisted.

"She really might have tampered with the balls?" the groundskeeper asked anxiously.

"She might have," Tommy said. "Or her husband might have. It is a complicated business."

He hoped the groundskeeper would not start to wonder how the Mackintoshes had got hold of the balls in the first place, as they had no reason to have them at their shop. Tommy did not want to have to bring up Reed's mitt. He was also hoping the groundskeeper did not know it was Mr Mackintosh who repaired Reed's glove for him.

"Seeing as the honour of my team is at stake," the groundskeeper said carefully. "I shall speak out about things, though I would usually prefer to be more reticent when it comes to discussing a lady's personal business."

"You are making me curious," Tommy said, finally

feeling they were getting somewhere.

"Mrs Mackintosh I know because I have taken some of the players' shoes to her husband's shop for repairs. We used to go to Mr Peebles' shop. His father was a keen supporter of the team, but recently I was told we would be using Mackintosh instead."

"Did you wonder why?" Tommy asked.

The groundskeeper shrugged.

"I didn't let it trouble me. Maybe Mackintosh gave us a better deal on the shoes? In any case, I have been in his shop enough times to know what his wife looks like."

"Go on," Tommy pressed him when he fell silent once more.

The groundskeeper sighed.

"For about a year now, I have noticed Mrs Mackintosh visiting the clubhouse. I wondered about it at first as I had not thought she was interested in cricket. She never attends a match."

"Why was she here then?" Tommy asked him.

"I can't say I know," the groundskeeper replied, dipping his head to one side as he did.

He was lying.

"I think you do know," Tommy insisted. "I think a clever man like you would have worked it out. You would want to know why a stranger was loitering around."

Playing to the groundskeeper's vanity, Tommy hoped it would be enough to elicit the information he was after. If not, they would have to leave empty-handed.

The groundskeeper fumbled with his conscience, trying to decide what was worse – exposing a lady or seeing his cricket team ruined. There was really no contest, especially as he had never really cared for Mrs Mackintosh, but that did not eliminate all his problems.

"What will you do if I tell you?" he asked.

"I shall try to determine if Mrs Mackintosh is truly responsible for tampering with the balls, or whether this is all coincidence. If she had no involvement, then no one shall know what you told me."

The groundskeeper was still indecisive. He flicked his hat at this lawnmower and scowled at the uncut grass.

"You see, if she did this, it would be because she thought she was helping out the team, right?"

"Yes," Tommy said.

"Then that means she thought she was helping her friend here?"

"I suppose," Tommy agreed.

The groundskeeper huffed and puffed a little more before he came to a decision.

"You shall have to talk to our chairman, Mr Juniper," he said. "She came to see him. Every single time."

Chapter Eighteen

"Engineer White!" Captain Blowers entered one of the many compartments of the liner, this one packed with pipework that meant it was necessary for even Clara to duck so as not to bang her head. The tight little cabin had one wall lined with dials, the needles gently bouncing in place, while an older man dripping with sweat kept busy turning various control wheels. Precisely what he was adjusting and for what purpose was a mystery.

He startled at the sound of the captain's voice, bounced up and hit his head on a pipe above.

"Ow! You bloody…" he caught himself as he realised it was the captain who had interrupted his happy seclusion.

"At least someone is where they are supposed to be during their hours of work," Blowers huffed. He was still reeling from the news that a number of his crew where playing cards when they should be working and his encounter with Gunther had not cheered him up at all. Gunther was now locked in a sizeable cupboard next to the captain's cabin. Blowers was fairly certain air could get into the cupboard, but as long as he checked on the man often enough, it should not be a problem.

"Captain," White said, anxious now. He never saw the

captain down here.

"We want to talk to you about the night Alf Matlock died," Inspector Park-Coombs stepped in.

White's gaze slipped his way. He was still rubbing hard at the spot on his head he had bumped. He was going bald on top, which had meant there was no cushion between him and the pipework.

"Alf?" he said, his anxiety increasing.

"Where were you that night?" Park-Coombs asked.

White had a hint of panic in his voice as he answered.

"Other side of the ship, where I was meant to be. Covering an early shift in the boiler room. Passengers had complained they were not getting hot water, so I was fixing the problem."

His eyes flicked between Park-Coombs and the captain, he had yet to notice Clara.

"Did you, at any time, come to the other side of the ship?" Park-Coombs asked.

Still the eyes flicked. Clara was watching him intently.

"No, why would I?"

"Perhaps to fetch something you had misplaced?" Park-Coombs said calmly.

"I never go over the other side of the ship. You know how vast this vessel is. My shift work is confined to the port side, there is another fellow works the starboard section. We have our hands full as it is."

"Shaun Gunther seems to think you went to the starboard side that night," Park-Coombs said, laying his trap neatly. "He says he saw you."

White's eyes were moving so fast now, Clara was expecting them to roll out of his sockets.

"Shaun?" White coughed and spluttered over the name. "He is mistaken."

"That is very serious then," Park-Coombs said casually. "Seeing as Gunther is under suspicion for being responsible for Matlock's accident."

White startled once more and nearly hit his head again. He had become increasingly jumpy with each passing moment. There was something on his conscience, that was for sure.

"Shaun would never hurt someone," he said, pulling a smile onto his face. There was nothing genuine about it. "Him and Alf, they got along like a house on fire."

"He seems rather worried for someone who was such good friends with Alf Matlock," Clara finally spoke up.

White swung around and spotted her at last.

"Didn't see you there," he said, twitchy at her presence. "You must be that private detective everyone is talking about."

"That would be me," Clara smiled. "The one who Gunther wanted threatened because she was sticking her nose in places it should not be."

She said this in a jovial tone and White was not sure how to respond. He made that nervous cough again.

"We know about the card games," Captain Blowers said, in a disappointed voice.

"I never went to them, Captain," White hastened to say. "I knew about them, but I kept my nose out of things."

"Then why did Shaun say you were over the other side of the ship that night?" Blowers demanded of him.

White was having trouble lying to his captain, lying to a policeman or a private detective was much easier. Lying to his captain was almost impossible. He respected Captain Blowers and there was a loyalty among a liner's crew it was hard to describe.

"I'm not sure I was," White hedged, trying desperately to think of a way out of the situation.

"You are not sure?" Park-Coombs asked. "A minute ago, you were certain you had not been there."

"Well, I started to think it over," White said, the sweat pouring between his eyes and down his cheeks. He grabbed up an oily rag and wiped his face, leaving a grey smear over his skin. "You see, I did have to go over that side one night. My radial gauge broke, and I needed to borrow one. Only person I knew might have one was on the starboard side. So, I went to find him. But I am not sure that was the night

Alf was killed."

"Did you see Gunther?" Park-Coombs went on.

White was battling himself, caught between a rock and a hard place.

"All you need say is the truth," Captain Blowers said in a grim voice. "If you can recall what that is."

White gave a nervous laugh.

"I saw him," he said. "But I don't think it will help him that I did, because we were not far from watertight door nine."

White knew the implication he was making; he dropped his head.

"Gunther and I, we go way back. I would do a lot of things for him, but I won't lie to my captain."

"Do you know what time it was?" Park-Coombs asked.

White began to shake his head, then he stopped.

"I suppose it was around half two in the morning," he said. "I don't have a watch, but there are little things that happen around the ship at set times you can learn to tell the time by. Such as when some of the pumps turn on, or certain systems engage. That was how I knew the time."

"Half two," Park-Coombs pricked his ears. "How long were you talking?"

"It was just a passing conversation," White shrugged his shoulders. "More of a quick greeting then I carried on to find the fellow with the radial gauge. He was in one of the service rooms. I suppose we were talking around the time poor Alf bought it."

"Are you sure about this?" Clara asked him.

It seemed a little odd to her that Gunther would suggest a witness who could place him so near the scene of Alf's death, at just about the time the poor lad died.

"Yes," White said firmly.

"Did you know about the card games Gunther and some of the others were playing when they should have been working?" Captain Blowers asked sternly.

White put on a good pretence of looking shocked by the

news.

"No! They were doing that? How awful."

Even Park-Coombs did not believe him.

"What was Gunther doing when you saw him?" Clara asked.

"I supposed he was walking to somewhere he needed to go to do something," White answered, settling into his rhythm now. "As I say, we just casually passed one another."

"All right," Park-Coombs sniffed. "Can you suggest any reason Gunther might have wished Matlock harm?"

"No, none at all," White replied, though now he was sounding less sure. "I mean, they were friends."

"We heard they had fallen out," Clara said.

"Oh, well, there had been a little something. A while back, when we were in the Pacific," White sounded as if it did not matter, but then his expression hardened. "They had quite a barny. Don't know what it was about."

"Mr White, your words confuse me," Clara drew his attention to her. "One moment you say the argument they had was nothing, a minor thing. The next it is a big argument 'quite a barny,' in your words. Which was it?"

White shrugged his shoulders again.

"Probably something over nothing," he said.

"Did they fight?" Park-Coombs asked.

"There was a lot of yelling, but Alf was not a fighter. Can't imagine him lifting his fists to anyone."

"What about Gunther?" Clara said solemnly.

"That I can answer," Blowers interceded. "Gunther has been into my office more than once due to brawling. I have marked his card on the matter. Though, it is the first time I have locked him in my cupboard because I thought he could be responsible for someone's death."

White startled as he heard this.

"This is very serious," Park-Coombs said to the room at large. "We need to speak to Gunther again and determine precisely what he was doing in that area, and what this falling out with Matlock was all about."

White had recovered from his surprise, now he just seemed sad.

"It is such a shame. Alf and Shaun at one time were real mates, good, good friends. Shaun took Alf under his wing when the lad started. Said the lad reminded him of his brother who he lost in the war. Never would have thought he would harm him like that."

"Mr White, you appreciate that no one has yet proven Gunther had anything to do with Matlock's death," Clara said urgently. "You are not to start spreading talk that he is being considered a suspect."

White nodded at her, but there was something false about his manner.

"I fully understand. I shall not say a word. It is such a shame, though, such a shame."

"White!"

White's head snapped around to his captain and the insincerity fell away, replaced by a look of anxiety.

"White, you will not say a word about this, that is an order!" Captain Blowers told him squarely.

"Yes, Captain," White tried to stand up to attention and bashed his head again.

He whimpered to himself and rubbed at his bruised pate.

"Are we done?" Blowers asked the inspector and Clara, no longer interested in the whimpering engineer.

Park-Coombs glanced at Clara. She nodded.

"We are done," the inspector said. "We need to speak to Gunther again."

"We do," Blowers said, though he was not happy about the notion. "Come on then."

They had barely stepped into a corridor when a hurrying crewman stumbled into the captain.

"Captain!" he said in alarm.

"Whatever is the matter, man?" Blowers asked him. "You were running like there was a demon on your tail."

"Captain, pump three is overheating again and is

sparking," the crewman said in a rush. "I was running to get one of the water hoses to sluice it down."

"Pump three!" Blowers spat. "I best take a look. My apologies Inspector, Clara, but this is an emergency. Pump three is in need of replacing, but the time has not been found yet to do so. You are welcome to go wait in my cabin for me."

Park-Coombs and Clara both cast their eyes down the maze of corridors and gangways. Neither had a clue how to find their way back to the captain's cabin.

"We shall stick with you, if that is all right?" the inspector said. "No rush."

Blowers did not argue and led them to one of the ship's pump rooms, which was rapidly filling with smoke. Two engineers were hurrying to shut down pump three, but it seemed it had already overheated, and something had caught fire.

The calamity took close to an hour to resolve, Blowers chipping in to save the situation. Clara and Park-Coombs stood back and watched, impressed by the calm way the crew dealt with what could be a serious malfunction.

Once pump three had been stopped, the fire put out and the whole thing cooled with lots of water, leaving the floor like a very shallow pool, a debate began whether they could carry on without it for the time being, or whether it should be restarted.

Clara lost track of what was being discussed and let her mind wander. Eventually, it was decided they would try to go along without pump three and hope the other pumps did not become overloaded, or worse, breakdown. At last Blowers had his mind back on the matter of Alf Matlock and he took them back up to his cabin to question Shaun Gunther again.

"I still find it odd that Gunther would send us to a person who would effectively cast more suspicion upon him," Clara said as they walked.

"I must say, it was not the brightest thing to do," Park-Coombs agreed. "But criminals are rarely bright."

Clara was not satisfied with that, she felt sure she was missing something.

"Why not tell us to go speak to the fellows he was playing cards with that night?" Clara added. "Would that not have made more sense?"

"He didn't want to admit to the cards," Park-Coombs replied.

"You mean, he thought it better to hide the fact he was skiving from work, than to prove himself innocent of murder?"

Park-Coombs scratched his head. Whenever he got into these sorts of discussions with Clara, he always ended up feeling very confused. She always seemed to see things in a different light, in a way that eluded him.

"Well, people have odd priorities," he concluded, though it was a poor summation.

They were at the cupboard and the captain was working through a fat ring of keys to find the right one.

"I never pegged Gunther as someone who would kill another," he said. "He got into fights, for sure, but it was never anything serious. A couple of punches and then it was over. I once saw him taking a bunch of flowers to a fellow he knocked out and who we had to put in the medical bay. Gunther was not the sort to hold a grudge, if you ask me."

"Yet, he wanted me off the ship," Clara reminded him. "Threatening ladies, even if they are very exceptional private detectives, is a cowardly thing to do and does not rank him highly in my regard."

Blowers sighed again, fudged out another key, tried it and found it was the wrong one.

"Air can get into that room, can it?" Park-Coombs said, noticing how tightly the cupboard door fitted and that it was another metal one.

"I am sure there is a vent, or something," Blowers said, though he started to run through his keys faster.

"White had a lot to say, once he knew he was not in trouble," Clara noted. "What is a radial gauge, anyway?"

"You are asking me?" Park-Coombs barked with laughter. "I am lucky if I can pick out a nail from a screw. My wife is constantly telling me that the modern man ought to be an expert at this new trend for 'do-it-yourself.' She thinks I ought to be able to fix up kitchen cupboards and repair the banister where it is loose. I want to know what she thinks she is doing putting regular carpenters out of a job."

Park-Coombs waggled his moustache.

"It is because she doesn't care for my fishpond. She says I spent too much time fussing over it. She thinks I could do more around the house if I didn't have my fish."

"That would be a shame, Inspector," Clara said sympathetically, patting his arm.

"That is precisely what I think Clara, but you cannot argue with my wife. She is certain I can put up kitchen cupboards. She has forgotten when I tried to install new curtains rails around the house and fell off a ladder. I bruised my coccyx."

"You have endured so much," Clara said, trying not to chuckle.

Park-Coombs failed to realise she was being ironic.

"She doesn't appreciate the life of a police inspector. Look at me now, out at sea!" Park-Coombs waved his hand in the general direction of the ocean. "I was not meant for a seafaring life. I like firm ground beneath my feet."

He could have gone on, but Park-Coombs was not a man to wallow, and his mind had clicked back to the moment.

"Have you found the key yet Captain?"

"It is this one," Captain Blowers said firmly, placing a key in the lock and giving it a firm twist. There was a reassuring clunk as lock levers disengaged. "Well, that is a relief."

He pulled open the door, warm air tumbling out.

"Oh, good heavens!"

Clara ran to his side and glanced into the cupboard. The air was muggy and warm. Not unbearable, but not ideal.

Lying on the floor was Shaun Gunther, apparently unconscious.

"I asked if this room got air!" Park-Coombs snapped at the captain.

"I thought it did!" Blowers protested.

Clara had slipped past him and was kneeling beside Gunther.

"Is he all right, Clara?" Park-Coombs called out from the doorway.

"No, he is not," Clara said sadly. "He is dead."

Chapter Nineteen

Mr Juniper thankfully did not live far from the cricket club, within walking distance, in fact. It was one of the reasons he had remained chairman for so long, he was so conveniently placed for any emergencies pertaining to the cricket club and could be summoned at a moment's notice. That afternoon he had been attending the cricket match in Brighton, but he had arrived home some time back, somewhat alarmed and disappointed the match had come to an abrupt halt. As chairman of the Hove team, he could have involved himself in the affair, but Mr Juniper had not been in his post for this long without learning a thing or two about management – namely, don't get involved unless you are asked. He had dawdled a while, just in case someone wanted him, though not too near the clubhouse or in plain view – no need to give people ideas, after all. Then, when no one had rushed to fetch him, he had decided to go home.

His comfy deckchair was calling, and he was quite content to half-heartedly read a book while awaiting the arrival of sleep. He was happily enjoying his nap when the doorbell rang. He ought not to have heard it, he was out the back, after all, but Mr Juniper had one of those 'helpful' neighbours who cannot resist assisting.

His name was Mr Browning, a schoolteacher by profession, a busybody by choice.

"Mr Juniper! Mr Juniper!"

Juniper winced as the shrill voice of his neighbour disturbed him from a very pleasant doze. He lifted the brim of his hat and glanced over towards the fence where Mr Browning was stood. One of these days, Juniper was going to have the height of that fence increased, he was just trying to find a reason for it that would not look as though he was deliberately trying to ostracise his neighbour.

"Mr Juniper," Browning persisted, "there were people at your door trying to get hold of you. When I saw them, I went out and told them you were in your garden. I said for them to come through my garden rather than wait at the door."

Juniper now saw there was a young couple stood just behind Browning. He could not fathom what they would want with him.

"It is Saturday afternoon," he said, but as he was grumbling, he noticed the young man was dressed in cricket whites and he had a sinking feeling. It looked like he was going to become involved in the Brighton scandal after all. "What has happened?"

"Could we talk privately, Mr Juniper?" the young man asked.

Of course, upon hearing that Juniper's stomach sank further.

"You best come inside then," he said, preferring Mr Browning heard no more of this conversation.

Mr Browning was nosy as well as 'helpful.'

"If you come around to the front door, I shall let you in."

Juniper went through his house and a moment later was showing the young couple through to his sitting room, having had to chivvy Mr Browning back to his own home – the man had quite assumed the invitation had extended to him as well.

"Please be seated," Juniper said. "Have you come from Brighton?"

"We have," the young man informed him. "I am Tommy Fitzgerald, this is my wife, Annie."

Juniper took them both in, wondering what was going to happen next. He was a man who preferred a quiet life these days, being in his twilight years and gladly retired from a strenuous life in the world of investment banking. He did not need a cricket scandal, especially one revolving around accusations of cheating. He only had a vague idea of what had occurred to halt the match, but there had been plenty of rumours flying about. Annie had not been precisely quiet about her accusations.

"Well, I best hear the worst of it," Juniper said, sitting down opposite them.

"Mr Reed has been accused of cheating during the match," Tommy explained. "It has been discovered that his special cricket mitt was tampered with, as was one of the match balls. Reed denies everything and, quite frankly, there is clear evidence of another person's involvement. We are just not sure who."

Juniper groaned as the news was imparted to him. He could have heard worse, he supposed, no one was dead after all, but this could be the end of the current Hove Cricket Bats team. It could be the end of him since all things seemed to eventually stop at his door.

"This is very serious," he said.

"It is," Tommy nodded.

"What do you want from me?" Juniper asked. "I don't see how I can do more than offer my sincere apologies and state I shall conduct my own investigation into this affair within my cricket club. If there is cheating on the team, I shall determine it."

Juniper was being honest. He did not like what was occurring, but there was not much else he could do except to offer his aid. The look Tommy gave him unsettled him.

"We have been trying to find out who might have been able to alter the mitt. The work was skilled," Tommy elaborated. "Certainly, it was not the work of Mr Reed. We know that his mitt was in the care of Mackintosh the cobbler before the match, it seems logical the alteration was made during that time. Mr Mackintosh denies it."

"Naturally," Juniper said, trying not to look perturbed by the name. "It could ruin his business."

"It is also possible he is telling the truth. Mackintosh does not seem to have a motive for rigging the mitt. His connections to the cricket team are slim to say the least. But perhaps the connection was not so much to the game itself, as to someone involved with the club?"

Juniper swallowed hard. He was regretting being so polite and inviting them into his house.

"I do not understand," he said, lying.

"You know Mrs Mackintosh, I understand," Tommy continued. "She visits you often."

There it was, the accusation. Juniper felt a thin trickle of sweat running down his back. How could it be that just a few minutes ago he had been contentedly dozing in his garden and now he was being confronted with his own unchivalrous behaviour.

"She is a friend," he said, the words sticky on his tongue. He was not a natural liar.

"A very good friend, it would seem," Tommy pressed him. "One who would perhaps do you a rather big favour if you asked."

Juniper initially thought he was talking about intimacy, and he was shamed that he found himself blushing. Then Juniper realised Tommy was suggesting something much worse. As he joined the dots together, he gagged on the idea.

"You think I was behind the cheating?"

"You could have asked Mrs Mackintosh to alter the mitt in secret," Tommy replied.

"But I didn't," Juniper insisted. "Why would I do something like that?"

He saw Tommy hesitate and Juniper relaxed.

"You don't have an answer."

"People cheat all the time," Annie interjected. "They do so simply because they wish to win."

"An important match, perhaps," Juniper agreed. "But this was a little local friendly affair. A chance to get back into the habit. Nothing significant rested on this match."

"Then perhaps you were using it as an opportunity to test out the new mitt and see if it was effective," Annie countered.

Juniper gaped at her.

"I have never cheated in my life, and I don't intend to start now I am in my seventies!"

"But you are having an affair with Mrs Mackintosh," Tommy pressed him.

Juniper wanted to deny it, he just knew he could not.

"How did you find out?" he said at last.

"There are rumours going about town," Tommy told him. "You have not been terribly discreet."

"Rumours?" Juniper was horrified. "Good heavens."

"Now is the time to be honest with us," Tommy added. "We need the truth. We might even be able to help you."

Juniper was trying not to panic that his secret was out. It had been a casual enough affair, more about companionship than anything else. Mrs Mackintosh was lonely and so was he. Her husband worked long hours and largely ignored her. He would prefer she stayed out of the way, up in their flat for fear her pretty features would attract male attention to her and cause her to commit adultery. His obsessiveness had been the spur for her to do exactly as he had feared.

"It began one Saturday afternoon," Juniper said, seeing no reason to hide any longer. "The cricket match had been rained off and nearly everyone had gone home. I was finishing up some paperwork when Mrs Mackintosh knocked at the clubhouse door. She was bringing over a pair of shoes that one of our players had left with her husband. He had mentioned wanting them for that afternoon, but they had not been ready when he had called for them. Mackintosh hastened to finish them and sent his wife to deliver them. He would have preferred she stay at the shop, but he had been busy that afternoon and had promised to have the shoes finished on time. That was the first occasion he had been asked to repair anything for our cricket team, and I suspect he wanted to make a good impression. Neither of them realised the match would be postponed due to the rain."

Juniper found it best not to look at either Tommy or Annie as he spoke. He pretended he was just explaining something dull and innocuous to them, rather than discussing his personal life. It was the only way he could carry on.

"She was soaked through when she arrived, and I had her come through to my office to dry off. I made her a cup of tea, and we just began to chat. I was struck at what a handsome woman she was, and I won't deny I was immediately attracted to her. We talked a long time. She admitted she did not have the chance to speak to people often outside of the shop. Her husband kept her busy, she often helped with his work as he had so much to do.

"At some point we both confessed we were lonely. I never married and I have felt the effects of that choice more and more these last years. We seemed kindred spirits in our shared unhappiness. The next thing I knew, I was suggesting she come by again, that it was good to have someone to talk to, and she agreed. One thing led to another. She began to visit more often, usually on a weekday afternoon when no one else was around."

"What about the mitt?" Tommy asked.

Juniper was angry they were back to that. He had just made a significant confession, but apparently it was not enough.

"I know nothing about this tampered mitt," he snapped. "I have never asked Mrs Mackintosh to make alterations to anything we have sent to her husband's shop. I believe in the Hove team, Mr Fitzgerald, and cannot see the need to cheat. Besides, if it was discovered, as it has been, the consequences would be dreadful for us all. I would not risk that."

"Someone did, however," Tommy persisted. "And you must say it looks suspicious that you were having an affair with the wife of the cobbler who is the most likely candidate for altering Reed's mitt. You were also at the match this afternoon."

"As were many others!" Juniper snapped. "Look, you can suspect all you want, but there is no truth to this and nothing you can do to prove it. I am guilty of seducing another man's wife, but that is it."

Juniper held his ground. He knew he was in the right and he was not going to be swayed.

"You have no proof," he added.

They could not deny it.

"You do appreciate how serious this is?" Annie asked him. "If Reed is innocent, he does not deserve to lose his place on the team."

Juniper relented a fraction at her soft tone.

"I am glad you are looking into this," he said. "It is important we find the culprit, but I did not have a hand in this."

Juniper realised the accidentally pun he had made too late.

"Mrs Mackintosh is a good friend. I would never place her in such a position. I had no reason to."

He knew he had them there. They couple paused, nothing else to offer.

"This is very troubling," Juniper added. "It places us all in a terrible situation. I keep thinking of the scandal of it all. I cannot fathom any of my team being so reckless as to endanger their entire amateur careers in such a way. These men are passionate about the sport, they just love to play. This matter could ruin that."

Tommy was frowning at Juniper's words.

"It could ruin a lot of people," he said thoughtfully. "The cricket team could be seen as collateral damage. The primary victim would be Mr Mackintosh. His business would be likely to go under when people heard what he had done."

"Mackintosh would be devastated about that," Juniper agreed. "He has worked so hard to create a viable concern in the town. It is not easy, what with so many rivals, some of them very well established. He is the newcomer to cobbling in Hove, his wife has told me as much, and he is often considered an outsider by his fellow cobblers."

Tommy was confused by it all. Juniper saw this and felt a little desperate.

"I dare say it is as hard to prove me innocent as to prove me guilty," he told them. "I can only express my honesty to you. I have better things to do than rig cricket matches. Besides, the team we have currently is the best team we have had in years. You must know that Mr Fitzgerald."

Tommy pulled a face.

"The papers have been making a lot about them. There are some very good players on your team. Some could have gone professional."

"That is not to diminish the Brighton team," Juniper hastened to assure him. "My point is, with a team so strong, why risk cheating? People cheat when they fear the potential of losing, none of my side feared that. The players were going from strength to strength, even Reed with his missing hand. That young man made such an effort to learn how to bat again, it is utterly remarkable."

Tommy's frown deepened.

"Do you believe me?" Juniper asked, anxious. If they left his home under the impression he had organised this cheating, he was sure his time as chairman was finished.

"I don't know," Tommy admitted. "I want to believe you, but the circumstances…"

Tommy hesitated and licked his lips.

"We need to speak to Mrs Mackintosh."

Juniper feared they would say that.

"I best come with you then," he said, miserably.

Chapter Twenty

"Dead?" Captain Blowers repeated the word in horror.

"You suffocated the man, you fool!" Park-Coombs barked at him.

"Actually, he was shot," Clara said before Blowers could react.

That brought them all to silence.

"In the chest," Clara said. "Looks like it was pretty much point-blank range."

Captain Blowers gazed at her, stunned.

"But I had the key," he suddenly realised how that sounded. "And I was with you the whole time!"

Park-Coombs headed into the cupboard.

"Is there a light?"

Captain Blowers indicated a string hanging from the ceiling, which caused a bulb to illuminate over their heads, supplementing the limited light coming from a tiny slot window in the wall. With the light on it was possible to see clearly the gunshot wound in Gunther's chest.

"Well, this throws a new angle on everything," Park-Coombs scratched at his chin in thought. "Makes me think something very serious is going on here."

"It all links back to Alf," Clara agreed. "Maybe he knew

something he should not, and that was why he died."

"Then Gunther knew too much and has to perish too," the inspector nodded.

Stood in the corner of the cupboard, near the light switch cord, Blowers stared on unable to speak. Shocked at the sight before him.

"We need you to fetch the doctor," Park-Coombs told him. "I would send for Dr Deáth, but that will take ages and I am starting to think we need to hurry up with this matter."

Blowers might be stunned to silence, but he had not forgotten he was captain, and he knew his responsibilities. He went to fetch the doctor.

Clara took a good look at Gunther. It was easy to say he must have known the person who shot him, that was how they got so close to him. Of course, he had been in a confined space at the time, not really possible to escape. He did not seemed to have fought his attacker or put up much of a fight, which knowing Gunther's character seemed odd.

Park-Coombs rifled through his pockets, hoping for a clue.

"What on earth could be going on in this ship to warrant the deaths of two men?" Clara said to him. "The only slightly illicit activity we know of is the card game during a work shift."

Park-Coombs had pulled out a comb from Gunther's pocket, it was tangled up in a slip of paper.

"Numbers," he said, reading the slip. "A telephone number?"

Clara looked at the string of numbers.

"Too many for a telephone number," she said.

She paused, then turned the piece of paper upside down.

"Look, turn it this way and that number seven at the end could be an L."

Park-Coombs took the paper back from her. The numbers on the paper, aside from the seven, were possible to read either way up and still make sense. The inspector stared and stared at the paper.

"Ships have numbers, and they always begin with a letter," he said.

"This could be the identification number for a ship," Clara nodded. "But which one, and is it at all important?"

There was nothing else in Gunther's pockets that assisted them. Loose pennies, an odd bolt and some strands of twine did not appear to be clues as to who killed him. They had just finished their search when Dr Gulliver appeared in the doorway.

"Good heavens!" the doctor stared at Gunther, appalled at the scene.

"Captain Blowers said Gunther had suffered a mishap."

"If you consider being shot by someone in the chest a mishap, well, yes," Park-Coombs replied.

The doctor walked into the room and knelt by the body.

"What do you want me to do? He is dead."

"It is a formality to have the body seen by a doctor," Park-Coombs explained. "However, anything useful you could tell us about the way he died would be appreciated."

"He was shot," Gulliver looked at the policeman as if he could not believe his ears. "What else do you expect from me?"

Park-Coombs valiantly refrained from sighing at his frustration with the man.

"I would normally call our coroner and police surgeon, who is very useful in these matters," he said. "He would offer some information on the time the man died and if there was anything interesting about the wound. He might note some detail concerning the way the man fell, that sort of thing."

Dr Gulliver gave them a tight smile and then shook his head.

"Well, I am not a coroner."

"Do your best," Clara nudged him gently. "Any information you can offer us would be useful."

Dr Gulliver did not look so sure, but he began an examination of the victim, nonetheless.

"The bullet went straight to his heart," he said. "Hardly

any bleeding, so his heart stopped almost at once. I don't see any other wounds. His hands are untouched and nothing about the neck."

"As we already suspected, he didn't put up a fight," Park-Coombs mulled.

"I am sorry, but what else can I tell you?" Dr Gulliver asked them, looking fraught.

"Earlier, when I spoke to you, you seemed very concerned about Alf Matlock's death being attributed to carelessness on his part," Clara said to him. "You seemed quite anxious about the idea."

"Alf was a good worker," Dr Gulliver shrugged. "It would be a shame to cast aspersions over his abilities and suggest he was doing something foolish which cost him his life."

"And that was all it was?" Clara pressed him.

Dr Gulliver did not reply, he did not meet her eyes either.

"It is quite obvious that Gunther was murdered," Clara continued. "Which makes me think Alf's death was also murder. Otherwise, why was Gunther targeted? We had brought him here suspecting he was responsible for Alf's death and before he could talk to us, he was killed."

"Gunther might have killed Alf?" Dr Gulliver asked, alarmed.

His response seemed genuine enough.

"It looks that way," Clara told him. "Or at least he knew something about Alf's death, something he was not supposed to tell us."

"I know very little about Gunther," Dr Gulliver began to open up a little. "He had been to my office perhaps once or twice for minor complaints. His medical records were unremarkable though he did suffer from a slight inner ear problem due to an accident on another ship. Nothing significant however, or that would stop him from working. He could be a little deaf, that was all."

"And Alf?" Clara asked. "You knew him a lot better."

Dr Gulliver winced, really not wanting to delve deeper

into his memories of his friend yet owing it to Alf to speak up.

"Alf shared some of my interests, namely a fascination with sea life, particularly whales and dolphins. The reason I came to sea was in the hopes I might catch glimpses of these creatures. I have not found many sailors who shared my passion, most are of that antiquated manner that see something superstitious or ominous about whales and dolphins near a ship. Some would rather harpoon them. Others are utterly convinced they are the souls of seamen lost at sea made into physical form. Really, in this day and age such nonsense is remarkable."

Dr Gulliver snorted at the gullibility of some of the crew.

"Alf was different. Once he found me on deck with my binoculars. We were sailing around Canada, and I had heard there were whales in the area. He was curious enough to ask what I was doing, and I explained. He admitted he too liked whales and dolphins and we began to talk. After that, we became friends. Sometimes, on a dark night, we would clamber up to one of the upper decks and watch out for signs of whales while drinking from a bottle of whisky. We never saw one, of course, but it was pleasant, nonetheless."

"Sounds like Alf was a good friend to you," Park-Coombs spoke. "The sort of friend you owe it to, to find out how he died."

Gulliver gave a solemn nod of his head.

"I knew Alf well, well enough to say for certain he would not do something foolish like play games with a watertight door. He was a sensible fellow."

"Was anything troubling him in the last few days?" Clara asked.

Gulliver thought about her question, his brow folding into a deep frown.

"I would like to say I noticed something," he said. "I have run events thought my mind over and over again. I thought Alf could talk to me, but if something was bothering him, he made no mention of it the last time we were together."

"There was nothing at all?" Park-Coombs asked, disappointed.

Gulliver paused to think a while longer.

"Alf kept things close to his chest. He was a man who knew how to keep a secret if you told him one. I suppose, there might have been something, but I am not sure if I am making it up in my head."

"Tell us anyway," Clara said. "Just in case."

Dr Gulliver did not look happy about this, but his attention drifted back to the fallen Gunther, and this strengthened his resolve.

"The night before he perished, Alf joined me for one of our nightly whale watches. Actually, we were hoping to see some seals as a few of the crew had mentioned them about the ship. We drank some whisky and watched the waves. Alf was a little quiet, not remarkably so, but just enough that I did ask him if everything was all right. He replied that things would be good in a day or so. It was an odd thing to say, so I asked him about it. He laughed, said it was a slip of the tongue and meant nothing, then he changed the subject.

"I have considered that conversation over and over, but I cannot decide if it means anything or not. Perhaps I am just trying to find some clue, some sign in a situation that was just completely innocent."

"What would have happened in a day or two?" Park-Coombs asked. "Can you say what Alf was referring to?"

"Well," Gulliver said, "had Alf not died, in a day or two we would have made harbour."

Park-Coombs glanced at Clara.

"Then perhaps that was what he was waiting for, to reach shore and do something or learn of something that would change things for him," the inspector said keenly. "And someone knew that, so it became imperative to kill him before he could get to land."

"Then, it was important?" Gulliver asked, more

horrified at the thought than pleased. "If I had just paid attention…"

"Doctor, you cannot overthink these things," Clara patted his arm gently. "You were not to know. As you say, it was such a throwaway remark, it could have meant anything."

Dr Gulliver was not terribly consoled.

"At least my feeling that someone had caused Alf to end up in that door was correct," he said, though he did not look much pleased with the notion.

"I must ask that you put Gunther's body with Alf's," Park-Coombs told the doctor. "He is a murder victim too. I would also ask you attempt to remove the bullet. I think it is still in the man."

Gulliver's eyes widened.

"Sorry, what did you say?"

"We shall need the bullet," Park-Coombs repeated. "It will tell us much about the gun and help us to locate the killer. The one good thing about being on a ship in the middle of the ocean is that our suspects are all trapped with us."

"Hm, but the killer could have thrown the gun out a porthole," Clara reminded him. "An excellent way to dispose of it."

"I like to think more positively," Park-Coombs countered. "The amount of killers who retain the murder weapon they used is remarkable. It is something at least. In any case, even without a gun, if we can learn who has a certain weapon aboard this ship it shall narrow things down."

"Wait a minute," Gulliver interrupted. "You want me to grope around in this man's chest and retrieve a bullet?"

Park-Coombs smiled at him.

"Yes."

Dr Gulliver opened his mouth to protest, but it was difficult to argue before Park-Coombs' best smile. It was the sort of smile that made you feel both that someone valued you and also that letting them down would not be a good idea.

"Oh," Gulliver said in the end.

"It really is not so bad," Clara assured him. "We have asked a lot worse."

Gulliver did not have a reply.

They left the doctor with the corpse and went to Captain Blowers' cabin next door. The captain was pacing back and forth, wearing a track in the fluffy pile of his rug.

"He really is dead?" he asked them as they entered. "He was not just knocked out, perhaps?"

"His heart stopped. He is dead," Park-Coombs informed him.

Blowers was despondent.

"This is terrible. He was in my care, and he was murdered, just like that," Blowers snapped his fingers. "I have been thinking about keys. I have a spare, you know, just in case. I keep it in my desk drawer on a bunch with lots of other keys."

Blowers opened the drawer and revealed the bunch.

"Who knows about the spares?" Park-Coombs asked.

Blowers groaned.

"I could make you quite a list. All my officers for a start. My steward and anyone who has been asked to fetch them in the past. I never made a secret of them, why would I?"

"No captain, why would you," Park-Coombs agreed, trying to console him.

"We found a slip of paper in Gunther's pocket, and it had a number on it, we think it is a ship's number," Clara tapped Park-Coombs' arm and he retrieved the paper. "We don't know if it is important, but we thought perhaps tracking the ship would be useful."

Park-Coombs handed over the slip of paper. Blowers stared at it, still dazed at everything that was occurring.

"How easy would it be to trace this ship by its number?" Park-Coombs asked.

"Very easy," Blowers said, looking miserable. "As I happen to know this ship."

"Really?" Park-Coombs was eager. "Tell us about it,

where does she sail?"

"Nowhere, not anymore," Blowers said. "This was the number for our sister ship, another liner just like this one."

"Was?" Clara picked up the use of the past tense.

"Yes. She sank," Blowers explained. "It is a year ago now. It was a terrible tragedy, lots of passengers drowned. One of the watertight doors was faulty, let water seep into the lower decks and flood the engines."

Blowers handed back the paper gloomily.

"I don't know why Gunther would want to remember such a thing," he said. "He nearly drowned that day. He was in the engine room. He always told me he made every effort to forget all about it."

Chapter Twenty-One

Mr Juniper was very impressed by the car. He made noises of approval as he slipped inside it and touched the leather seats with great care and awe.

"You must have money, Mr Fitzgerald," he said, his respect for Tommy increasing.

"Not personally," Tommy answered him – he was sitting in the seat beside Juniper. "But I have a good friend who does, and he has kindly loaned us this car due to the distance we needed to travel to resolve this affair."

"An important man, your friend," Mr Juniper said to himself, considering only important people could have cars. He was thinking it was very crucial he worked with Tommy, seeing as he had influential friends. "You must make it plain to him that I had nothing to do with this cheating business. It would be terrible for me if someone significant in Brighton was to imagine I condoned the fixing of matches."

Tommy did not disabuse him of this idea. He needed Juniper to be cooperative and the best way to ensure that was to make him feel his reputation and position as chairman of the cricket club was on the line. People always were more talkative when they feared keeping quiet could be bad for them.

They arrived back at the shop belonging to the Mackintoshes. It was closed, as before. Mr Juniper started to shuffle in his seat, looking anxious.

"Mr Mackintosh... he does not know, you see?"

"He will know shortly," Tommy said, not interested in the man's sudden reticence. "This is now beyond just the deception of a husband. We need to know if it has led to the disruption of a cricket game."

"I do appreciate that," Mr Juniper said, fidgeting in his seat and wondering why he ever allowed himself to be smitten by a pair of pretty eyes. "We cannot allow the good name of cricket in this county to be foully ruined. It is just... well, Mr Mackintosh is going to be in for a shock."

"Mr Mackintosh is looking out the window," Annie remarked.

She had been looking at the shop, letting Mr Juniper's chatter wash over her. She had seen the upper window swing open and Mr Mackintosh put out his head.

"He must have heard the car pulling up. He has a very sour look on his face."

"We best get out," Tommy told Mr Juniper firmly.

Juniper grimaced but obeyed. He stepped out into the road, while Tommy exited onto the pavement. Mr Mackintosh saw Tommy first, as a consequence, and was going to yell something at him for daring to come back. Then he saw Mr Juniper walking around the back of the car and his words dried up on his tongue.

"Mr Juniper?" he said. "Don't tell me they have embroiled you in this ridiculous fiasco?"

Juniper smiled up at the cobbler. It was a sad smile, masking a deep sense of guilt.

"It would be a good idea for us to talk," he said.

Mackintosh frowned at him in confusion.

"Right now?"

"Right now," Juniper nodded.

Mackintosh was reluctant. He gave a stern look at Tommy, not wanting to ruin the rest of his Saturday by being further accused of tampering with a cricket mitt. Little did he know just how ruined his Saturday was about to become.

"Please, Mr Mackintosh," Juniper called up. "The reputation of the Hove Cricket Bats is at stake. There can be nothing more paramount than preserving it."

Mackintosh sniffed. Cricket did not particularly interest him, but he did like the trade the club regularly sent his way. He had worked hard to ensure he was the first name they thought of when they were considering who to send their shoes or other leather goods to. He could not afford the loss of such a profitable side-line. Like so many people, Mackintosh was ultimately driven by financial prudence and a selfish desire to ensure he was not 'done down.'

He disappeared from the window without a word, and they had to wait impatiently to see if he was going to come down to the door, or merely ignore them.

"I have wronged this man greatly," Juniper said, suddenly developing a conscience.

"A little too late for such thoughts," Annie said.

She was ready to act as a buffer between Mrs Mackintosh and the accusations she was about to face. Annie had little time for a woman who cheated on her spouse, but she would never see a member of her sex being confronted on such a subject without some female support. She would be on Mrs Mackintosh's side out of principle.

Mackintosh seemed to take a long while to reach his front door. He opened it and ushered them in, glancing about to see if anyone was watching. In a place like Hove, there was bound to be someone who saw something and would gladly talk about it.

"Thank you, Mr Mackintosh," Juniper said, very humbly. Mackintosh did not notice the way the man was trying to grovel to him. "Could we perhaps talk upstairs? You wife ought to be present."

"My wife?" Mackintosh frowned, a sudden pang of unease catching at him.

"It is essential, in fact," Juniper insisted. "There are

some dark rumours abounding."

Mackintosh's frown deepened and he hesitated. For a moment he almost seemed to sense what was to come, then he shook it off like a wet dog shakes off water.

"This stupid business about Reed's mitt," he spat. "I had nothing to do with that. Why would I risk my reputation, my business in that way?"

"Yes, of course," Juniper smiled in a placating fashion. "You do see, however, that it is imperative we discuss this business and determine who did tamper with the mitt, so as to avoid being further accused of the crime."

Mackintosh did not see; he thought his word should be good enough. He huffed to himself, then consented to letting them up into his flat above the shop.

"I ought to be reimbursed for wasting my time," he told Juniper, though the remark was intended for Tommy. "This is my Saturday afternoon off."

"I appreciate that, Mr Mackintosh," Juniper said, all too aware that very soon this mild camaraderie he had with the man would be destroyed.

"I don't often get a Saturday afternoon to spend with my wife," Mackintosh continued. "She usually goes to see her mother on a Saturday afternoon. It just happened that this week the old lady was being visited by her sister and my wife could stay home."

"Yes," Juniper said, his deceit beginning to eat at him. He cast his eyes at Tommy who tried as best he could with a return glance to convince the man to stay strong.

They arrived in the sitting room of the flat. Mrs Mackintosh was sitting by the unlit gas fire working on darning some socks. She watched them enter without a flicker of concern. Her calm was almost alarming. She was a decidedly good actress, and that made Tommy begin to wonder how they would ever be able to determine the truth from her.

"What is this all about?" Mackintosh asked, collapsing into a worn armchair without asking his guests to sit.

Tommy preferred to remain standing anyway, and

Juniper was inclined to pace.

"This terrible business with cheating," Juniper began, doing a fine job of not looking in Mrs Mackintosh's direction, even though his statement could have a double meaning. "It has reached out and touched us all and we must nip it in the bud."

"How many times do I have to say…" Mr Mackintosh began again, leaning forward in his chair.

Juniper stopped him before Tommy could.

"This is not about you," he said and now he was serious.

Mackintosh sensed the change in his tone and moved back, worried.

"There is a suggestion that your wife could have tampered with the mitt," Juniper said, before Mackintosh could splutter out 'what do you mean?' and interrupt again, Juniper soldiered on valiantly. "The implication being she did this as a favour for me, and that I, in turn, wanted this done to ensure the victory of my cricket team. This is incorrect, but we must resolve this matter and get to the bottom of things to prove we are innocent."

Mrs Mackintosh was watching Juniper intently. It was difficult to judge her expression, but Tommy would suggest there was both anger and betrayal in her gaze.

"I don't understand why anyone would suppose my wife would do this," Mackintosh laughed. "She doesn't even know you, Mr Juniper, other than to maybe serve you in the shop from time to time."

"That is where you are sadly mistaken," Juniper said, in his stride now and determined to brazen out the worst. "Your wife and I have been…"

"Stop it!" Mrs Mackintosh barked out. "If he has to be told, let me tell him."

Her eyes were blazing with fury, and it was enough to cow Juniper who fell silent. Mrs Mackintosh turned her gaze to her husband. The fury diminished, she tried to look kind. She was not after sympathy, but she wanted the news to fall as lightly as possible on her husband's shoulders.

Mackintosh was deeply worried now.

"My dear?"

"I have been having an affair with Mr Juniper," his wife said bluntly. "There, it is out."

Mackintosh was shocked into silence. His worst fears had finally come true. He had always known his wife was pretty and he was dull, he had always lived in anxiety of her running off with another man. What he had never imagined was that it would be with someone like Mr Juniper.

"Him?" he said in astonishment, pointing a finger at the aging chairman. "He is much older than me!"

Juniper winced at the comment, though it was the truth.

"I like him," Mrs Mackintosh shrugged. "Or I did, when I thought he could keep a secret."

Juniper hung his head, morose at losing the one person who had brought a little light to his life.

"Back to the point at hand," Tommy interjected, not wanting to get hung up on the details of the affair. "Mrs Mackintosh, the suspicion is that you tampered with Reed's mitt as a favour to Mr Juniper."

"What nonsense," Mrs Mackintosh said derisively. "What do I care about the cricket team?"

"It is not about the cricket team," Tommy persisted. "It would have been about helping out your... friend."

He had almost said 'lover' but had not been quite prepared to say such a thing aloud and rub salt in Mr Mackintosh's wounds.

"Well, I didn't," Mrs Mackintosh snapped. "I hardly consider this fling I have been having with Juniper worthy of such action."

Juniper was lashed by her disregard.

"We have limited options as to who could have done this thing," Tommy carried on. "If not you, or your husband, who?"

"Who told you about my association with Mr Juniper?" Mrs Mackintosh demanded.

"It came up in a conversation," Tommy said.

"A conversation with who?" Mrs Mackintosh insisted.

"I have worked hard to keep this a secret. Few people know of what I have been doing. I want to know who saw me and told you."

"I am afraid your secrecy has not been terribly effective," Annie interceded. She was fed up with Mrs Mackintosh. It was natural enough for the woman to be defensive, but that did not make Annie feel any rosier towards her and she did not like the way she was haranguing Tommy. "The rumours are everywhere. The groundskeeper had his suspicions, even."

"Who told you specifically?" Mrs Mackintosh pressed them, refusing to let them dodge the issue. "I want to know who was the one who laid this out for you. Who made you start looking my way?"

Tommy sighed.

"It was Mr Peebles who gave us the nudge," he said.

"Peebles!" Mackintosh spluttered, he nearly seemed about to have a fit. "He is the worst sort! He hates me because I have made a name for myself! I had to work for every scrap of business I have, and he resents that. He thinks just because his father and grandfather were cobblers in this town he should have a monopoly on business, even if he has a ratty old shop down a dark alley and barely anyone knows where he is. He does not advertise, and he does not have schemes in place for his repeat customers like I do. He berates me for being proactive when he is just... just lazy!"

Mackintosh seemed more furious about his rival's words than he did about the actual affair his wife was having. A thought suddenly struck him.

"He is lying!" he said. "This is all nonsense spread by my rival!"

It was a remarkable act of mental logistics, considering Mackintosh had just been told to his face by his wife that she had been having an affair.

"I don't believe it, hah! Peebles was trying to pull one over me and cause me to lose sight of my business, hah!"

Juniper looked dazed by the man's change of direction.

He opened his mouth but was waved to silence by Mrs Mackintosh.

"Look, you have our word we did not alter that mitt," she told Tommy while her husband smiled to himself, in his bubble of self-delusion. "But you will not believe us, will you?"

Tommy shook his head.

"Someone did this and all we have are denials."

"Very well," Mrs Mackintosh focused on him, proving herself more astute than her husband. "Let us consider this more fully. The alteration of the mitt could have occurred here, yes? What was the alteration?"

"The mitt had a magnet stitched inside it," Tommy answered.

"And how did that influence the game in the Cricket Bats' favour?" Mrs Mackintosh continued.

"Well, one of the match balls had a lump of metal in it so it would be inclined to fly to Reed's mitt when near enough," Tommy explained.

"Therein lies how we shall prove our innocence!" Mrs Mackintosh cried out. "For, if I am correct, the match balls are supplied by the team hosting the game?"

"Yes," Tommy concurred.

"Then, to insert a tampered ball, it must have been done at the match when the balls were produced by the Brighton team. How could we simply send a single ball to that match? It would be most odd. Someone had to place that dummy ball at the game."

Mrs Mackintosh was pleased with her assessment, she felt it proved her innocence. There was a hole in her theory, however, and Mr Juniper saw it at once. In a morose voice he declared.

"But I was at the cricket match, people will say I placed the bad ball, and they shall say I had you alter it for me," Juniper looked as if his world had crashed down around his ears. "It all comes back to me, over and over again."

Chapter Twenty-Two

"She was called the Sussex Princess," Captain Blowers explained. "Beautiful, like this liner. A gem of a ship. We plied the waters in tangent, often entering and exiting ports together. We would salute one another as we passed."

Blowers glanced over at a cabinet and went to fetch himself a drink. He did not feel it was wrong to be drinking at this time of day considering the shock he had had.

"Her captain was a good friend. I never doubted his abilities," Blowers added. "That all came up at the inquest, of course. The company did not want to imagine it was something in the design or construction of the liner that had caused the catastrophe."

"Did the captain perish on his ship?" Park-Coombs asked gently.

Blowers nodded his head.

"Captain Vernon. He stayed until the last, trying to get off as many people as possible. Not just passengers either, he looked out for his crew too."

Blowers realised he had consumed his drink already, but it had not helped at all. He stared at the empty glass and put it down in disgust.

"It was a messy business. Those that survived from the crew blamed the ship. The surviving passengers blamed the company, and the company blamed the crew. Ultimately the inquest proved there was a fault with the watertight doors. They believed they had failed and had allowed water to leak through."

"There must have been a reason the ship started taking on water in the first place," Clara said.

"Yes. They hit a mine. It was not long after the war and you know what the seas were like. Crikey, they are still full of mines. Only got to have one drift into a shipping lane and you have had it," Blowers sucked air through his teeth at the thought. "I served in the war. I saw what a mine does to a ship. It's not something you care to dwell on."

"And once the water was rushing in, with the failure of the doors the ship began to sink," Park-Coombs extrapolated. "This reminds me why I have never agreed to going with the wife on a ferry to Jersey for a holiday."

"The pumps flooded," Blowers continued. "Once they were down it was only a matter of time. The engine room was overwhelmed by water. The engineers battled on until the last to try to buy time to get the passengers off. Many perished in the effort."

Clara winced at the thought of the crewmen drowning down below, unable to escape the suffocating corridors and the swell of water.

"She went down too fast. The crew did their best to get the passengers off, but I don't need to tell you what people are like. They dither and dawdle, don't believe the situation is as dire as you are telling them, try to take papers and personal items with them. Then there are those that are physically unfit and need to be assisted off the ship. At least there were plenty of lifeboats. Those who made it to them were rescued twenty-four hours later by a French liner. Distress messages had been issued, but the lifeboats drifted from the site of the sinking and were hard to locate. No one knows what became of Vernon. He was last seen on the deck helping with the evacuation, but he never made it to the last lifeboat which took off the rest of the crew. It was assumed he had either been swept overboard or had gone to the bridge to go down with his ship. It would have broken his heart to know so many in his care had perished that day. I think he thought the only honourable thing to do was to go down with them."

It was grim talk, somehow made worse by the pleasant sunshine drifting through the window of the captain's cabin and the calm seas that seemed to deny such a ghastly thing could ever occur upon them.

"What about Gunther?" Park-Coombs asked after there had been a suitable length of silence in respect of those who had never made it off the liner.

"He was trying to close one of the watertight doors in a desperate attempt to stop the flood. He couldn't get it to seal, but refused to give in. He was being yelled at by his mates who were already on the gang ladder to the next deck. Then there was a wash of water, and he went under. He ought to have drowned, but one of his mates went under and dragged him out. He was a lucky man, with very good friends that day."

"Did he speak at the inquest?" Clara asked.

"He did, but I don't recall his specific testimony," Blowers shrugged. "I just recall his miraculous escape. He was bitter about the loss of so many."

"After an experience like that, makes you wonder how he could face a return to the sea," Park-Coombs said thoughtfully. "I would certainly reconsider my career path."

"The company offered him a place on this liner as compensation for his heroic efforts," Blowers shrugged. "The inquest concluded there had been a problem with the doors, the rubber seals had deteriorated. The final blame was laid at the feet of the company that had supplied the rubber and which was deemed inferior to what it should have been. We had all our doors refitted at that time, just in case."

"But the company blamed Vernon?" Park-Coombs asked.

"It was the easier option for them," he said. "Blame a dead man rather than a rubber maker that did not even exist anymore. Though the inquest found Vernon not to blame, our company hung to the belief that he had strayed out of a shipping lane and encountered the mine as a result. Without the mine, the ship would not have sunk and if Vernon had not hit it, there would have been no tragedy."

"Was the ship out of its shipping lane when it hit the mine?" Clara asked.

Blowers gave her a sad smile.

"Not according to the inquest, but our superiors ignored that."

"You did not take offence and consider leaving the shipping line?" Park-Coombs added.

Blowers gave him a smile at his naivety.

"Where else would I go? In any case, the captain always gets blamed for these things. No point fretting about it. Same happens in the Royal Navy. You think the Admiralty cares to be deemed culpable for poor ship design or sourcing products of inferior quality? You dig deep enough, you just know someone at the shipping line went with that rubber maker because they supplied their product at a cheaper price and that makes them just as culpable."

Blowers folded his arms and leaned against his desk. He was a realist and he saw how the world worked. He did not feel anguish over it, he just accepted it.

"Curious how all this comes back to watertight doors," Clara mused. "I always find coincidences interesting."

"It still does not explain why Gunther was shot, or who did it," Park-Coombs remarked. "Who was so worried about Gunther speaking to us?"

"We need to search the ship for the gun, but who can we ask to help us conduct the search?" Clara frowned. "Anyone could be responsible and by the time we have policemen brought out here, the culprit would have realised our intention and disposed of the gun, if they have not done so already."

Blowers looked morose at the statement but did not argue that his crew could not be trusted. He had lost faith in them around the time he realised Gunther was keeping secrets and was prepared to have people threatened. He did not have the energy to argue.

"We need to conduct a search of the crew quarters swiftly and discreetly to avoid the shooter getting a heads-up," Park-Coombs spoke his thoughts. "If we can catch them unawares, we may get lucky. Even if there is no gun, we might find something else, such as blood on their clothes."

"Just the two of us…" Clara paused and corrected herself, "the three of us, is going to mean we take a long time to search this ship."

"Then we ask for help from the passengers," Park-Coombs argued. "They are not likely suspects, not with all this seeming to link back to another sunk liner. Besides, if a passenger was wandering around down below, someone would have noticed."

Clara agreed with his argument. She ran through in her mind the possible consequences of involving passengers. They already knew about the death of Matlock but had been told it was an accident. Involving them in a search for a gun would naturally lead to everyone knowing a murder had been committed. But it might also assist in organising a search party, as the passengers were keen to get to shore and the only way to achieve that was through resolving this matter.

"We have to ask the passengers to assist us," Clara agreed after a lot of considering. "Captain Blowers, do you understand and agree?"

Blowers had sunk his head down to his chest, lost in thoughts of the nightmare he had stumbled into.

"I suppose I have no choice," he said.

"Were any other members of your crew once part of the crew of the Sussex Princess?" Clara asked.

Blowers was silent a moment, before he gave the

inevitable answer.

"Yes. I would have to write you up a list if you want names."

"I know this is a shock, Captain."

He looked up at her, his face a picture of misery as well as acceptance.

"People deserve answers, don't they?" he said. "I always thought that at the time of the Sussex Princess disaster. I wanted answers, I wanted to know what had happened to my friend. Partly you want to know so you can avoid the same mistakes, but mainly it's because you just need to learn what happened to a person you cared about. He was a good captain, was Vernon, and a hero in the war. You don't expect to survive four years of hell on water and then die on a civilian liner. It isn't the way it should happen."

Clara would have liked to have offered some sort of reassurance to Blowers, some declaration that they would find this murderer no matter what, but what could she say that sounded anything other than pointless platitudes? Whatever the outcome of all this, it was going to leave a hole in Captain Blowers' soul and spoil his remaining years in command of the liner.

Blowers, however, was a man with an iron core and though he was shaken, he was far from defeated. He would need a couple more glasses of scotch that evening to completely right him, but then he would find his path once more.

"I am not blind to the irony that I was prepared to blame my crew, or more specifically Alf Matlock, for our fate here," he said, the scotch at last opening him up. "I am no better than the shipping line, after all."

"That is somewhat unfair to yourself," Clara told him gently. "At first glance, this did look like a terrible accident."

"But I resented the appearance of the police and hired you, Miss Fitzgerald, to prove this was an accident. I was so determined to have this matter brushed aside," he hesitated, the full implication of what he had been thinking and attempting finally coming to him. "I did not want to be the one at fault. I did not want to be Captain Vernon. My selfish desire to save myself blinded me to everything else and I cannot ignore that. It makes me despise myself."

"You are really being too harsh," Park-Coombs joined the debate. "You are forgetting the shock you had received. Shock makes people act differently and often more instinctively. It makes you rush to protect yourself. Only after it has faded can you begin to appreciate the fuller situation."

"It has taken far too long for me to see there was more to this than just a sad accident," Blowers refused to be let off the hook so easily.

"We don't have time for this," Park-Coombs grumbled, his tolerance for self-pity quite slim and already at an end. "We must organise a search party. You, Captain, must have the most able passengers assemble to be assigned this task. I rely on you to weed out any who might be undesirable to the task."

Park-Coombs did not specify what this meant, leaving it up to Blowers' judgement. His tone was hard, but it seemed that it was what Blowers needed to hear at that moment and he straightened up.

"Yes, quite, I can do that. Anything else?"

"I am going to have some constables summoned across," the inspector added. "It is high time we had a bit more police presence, considering the circumstances. This matter is getting dangerous."

His words hung over them all. Things were getting dangerous, but who was in the most peril next? Need they fear for themselves or was another crew member about to perish in mysterious circumstances?

"I shall have to notify the company about all this," Blowers said, mostly to himself. "At least I can now demonstrate we need further time, though I imagine I shall receive further blame for allowing the situation to occur in the first place. In all matters, things end at the captain."

Blowers paused, his eyes drifting out to the sea. He had

made his life on the waves, had never known anything else and had been happy with his choices until that very day. Now he saw everything differently. What had he done with his life, really? He had devoted it to the sea and to a shipping company, for what?

"Vernon had the right idea, you know? Go down with the ship, commit one final act of honour and choose your own way of ending things," Blowers pulled a bleak smile onto his face. "I guess I do not have that choice."

Chapter Twenty-Three

"What do we do now?" Annie asked the room.

It was a good question, what were they supposed to do now? The Mackintoshes denied they had tampered with the mitt. Mr Juniper denied he had anything to do with the matter despite the implications of Mr Peebles, and back in Brighton Jim Reed was denying he had plotted to cheat at the match. They all sat in silence a while, considering the problem.

"I could have done it," Juniper said miserably. "I am not saying I did, but I could have. I was at the match and could have placed the tampered ball in among the others. How can I prove I didn't do it?"

He looked hopelessly at them all.

"This is going to ruin me!"

"What about me?" Mackintosh snapped at the chairman. "You have stolen my wife away from me and placed my business in peril!"

"And what about me?" Mrs Mackintosh glared first at her husband and then at Mr Juniper. "What of my reputation?"

No one had much of an answer for her since her problems stemmed from her own decisions. They were at an impasse.

"I suppose it all has to come down to motive, in the end," Tommy said. "Why was this thing done? Mr Juniper denies his team needed the help to win the match and, knowing the quality of the Hove Cricket Bats, I must say he has a point. It would be far too risky to cheat at the match when they were almost certain to win anyway. Both you, Mr Mackintosh, and your wife, only had reason to tamper with the mitt if you were asked to do so by someone important, willing to pay you. That would likely be Mr Juniper again, which brings us back to the same problem."

Juniper was nodding in understanding.

"I see how this all sits," he said. "But are you sure Reed did not pay Mr Mackintosh to tamper with the glove? Reed may have started to doubt his own competency as a fielder."

"I already said I did not do it!" Mackintosh yelled at them, his temper up. "Reed never asked me to do anything to that mitt!"

Tommy held up a hand to placate him. Mackintosh did not want to be placated. He wanted to be left alone, to contemplate the crime that had been committed against him by his wife, as he saw things. The trust she had broken, and the treachery shown him by a fellow man. This had to be the worst Saturday of Mackintosh's life and he was not going to forget it soon.

"Look, let us stop speculating and try to focus on facts," Annie interjected, trying to get them back on track. "The problem we are faced with, Mr Mackintosh, is that the mitt had to have been tampered with while it was at your shop. If it had been tampered with before, you would have noticed the alteration, and once the mitt was returned to Reed it would be very difficult for anyone to access it and change it. Therefore, the likeliest time something happened was while it was here."

"Again, I did not…"

"Mr Mackintosh, I am not accusing you directly, I am saying you need to think hard and consider if there was any time when the mitt could have been accessed by someone else?" Annie persisted.

Mr Mackintosh opened his mouth and shut it like a fish out of water. He was a proud man and for so many reasons he did not want to admit to being negligent when he was looking after the mitt yet denying anyone could have gained access to it was placing him in a terrible position.

Mackintosh fell into silence, sucked in his lower lip, and gnawed on it. His wife was watching him intensely but did not come to his aid.

"This is pointless," Juniper sighed. "Why would anyone do this after all? I shall have to accept my fate, even though I am guilty of nothing except feeling rather lonely and reaching out to another person."

His words were for Mrs Mackintosh, a vague attempt to win her back to him. It did not work. She had hardened to him as he had revealed their secret and she would not even meet his eyes. Tommy felt that if anyone was cold enough to calculate how to tamper with a mitt and do so without regard for the people it would implicate, it would surely be Mrs Mackintosh and he found himself almost convinced she had done it. They just needed a little more proof to wrap things up.

Several minutes had passed, no one sure what to say or do. Tommy was about ready to leave, feeling that nothing more could be done here.

Then Mr Mackintosh looked up.

"There was one thing," he said, his voice hoarse as he was forced to reveal his secret. "We had a break-in one night. Nothing was taken. I thought the culprits must have been after money and could not get my safe open."

"This was while the mitt was here?" Tommy clarified.

"Yes," Mr Mackintosh nodded. "I had no reason at the time to suppose the mitt had been touched. I keep all my work in a set of pigeonholes screwed to the wall. The mitt was in the same hole I had left it in the night before."

"You never told me about a break-in," Mrs Mackintosh

glanced at her husband suspiciously.

"I did not want to worry you and, as I said, nothing was taken," he replied.

Tommy was not sure he believed this convenient story.

"How did the intruder get in?" he asked.

"They forced the lock on the back door. They were clever because I heard nothing. I have since replaced the lock," Mackintosh was beginning to see his way out of this mess. "Let me show you."

He took them all downstairs and into his workshop. There was a corridor running along the side of the room and at the end of this was a door leading onto the yard beyond.

Mackintosh pointed out where he had removed the broken lock and replaced it with a new one. The change was obvious, the new lock not sitting precisely in the same place as the old one.

"I never really gave it a thought," Mackintosh explained. "The safe was still locked, after all."

Tommy ran a finger around the new lock, noting where paint was missing beneath and indicated the site the old lock had sat.

"Supposing whoever broke in was not here for money," Mr Mackintosh continued. "But was here to alter the mitt. I never would have known."

"It is very possible," Juniper said, only too keen to jump onto this idea which would protect him from scandal too.

Tommy opened the door out of curiosity and looked into the yard. Evening was fast setting in, and the small yard was glowing with orange light. There was a gate at the far end, probably unlocked, even if it was locked, the walls were not so high and the sort that were straightforward to climb over.

"The intruder could have used my tools," Mackintosh pressed on, seeing he had not quite convinced Tommy. "What a perfect ploy! They could make it seem that only I had the opportunity to tamper with the mitt! It is very cunning."

"Someone needed to be capable of the leatherworking skills necessary to alter the mitt without the changes being obvious. Not just anyone could do this," Tommy said. "Once again we are back to asking why someone would want to mess around with the mitt?"

Mr Mackintosh tapped his fingers together anxiously, he wanted to offer them a culprit, he just did not know who he might suggest.

"I wonder where the cricket balls used for the match came from?" Annie said abruptly. "I presume all cricket balls carry their maker's mark upon them? So you can know who made them. The person who tampered with a cricket ball would need to have known that, so they could slip in the altered ball without it being spotted."

It was a good point.

"We buy our balls from Willis and Co.," Tommy explained. "We have always gone to them. They send them down from London."

"The Cricket Bats prefer balls from Farndon and Sons," Mr Juniper explained. "We have an arrangement with them which goes back many years."

"Then, whoever changed the ball, had to know to use a Willis and Co. one," Annie said. "I raise this point because, quite frankly, I have no idea who makes cricket balls, and I would likely not even think about checking I had altered a ball from the correct manufacturer."

"You are suggesting someone with inside knowledge of how cricket games work did it?" Mr Juniper said miserably, because once again the finger of blame had swung in his direction. He was an obvious choice for knowing what company the Brighton Badgers bought their balls from.

"This is not helping," complained Mrs Mackintosh.

"I don't know, I think it does a bit," Tommy corrected her. "You see, Mr Mackintosh has already stated he lacks any interest or knowledge of cricket. Yet, whoever did this was very aware of how the game worked and the intricacies of the games' arrangements."

"Mackintosh could be lying," Annie reminded him.

"Now a man's word is not good enough!" Mackintosh snapped at her.

Annie ignored him. Tommy was thinking hard. None of the evidence he had seen explicitly got Mackintosh off the hook, but it did raise possibilities.

"Who has a strong enough grudge against you Mr Mackintosh to wish to see you in trouble?" Tommy asked.

Mackintosh was startled.

"What do you mean?"

"We seem to have ruled out that the game was rigged because someone feared the Cricket Bats could not beat the Badgers. If we eliminate the motive of seeing the Bats win the game, then we must ask ourselves what was the point?" Tommy looked directly at Mackintosh. "It seems to me that there is one other reason someone would go to such trouble. They wanted the cheating to be discovered and they wanted the blame for the tampered mitt to fall on you, Mr Mackintosh. They wanted to ruin you."

Mackintosh was startled by this information, but he had to admit it did make a sort of sense.

"You mean, look at one of our rivals?" Mrs Mackintosh was quicker to catch up. "We are not popular among the long-established cobblers in Hove. They see us as intruders who have slipped in to steal their trade."

Tommy nodded.

"Jealousy can lead a person to do remarkable things. Desperate, terrible things."

Mackintosh was looking alarmed by this discovery. He glanced at his busted door and thought of that morning he had come down and found it open. It had been nearly ten before he had noticed, and the only reason he had become aware the door was damaged was because he heard it banging in the wind and went to look. It had given him a shock, but it had always seemed odd that nothing had been taken. He could understand the safe being too difficult for the thief to break open, but they could have taken tools or other small items to sell. After noticing the door, he had gone through his whole workshop looking for anything missing, but there was nothing, nothing at all.

"There are plenty of other cobblers in town," Mrs Mackintosh said grimly.

"How many are angry enough to do something like this?" Tommy persisted. "So angry they would concoct this elaborate scheme and go to all this trouble, in the hopes blame would fall back on you? They must have spent hours plotting it all out and they had to rely on a number of coincidental things occurring to see it through. For a start, if we had not realised Reed could not possibly have made the alterations himself, well, he would have been blamed for the cheating and no mischief would have befallen you, Mr Mackintosh."

Mackintosh was frowning, trying to appreciate what they were telling him. It was the most curious thing he had heard. Someone had gone to all this effort because they disliked him and his shop?

"What could I have done to offend someone so?" he said. "I have never bad mouthed my rivals or deliberately stolen their trade. I just get on with my work and strive hard to ensure people notice where I am. Is that so wrong?"

"There is enough trade to go around," Mrs Mackintosh insisted. "Besides, we are about the only cobblers this side of the town and thus we are stealing trade from no one."

"Except for Mr Peebles," Annie said quietly.

Her remark could have been easy to miss, it had been spoken in such an undertone as if she was just thinking aloud, but once it was out, it held everyone's attention.

"Peebles," Mackintosh hissed the name. "He thinks I am to blame for him ruining his father's business. Have you seen his shop? It is this dingy cavern down a back alley. Why would anyone rush there?"

"It was Mr Peebles who told us about Mrs Mackintosh having an affair with Mr Juniper," Annie added.

Mackintosh growled because he had forgotten that in the commotion.

Tommy was rubbing at his chin, thoughtful.

"Peebles does have a vendetta against you, Mr Mackintosh. He sees it as a personal affront that you set up shop so close to him. He thinks you are stealing his trade."

"Mr Peebles took it badly when we decided to remove our custom from him and switch to Mr Mackintosh," Juniper said. "The decision was not made lightly, but Peebles had been late a few times with repairs and there had been some remarks about the quality of his work. He did not have quite the mastery of his father or grandfather. We had some sample work done by Mr Mackintosh and were very satisfied."

"I was not aware that Peebles had previously supplied the cricket team," Mackintosh added. "It would explain his hatred towards me."

"Hatred enough to concoct such a complex scheme?" Juniper said.

"Well, to prove it was him we shall need something concrete," Tommy considered. "It would be useful if someone saw him at the cricket match, especially as he told us he dislikes the sport. He had to have been there if he was the culprit, to switch in the tampered cricket ball and to remove and hide it and the mitt in the pond when the crime was discovered."

Tommy was trying to recall if he had seen Mr Peebles at the match, but he could not say he had. Then again, he had not been looking for him, or paying much heed to the spectators.

"We should talk to him," Mackintosh said, looking fired up. "He has some explaining to do!"

Chapter Twenty-Four

Captain Blowers had the ship's stewards go from passenger cabin to passenger cabin asking any able-bodied male passengers to gather in the main dining room. Clara would have preferred if he had not specified only male passengers attend, but Blowers went over her head and she did not think it was the right time to press him on the matter of female equality. He looked like a man watching his world fall apart. She completely believed, if the opportunity arose, he would rather go down with his ship than be faced by this nightmare. She hoped there was no chance of that happening. Escaping a sinking ship was not on her agenda for the day.

Park-Coombs had gone to the wireless room and had a telegraph sent to the police station to summon as many constables as were free to the ship. He was expecting the summons to take considerable time. He wandered back into the dining room, taking a long look at the ornately arranged tables with smart glassware and cutlery. The sort of tableware a humble police inspector could never expect to dine off. Not a chip, not a scratch, nor a hint of tarnish marred any of the dinnerware in the room. It could almost make a man afraid to touch it.

"How the other half live," he remarked to Clara as he drew closer.

"This is the first-class dining room," she replied. "There is also a second class, and a third class. I checked. I am not sure quite which division I would fall into, though I rather fancy it would not be this level."

"Which class do you have to be in to need to bring your own sandwiches?" Park-Coombs asked.

"Steerage," Clara smirked at him.

"Sounds about right," he chuckled.

The passengers were arriving in dribs and drabs. They looked either anxious or angry to a man. They were still waiting on news as to when they would reach harbour and be able to get on with their lives. Despite asking for only able-bodied men to attend, Clara saw a number of elderly gentlemen and several women had opted to ignore the prerequisite. In the latter case, she was rather pleased.

As the dining room began to fill, the noise level increased with the muttering of the discontented. Blowers winced at the sight of them all. This was not a meeting he relished hosting.

When it seemed everyone had arrived, Captain Blowers had the stewards leave and close the doors behind them. Clara had convinced him that even his stewards were under suspicion, even Lieutenant Harper. He had been despondent at this information but had accepted it eventually.

"Gentlemen," he addressed the room, ignoring the presence of the ladies, or perhaps failing to notice them as his mind was rather occupied. "Thank you for coming. We have a pressing matter before us, and I need your assistance if we are to resolve it and have this ship moving again as soon as possible."

Silence greeted his announcement. Not even an angry remark disturbed the quiet. That made things all the worse. Captain Blowers cleared his throat and carried on.

"We are now certain there is a murderer aboard this ship. He is targeting the crew, not passengers," Blowers said this in haste when a ripple of alarm went through the crowd. "You have nothing to fear, however, we shall not be able to leave this place until the culprit is found. We cannot make port until we have a suspect in custody in case he jumps ship and eludes us. The police will not allow us to leave the shores of Brighton until we have our man in shackles."

Blowers motioned to Inspector Park-Coombs, quite obviously trying to deflect some of the passengers outrage. Park-Coombs did not care. He had a broad back and was used to people despising him.

"I need to ask for your assistance to resolve this matter," Blowers continued. "We need to search this ship for a gun. It may already have been consigned to the ocean, but if it is here, we must find it. It shall lead us to our culprit and speed up our departure."

There were mumblings in the crowd and people started to speak up.

"You are asking your passengers to search for a killer?" one man demanded.

"I cannot ask my crew, as we believe the culprit is among them," Blowers admitted. "I need this done speedily and quietly so that the murderer does not get wind of what we are doing until it is too late."

"Why can't the police do this?" someone else demanded.

Park-Coombs stepped forward to respond.

"I have summoned constables from Brighton, but it will take time for them to arrive and there will only be a handful to spare. Waiting for them will cause a further delay, which I thought you would prefer to avoid."

He threw the complaint back at them. The crowd of passengers rumbled with discontent.

"You will not just be looking for a gun," Park-Coombs went on. "We want you to keep your eyes peeled for anything unusual. Clothing marked with blood, for instance. We need something to lead us to our killer. He has to have left some clue behind."

The crowd was mollified, until another voice rose from

the midst of them.

"Why does this even concern us? It was a crewman who died, not any of us. Why should we care? I demand we are allowed to reach harbour. I have important business to attend to!"

Park-Coombs scanned the crowd until he located the man who had spoken up.

"I care," he said. "When it comes to my work, it does not matter to me how important the victim was, how much money he earned or what he did for a living. It matters to me he was killed, and I am responsible for finding his killer. You can either assist me, or you can go back to your cabin and wait. But you will not be leaving here until I find my murderer."

"This is preposterous!" someone yelled, and the crowd became restless, throwing accusations at Park-Coombs and Blowers that they were dragging their feet on purpose.

"The shipping company will hear my complaint! I shall never use this line again!"

"I shall have you struck off as a captain for allowing a murder to occur on your ship!"

"I demand compensation! I lost a lucrative business deal because of this!"

The insults and threats flew at Blowers, and he weathered them for about as long as he could before his strained nerves snapped. He was done with this, done with the temperamental passengers who did not want to help him, but only to make his life harder. He was starting to think there was no way he would get out of this situation retaining his position and that realisation dimmed his usual patience with irate passengers. When he next spoke, it was with a bellow that could have silenced a mutiny.

"I am done with you all! I would rather this ship had sunk like the Sussex Princess and drowned you ghastly people than to have to endure your petulance! Years ago, a dear friend and fellow captain went down with his ship making the effort to save people like you. He believed it was his duty and up until the last hour or so, I would have agreed with him. Now, I am not so sure I would not gladly see you all at the bottom!"

His outburst, blunt as it was, silenced them all. What could you say when the man charged with your safe passage confessed he would prefer everyone aboard drowned?

Clara decided it was time to intercede. She moved before Blowers before he could make the matter worse.

"This is a nasty business," she began. "A young man died in a dreadful fashion, and someone tried to make it look like an accident. We are not certain, but this may have a link to the sinking of the Sussex Princess when many people lost their lives. If that is the case, if somehow this tragedy is linked to that terrible event, then we are looking at a case of mass murder. Supposing there was someone aboard that ship who was instrumental in the failure of the watertight doors? I am not saying that is the case, I am not even saying I know how it would happen, but if that were true, then perhaps that person is now trying to cover their tracks?

"Innocent people, just like you, died that day. If you cannot bring yourself to search this ship for a killer, for the sake of a young, diligent man who was just trying to do his job, then perhaps you can do it for those people, those fellow passengers, who never made it off the Princess. They deserve justice, just as Alf Matlock does."

The room was still. Clara was stretching a point to link the sinking of the Sussex Princess with the death of Alf. She did not see a connection as yet, except for that slip of paper in Shaun Gunther's pocket and a hunch that something bigger was at play here, something more than just the awful death of Matlock.

No one spoke for a while, then a woman in her fifties, stout and wearing a dress a good decade out of fashion, gently pushed her way to the front of the crowd.

"My brother was aboard that ship," she said solemnly. "He was one of those drowned. I never felt there was a good answer for what occurred that day. It seemed as if no one wanted to be considered responsible. He was a good man, my brother, a very good man."

Her words hung in the air. There was an expectant pause, as if it was imagined someone else would come forward to tell their story of loss onboard the Sussex Princess, but no one did. It was Captain Blowers who finally added to the saga.

"A man has been murdered. A man who was a hero of that distant day. Shaun Gunther tried to buy the liner more time by dragging a watertight door shut. He nearly drowned in the effort and lost his hearing in one ear. He was also a hero of the last war. He never shirked his duty, even when it put him in peril. We should all consider that example."

His words were poignant and had the effect he had hoped. Combined with the woman's story of a lost brother, the tale had brought a new mood over the passengers, and they were no longer still surly.

Well, for the most part, and those who could not see beyond their selfishness were thankfully in the minority.

"Will you help me search this ship?" Blowers asked, his tone calm now.

He scanned his eyes across the passengers. He had resigned himself to losing his position, especially after his outburst. He just wanted to end on a positive note, successfully finding a murderer.

"I will help," a smartly dressed young man raised his hand. "I would rather be a part of helping us out of this situation than simply sitting around and complaining."

His pointed words sparked a plethora of offers to help. Captain Blowers was relieved. It did not take long to have a sizeable search party to hand. Those who did not offer to help, either because they did not care or were too frail to be of use, were dismissed.

Clara noted that nearly all the women who had come to the assembly remained and stubbornly stood among the men of the search party. This cheered her no end.

Captain Blowers turned to his search party, surveying

them as if they were new recruits to his crew. He was pleased at the number who had volunteered though, unlike Clara, he was rather concerned about the women present.

"There are enough of you to split you into groups to search each deck," he said. "Inspector Park-Coombs has advised that the focus of our attention will be crew quarters, looking for the gun or anything else that could be considered suspicious. I cannot outline what precisely that might be and must rely on your judgement. You shall also be looking in other areas, such as storerooms and along the corridors for potential places to hide a gun. We may be looking for a needle in a haystack, but I know you shall all be diligent in your searching."

As he finished, Clara stepped forward to speak.

"I would like you to keep your eyes open for anything that could relate to the Sussex Princess. It is rather a long-shot, I admit, but I have this inkling it is important we consider it. You may find certain of the crew were once aboard that vessel, if you come across anything of interest, please report it at once and who you found it with."

Clara nodded at Captain Blowers to indicate she had said what she wanted. He took a deep breath.

"I want to thank you in advance for your assistance. This is an unprecedented event for a ship's captain, but I feel if we work together, we shall have this situation resolved swiftly. None of us want to be stuck here any longer than necessary. That is why we are working together."

Captain Blowers started to split the passengers into smaller search parties. He assigned leaders for the groups, as best he could as he did not really know people, and arbitrarily told them which deck they would search. He would have liked to offer them maps of the lower decks, considering how labyrinthine they were, but he did not have any. The best he could do was explain the rough layout of the lower levels and advise how best to search through them.

This done, the search parties were all escorted to the

main gangway and then to their relevant floors. Clara and Park-Coombs held back, watching on. There was nothing more they could do now.

"I was thinking," Park-Coombs said. "We never really looked through Alf Matlock's belongings. There did not seem much point when we thought he had been the victim of an accident. Now I am wondering if there might be something among his things that could help us."

Clara nodded.

"It is worth a shot, though any clever killer would have already been through them and made sure there was nothing there."

"Even clever killers can miss things," Park-Coombs smiled. "Anyway, it will pass the time while we wait for our search parties to return."

Clara glanced over at the disappearing backs of the last of the passengers.

"Think they will find anything?" she said.

"I am not holding my breath," the inspector admitted. "However, you never know and right now, anything we do is better than doing nothing at all."

Chapter Twenty-Five

Mr Peebles was not happy to see them. They walked into his shop just before closing time, Tommy and Annie ahead so he could not see Mr and Mrs Mackintosh until it was too late for him to deny them entry. Mr Juniper came last, looking sorrowful and wishing he was not there at all.

Peebles opened his mouth to protest, his eyes blazing with fury at the sight of his rival. Tommy put up a hand to stop him before he began

"We have some questions for you, Mr Peebles. Difficult questions."

"I am closing up," Peebles reacted. "I am done for the day."

Mackintosh glanced around his shop in a dramatic fashion.

"I would say you are done for good," he said sniffily.

Tommy wanted to yell at him how unproductive such a comment was, but he bit his tongue instead and focused on the matter at hand.

"Mr Peebles, a serious incidence of cheating has occurred at a cricket match."

"You told me," Peebles said haughtily. "Someone

messed around with a cricket mitt and a ball."

His eyes flicked to Mackintosh.

"I also recall you were fairly confident who the culprit was."

"I never did this!" Mackintosh snapped.

"The mitt was in your care," Peebles shrugged. "Reed seemed to think you were a better choice to take care of it than someone with experience."

"Your father had experience, your grandfather had experience, you are barely fit to sew a button on a boot! You buy in your shoes!" Mackintosh waved his hand in the direction of the shoe display, a bone of contention he knew would get a reaction from Peebles.

"I can't help it if people want mass produced shoes these days!" Peebles retorted. "You have to move with the times!"

"But not move out of this dingy alley which might actually save your business!"

"My great grandfather help lay the bricks for this shop!" Peebles was up on his toes as he yelled at his rival. "He painted the original sign!"

"And his great grandson will be the one who takes it down when this place goes under," Mackintosh responded coldly. "Think about that."

"You are a nasty man, Mr Mackintosh. Just because you have come to this business new, and have no time for the traditional ways, you think that makes you better than the rest of us, let me tell you it does not! You are worse, with your fancy workshop and modern gadgets, your pigeonholes for all the work you get and your smart sewing machine. Latest model, is it? Must have cost a pretty penny, but does it sew better than I can by hand?"

Peebles's eyes seemed to be bulging as he made his accusation. Silence followed his outburst from Mr Mackintosh, but it was not because Mackintosh had been cowed, it was because he had heard something that puzzled him.

"How do you know what I have in my workshop?" he

said.

Peebles blinked.

"It is a workshop," he shrugged. "A cobbler's workshop."

"But you knew about my new sewing machine that I only got last month," Mackintosh went on. "I haven't mentioned it to anyone, why would I? It is very useful, but I am not the sort to brag. The only way you could know about it, is if you had seen it."

Peebles was now blinking very rapidly; his cheeks were puffing in and out as he tried to regroup.

"I guessed," he said, when no other excuse came to mind.

"No, you did not," Mackintosh said quietly. "How could you guess that? You must have seen it. You must have been in my workshop, and I certainly did not invite you."

Peebles was caught out and was desperately trying to think of a logical reason how he had known about the sewing machine. His mind had gone ominously blank, and he winced.

"When we discussed the possibility of you, Mr Peebles, breaking into our shop and tampering with the mitt, it seemed extraordinary to me," Mrs Mackintosh said softly. Her voice seemed to cut through the tension and had them turn her way. "I did not think it could be possible. Yet, clearly it was."

Peebles was weighing up his options and struggling to find any. Denial seemed his only choice.

"I have done nothing of the sort, what type of man do you think I am?"

"Mr Peebles, I am afraid none of us believe you," Tommy told him calmly.

Peebles glanced between their faces, looking for some indication of hope that at least one of them was having doubts about the accusations. He saw nothing to help him.

"Were you paid to do it?" Mackintosh asked. "Or was it just about making me look bad?"

Peebles opened and shut his mouth, helpless to explain

himself. With a shaking hand he wiped a bead of sweat off his forehead.

"Really, this is all preposterous," he muttered to himself. "I am a professional."

They waited for him to say something more convincing. He did not have anything to add.

"Mr Peebles, we need you to come with us to the Brighton Cricket Club. You have a number of questions to answer, and it would be best if we discuss this only once, rather than me reporting your words," Tommy told him.

Peebles laughed at them.

"I am not going anywhere. I have my shop to close, the takings to count…"

"You have takings for today?" Mackintosh mocked him.

Peebles pulled himself up proudly.

"You are a rude oaf Mr Mackintosh."

"And you tried to ruin me!" Mackintosh pointed an accusing finger. "Whatever you think of me, I have never done anything to deliberately affect your business."

"Except to open your shop just down the road from mine! You knew exactly what you were doing! You had every intention of stealing my trade from me!"

"Nonsense!" Mackintosh laughed, but there was something a little forced to the sound.

"You could have set up your shop anywhere, anywhere at all, but you picked a place close to mine so you would take my trade! Not just new trade either, but my regular customers too. Did you think I would not notice? Mrs Cartwright came in here and told me how you referred to my work as slipshod and unreliable and offered to undercut my price for the same work!"

"Mrs Cartwright failed to mention that she came to me because she was disappointed with the repair work you had done on her favourite pair of boots," Mackintosh retorted. "She showed me how the stitching you had done was coming apart and asked me to make the repairs. She did not say who had done the work, just that it was another cobbler. I told her the stitches appeared to be slipshod and sewn in an unreliable fashion without knowing they were yours, and I stand by that statement. As for the price, I charged her what I always charge for such work. I do not even know your prices, so it would be impossible for me to undercut them."

"Then why did she come to me and say all those things?" Peebles demanded.

"People are complicated," Mackintosh shrugged. "Perhaps she felt guilty about coming to me afterwards and criticising your work. But I bet you have had no further shoe repairs from her."

Peebles fell silent because Mrs Cartwright had not been to his shop for some time. She used to be quite a regular as someone who liked to get the most out of her shoes. She always had a new pair of slippers from him at Christmas, and she used to come in every couple of months for little things – a new pair of laces for her husband's dress shoes, stopping leaks in her wellingtons, and having her grandson's school shoes cleaned and repaired.

Peebles was also happening to think how the only reason she had come into his shop that day at all, was because she was picking up a pair leather work gloves he had been fixing for her husband. She had seemed out of sorts and fluttery, a touch nervous, in fact. Now he thought about it, she seemed to want to blurt out her story of going to Mr Mackintosh and having her shoes repaired, like she could only face him if she confessed her sin.

"Mrs Cartwright came into my shop just last week," Mackintosh drove home his victory. "She was after shoe polish."

Peebles' eyes went to the large display of shoe polish in his window. Getting dusty through lack of sales.

"If you had never come along, she would still be coming to me!" he said, missing the point and returning to an old hurt that soothed his guilty conscience.

"You mean, if she had no choice?" Mackintosh said coldly.

The insult hit home, and Peebles shut up. He curled his

hands into fists on the surface of his counter and pretended none of this was happening.

"I am going nowhere," he told them. "And you cannot make me."

In that regard he was perfectly correct. It was Annie who broke the stalemate. She stepped forward, right up to Mr Peebles' counter and looked him in the face. This required her to look up a fraction.

"Mr Peebles, I am in no doubt you did this thing. You condemned yourself by revealing details of Mr Mackintosh's workshop that only someone who had been there could know, and we all know you would not visit his workshop on friendly terms. It seems to me you did this all out of spite. You were upset that your own work had been criticised and wanted to hurt Mr Mackintosh by insinuating he would assist a man to cheat.

"Honestly, this petty rivalry between the pair of you is childish, and that may even be insulting to children," she glared at him. "You are grown men who make choices, and you have chosen to start this stupid war between each other."

"I have not declared war!" Mackintosh piped up.

Annie's surly gaze was spun upon him, and he regretted opening his mouth.

"You, Mr Mackintosh, opted to place your shop in a position where it could steal trade from Mr Peebles. You may claim it was a coincidence, but he is right, you could have gone further away. Instead, you set yourself up as his rival and I do not believe you have no idea of what he charges, so that you can charge just a little less."

Mackintosh was going to bluster out a denial. Tommy reached for his arm and shook his head. He understood his implication.

Annie swung back to Peebles who had been enjoying seeing his rival taken down a peg or two. He had a grin on his face which he rapidly lost when Annie faced him.

"As for you, Mr Peebles, I could say a lot of things, but it shall suffice to state that your actions have not only hurt

Mr Mackintosh, but Mr Reed who was wholly innocent in this affair."

"Innocent?" Peebles pulled a face of bitterness at the word. "He went to Edinburgh to have his mitt made. No cobbler in Hove was worthy of the task, apparently. He is just as bad as Mackintosh."

Peebles folded his arms and would not be moved on the subject.

"What about the Hove cricket team? Are all of them culpable to your mind?" Annie asked.

Peebles hesitated, just for a moment.

"That is not the same."

"It is the same, Mr Peebles. Because of your actions, the whole team will be tarnished as cheats. No one will believe that the other players knew nothing of the rigged mitt, just as no one believes Reed is innocent. Your actions are remarkably vindictive, all for the sake of…" Annie was going to indicate the shop, ask how a man could do something so awful for the sake of his business, but then she realised what she was saying. She softened her tone, lacing it with understanding and sympathy. "This is your family business, not just the cobbling, this very shop. Leaving here would seem like a betrayal of your father and grandfather, and great grandfather, wouldn't it?"

Peebles dipped his head.

"Yes," he said, licking his lips. "I grew up here. I can't just leave it."

"And you can't fail either, because that would be failing your family," Annie nodded. "Mr Peebles, family ties can put a lot of pressure upon us and cause us to do things that at any other time we would not consider rational. That does not make them right."

Peebles seemed to feel the shop like a weight upon his back. He looked around him, at the old fixtures and fittings, the display dummies that went back to the time of his grandfather. This was a place of memories, a means of connecting to his past. He would fight tooth and claw to save it because this was all he had left.

"You… you can't prove anything," he said. "You can't prove I was in Mackintosh's workshop."

"I don't think we need to," Annie told him. "You will come with us to see the players at Brighton and explain yourself."

"I won't!" Peebles snapped.

Annie just stared at him. He tried to match her gaze, but Annie had been schooled by a master of hard staring in the form of Clara. She had been naturally gifted in the matter to begin with as well.

"Then we shall bring the cricket team here, both cricket teams," Annie replied. "It shall be quite something, all those men in cricket whites on your doorstep. It will draw attention, especially when they start to get angry about what you did."

"You cannot…" Peebles had visions of angry cricketers outside his shop, making complaints that he had cheated them and having all the street hear it. "It would ruin me."

"We either do this privately and discreetly, or we do it in public," Tommy hammered home Annie's ultimatum. "You can choose Mr Peebles."

He did not add that the logistics of bringing both cricket teams here, along with umpires and Mr Hardcastle boggled the mind and he was desperate for Peebles to agree to go with them.

"You are cruel!" Peebles threw at them, flustered. "You are all cruel!"

No one responded. They waited.

Peebles dropped his head into one hand, feeling as if this had been the longest day of his life. He was not prepared to admit to what he had done. He did not feel the guilt Annie had tried to encourage in him. He was worried about bad publicity, however. He could not afford it, not with everything else that was happening.

He realised he was over a barrel, and he was not getting out without making a choice. He grimaced, angry at his accusers, angry at the world, but especially angry with Mr Mackintosh who seemed to symbolise every reason things were going wrong for him.

"Well, Mr Peebles?" Tommy asked him. "What is your decision?"

Chapter Twenty-Six

After his passing, Alf Matlock's belongings had been taken to the storage area of the ship and placed in one of the vast lockers were the passengers' luggage was held. Captain Blowers told them where to look, then went back to considering damage control for this whole hopeless voyage. Clara felt sorry for him, he really had been placed in a terrible position and though none of this was his fault, he would surely be blamed for it by his employers. She did not think she could arrange a happy outcome for Captain Blowers, no matter how hard she tried, the best she might be able to do would be to prove he was not to blame for this debacle and had done everything in his power to keep the voyage going.

They found the storage area was manned by a single steward at that time of day. He kept an eye on things, for on a ship so vast you could never rule out the potential for an opportunistic thief and there would be nothing worse than a passenger discovering their property had been pilfered while they were happily in their cabin. The steward was naturally suspicious of their arrival and hesitated to show them Alf's belongings, until Inspector Park-Coombs pulled rank and suggested he communicate with Captain Blowers if he needed further clarification.

The steward took a good look at Park-Coombs, considering whether he thought he looked like a police inspector or not. He came to the conclusion he did and agreed to show them to where he had put Alf's things.

"Not that he had much," he said as he escorted them, now quite talkative as he had decided they were acceptable in his domain. "None of those sorts have much."

"Those sort?" Park-Coombs asked before Clara could.

"Lower crewmen," the steward shrugged. "They only have a bunk to call their own, so they can't have much, can they? No space for it."

His comment, though poorly put, was apparently not malicious and rather a statement upon the conditions his fellow crewmen laboured under.

"They usually keep a bag of things," he continued. "You know the sort of haversack thing I mean? Swing it over a shoulder when you move on. Now, the likes of me, being a steward and with more responsibilities, I have a cabin. It is in down here in storage, admittedly, but it is still a cabin. I have a lot more belongings. It would take quite the effort to clear them all out."

The steward whistled at the thought.

"I have collected knickknacks from all the places we have visited, and I have them all about the cabin. Still, I suppose if I died suddenly, they would just lock up my cabin until they reached port."

He was quite cheerful about this notion, clearly satisfied it would never occur. He took them to a locker, which was the size of a small room and lined with shelving units that were fixed to the floor and walls. Each shelf had a rope running across its front to prevent larger objects from tumbling off in high seas. Smaller objects were arranged in wooden boxes, that looked like drawers from a dresser. These could then be placed on the same shelves and would be prevented from falling off by the rope.

The steward started to fudge around on a shelf, going through several sacks that looked similar to one another until he discovered the one he wanted.

"Alf's bag," he said, dragging out the canvas bag which had been labelled with a cardboard tag. "It is terrible what happened, you know. Dreadful. It should not have occurred, what with the doors closing so slowly."

"It is a mystery," Clara remarked.

The steward handed over the bag.

"Why all this fuss when it was an accident?"

"Was it an accident?" Park-Coombs asked darkly.

The steward stared at him. A man of plain thinking, the comment had thrown him. He did not do subtlety.

"That's what I said."

"You said?"

"It was an accident," the steward frowned. "Why did you repeat me?"

Park-Coombs opened his mouth to snap something, then decided to be nice instead.

"I meant, there is a possibility Alf did not die in an accident."

The steward's face fell as the horror of this caught up with him. It was apparent why he had the job down here. He was not imaginative enough to contemplate stealing anything, he would not have the first idea what to do with anything he took, and his black and white view of the world kept him, mostly, from being manipulated by those who were criminally inclined and might try to get past him.

"That is terrible!" he said at last and then looked like he needed to lie down.

"Is there somewhere private we could look through this bag?" Clara asked him, before he became completely lost in his thoughts.

"There is, well, my little office. I suppose."

The steward took them back the way they had come and to a cramped office that just about fitted in a narrow table and chair, along with a ledger for recording the property in his keeping and a large box full of cardboard tags that looked the same as the one attached to Alf's bag.

"Do you want me to stay?" he asked uncertainly.

"Only if you want to," Park-Coombs told him in a voice that plainly stated he would rather the steward left.

The steward, on this occasion, took the hint and departed without a murmur.

"Thank goodness for that," Park-Coombs groaned as he hefted Alf's bag onto the table and pulled open the buckles that kept it closed. "Still expecting to find something?"

"Inspector, I avoid expecting anything, as that is dangerous territory for an investigator of crime."

"Good answer," Park-Coombs smirked, then he started to pull out Alf's belongings.

There was a change of clothes, a few pairs of socks, some handkerchiefs, a smart cap for any occasion when Alf might be called on to be present before the captain and a spotted blue neckerchief with the word 'Blackpool' sewn into one corner.

"Another collector of knickknacks," Park-Coombs said as he laid everything out on the table.

Clara picked up the neckerchief and fingered it sadly. It was things like that, little tokens of personality, which brought a dead person to life and made their demise seem all the worse. They became a person, rather than just a name and a corpse.

More belongings came from the bag, which seemed somewhat bottomless. There was a pouch for keeping loose change, a wallet with photographs of family inside, a book of poems and another of seafaring adventures.

"Wanted to hunt whales and look for mermaids," Park-Coombs said wryly as he thumbed through the book, which had been well-read. "He liked the sea."

There was an engineering book, with Alf's name carefully written on the fly leaf. The book indicated it was given out when he took his engineering course for the shipping company, a prelude to working on a liner. From the flimsy nature of the book, it did not appear the course was particularly in-depth, just enough to weed out any complete idiots who would be liabilities at sea.

Further in the bag was an unopened bottle of

seasickness pills – presumably just in case Alf did not have sea legs. There was a bundle of letters beneath it. A quick glance showed they were from Alf's mother and sister.

"This is the tough part," Park-Coombs said, glancing at one of the letters and reading how Alf's mother looked forward to him coming home soon. "The family's grief is what always gets me."

"It is also the reason we do this," Clara reminded him.

She took the letters and scanned through them. There might be something in them, some hint of a concern Alf was fretting over, but after running through the most recent ones, Clara surmised Alf had kept his worries to himself.

"Is there anything else?" she asked, somewhat disappointed.

Park-Coombs had emptied the bag, but he felt around inside it, just in case he had missed something. That was when he felt a hard object in the lining. He pulled at it, but it had been sew behind a patch, a crude job but sufficient to keep it largely hidden.

"A secret compartment," he said. "Hang on, I should have my penknife."

He started to fudge in his pockets. Clara was looking at the patch and had noticed that there was a thread loose. She gave it a yank; in the off chance it might release the patch. She was as much surprised as the inspector when all the stitches came out with ease and a small notebook thudded out of the secret space.

"No need for the penknife, then," Park-Coombs said.

"Alf was many things, but he was not a good seamstress," Clara replied, picking up the object she had released. "A diary?"

"Something he wanted to avoid other people seeing," Park-Coombs answered. "That is obvious enough."

Clara opened the little book which was only the size of her palm. It was not a diary, as she started to read the contents, she realised it was a confession.

"This is the story of the sinking of the Sussex Princess,"

Clara said. "Told by a survivor of the disaster."

"Alf was not on that vessel," Park-Coombs frowned.

Clara flicked through the pages, right to the end. It was on virtually the last page she found the answer.

"This is the confession of Shaun Gunther."

"Wait, a confession about what?" Park-Coombs said. "Gunther nearly died that day trying to save the ship."

Clara was reading as fast as she could, without missing anything. The book was filled with small, densely packed writing that made unpicking the sentences difficult. She gradually understood the nature of the confession.

"Oh my," she said under her breath, then louder to the inspector, "Gunther stated that he and other members of the engineering crew were directly responsible for the failure of the watertight doors."

"How?" Park-Coombs asked, confused.

"For the convenience of the crew, they had taken to wedging open the doors so they could pass through quicker. The doors were fixed open when the ship hit that mine and so water flooded through with ease. The very thing that should have saved the ship had been disabled."

Park-Coombs winced as he understood the implication.

"All those lives lost, so that the engineering crew did not have to spend a few seconds opening watertight doors on their rounds," he groaned.

"You appreciate that if the company learned of this, they would haul every engineer who survived that ordeal over the coals," Clara continued. "They would find out who was most senior and gave the clearance to wedge the doors open and that man would be in serious trouble. Perhaps he would go to prison for the part he played in the sinking?"

"He bears all those deaths on his shoulders," Park-Coombs sighed as the thought came to him. "Including the death of Captain Vernon who went down with his ship thinking he had somehow failed his passengers. But why is this confession here at all? Gunther did not seem a fellow racked by guilt."

Clara examined the book a while longer, then she

glanced among the other belongings.

"Is there anything here with Alf's handwriting on it?"

Park-Coombs offered her the engineering handbook with Alf's name in the front. It was not much to go on, but after looking at the letters of his name compared to the writing in the confession, Clara felt confident it was one and the same.

"Alf wrote this confession. He and Gunther were friends until they fell out. Supposing Gunther was battling the remorse and guilt of the day the Sussex Princess sank and he reached out to a friend? Someone who was unconnected with that ship and who he perhaps hoped for sympathy from."

"And Alf wrote down every word he said," Park-Coombs said dryly. "Quite a breach of trust."

Clara turned the book over in her hands.

"We are looking at this the wrong way. What if Gunther asked Alf to write this down? His conscience had finally gotten to him, and he wanted to have a written record of that day when he and his colleagues condemned all those people to drown."

Park-Coombs thought about her suggestion for just a moment.

"It could be," he said. "Gunther tells Alf the story, has him write it down and take care of it. Then what? He kills him because he regrets saying all this? Then who murdered Gunther?"

Clara was thinking fast, piecing together all the things they knew.

"Guilt is a funny thing, Inspector, we both know that. It comes in waves and can just as easily disappear. Supposing, in a moment of sorrow and distress, Gunther asked Alf to take down his confession, but with this act done, he felt better and did not want to take the matter further. Alf hides this book away until such a time that Gunther decides he wants to reveal the truth."

"Or he confronts Gunther, tells him he must confess or else he will hand the book over to the shipping company,"

Park-Coombs said. "Gunther gets rid of him to prevent that but does not know where to find the book."

"No, that does not make sense," Clara countered. "Gunther's murder means someone else was involved and that makes me question why he was killed also. If he murdered Alf to keep his secret, then why did someone else feel the need to kill him? And he had that shipping number on him, remember?"

"He also had a big falling out with Alf," Park-Coombs said. "I see it this way. Gunther has a moment of weakness and confesses all to Alf. He even has him write it down. Then he sleeps on it and regrets what he said, realises the implications. He argues with Alf over the matter. Alf thinks the book should be given to the authorities while Gunther wants to forget all about it. Gunther begins to get nervous and one night he comes across Alf alone. They talk again, the same old story, and in the process, Gunther gets so agitated he forces Alf into a closing watertight door."

"Then who murdered Gunther, and why?" Clara argued.

Park-Coombs frowned.

"He must have felt guilty about the murder and confessed to someone else. Someone who had something to lose if the truth came out and that someone, when they saw we had Gunther, set about killing him."

Clara was not convinced by this scenario.

"What about the liner number we found in Gunther's pocket, what was that all about?"

"I don't know, but we are so close now Clara. We just need to work out who would be in the worst position should Gunther confess, and we shall have his killer."

Chapter Twenty-Seven

It was not easy to fit everyone in the car despite it being a spacious model. It necessitated people becoming rather friendly with one another, and there was consternation between Mr Mackintosh and Mr Peebles as to how they would arrange themselves. The matter was made worse when Mackintosh realised his wife was sitting directly next to Mr Juniper. This nearly erupted a fresh burst of outrage and Tommy had to hastily defuse the situation by placing Juniper in the front of the car. They ended up with the ladies and Tommy sitting on the back seat, while the two rival cobblers compressed themselves into the footwell before it, settled in for an uncomfortable ride. At least they were as far apart as possible and yet still able to glare at one another.

Jones took all this rearranging in his stride. Nothing much fazed him and when you spent time with the Fitzgeralds, you soon became used to having a car full of unusual people. He did not say a word during the reshuffling of everyone, though there might have been a slight hint of disapproval on his face when the cobblers wedged themselves into the footwell.

Uncomfortable as the ride back to Brighton was for

most of the people in the car, no one was inclined to talk and break the awkward silence that had fallen. They were happier to cast accusing glares at one another, knowing looks upon their faces.

Tommy was somewhat relieved when they found themselves drawing up to the cricket club. He just hoped everyone had remained and people were prepared to listen to his explanation. He spotted Mr Hardcastle pacing back and forth before the main entrance of the clubhouse, smoking a cigarette, and looking agitated. He glanced up sharply as he heard the engine of the car, anticipation mingled with both hope and dread in his expression.

Tommy released the passenger door of the car from the inside and Mr Peebles near enough fell backwards onto the hard gravel. He bumped his elbow and started to protest such abuse. Tommy was attempting to clamber over him so he could help him up, the man still had his legs wedged in the car and had twisted them as he fell making it awkward for him to stand up. On the other side of the car, Mr Mackintosh was attempting to extract himself and finding himself similarly stuck. The scene was rapidly becoming farcical, so it was fortunate that Jones stepped out of the car and went to the aid of Peebles, while on the opposite side it was Juniper who assisted Mackintosh. Mackintosh nearly resisted him, resenting his presence, then he remembered his situation and consented to allowing his cuckolder to help him to his feet.

For Juniper's part, the man was feeling racked by guilt over everything and was broken hearted that Mrs Mackintosh seemed to have cast him aside. He suddenly had developed a bizarre camaraderie with his lover's husband. He felt as if they shared in a wrong, though he would have been hard pressed to explain it.

"What is this?" Hardcastle came towards the car and scowled at Tommy, who was finally standing on the gravel drive. "Who are all these people?"

"I have brought you an explanation for the cheating," Tommy told him. "It is not what any of us expected and the culprit is right here."

Hardcastle turned to Mr Peebles.

"Peebles?" he said, looking the man up and down in astonishment. "What has he to do with any of this?"

"You know Mr Peebles?" Annie asked the chairman.

Hardcastle snorted.

"Of course I know him," he said. "The Peebles family have been supporters of the Brighton Badgers for decades."

Peebles ducked his head at the revelation. Tommy suddenly saw the last piece of the puzzle click into place.

"That explains why the Hove team took their business elsewhere when another cobbler opened up in the same area as you, Mr Peebles," he said. "They were aware of your allegiance to the Badgers and did not like bringing their leather goods to you. When they had to, they lived with it, but when there was an option, they gladly changed, and you lost valuable trade.

"It also explains why you did not bat an eye at aiding your home team to lose this match and why it did not worry you that they might be accused of cheating. You wanted them to be accused, because the only way for you to have your revenge on Mr Mackintosh was if the rigged mitt was exposed during a game."

"Peebles?" Hardcastle asked, looking astounded.

The cobbler could not meet his eye.

"We should go inside and let everyone hear this," Tommy said.

Hardcastle was still trying to get his head around what he had just heard, but he did not argue the suggestion and moved aside so they could head into the clubhouse. They found the majority of the cricketers still in the meeting room. They looked tired and fed up. Reed was sitting all alone in a corner, his ego bruised, his isolation a mark of the crimes of which he was suspected. He did not look up when Tommy returned. He had lost all hope a while back.

"I imagine most of you know Mr Peebles?" Tommy said as he entered the room.

His teammates observed the cobbler but did not show

recognition. It was the Hove Cricket Bats who responded.

"Mr Peebles used to mend our shoes and things," the Hove captain declared.

There were murmurs of agreement from his companions.

"I do not suppose anyone noticed him here this afternoon during the game?" Tommy asked.

"I saw him," Hardcastle stated. "I offered him some lemonade. It was during the early stages of the game."

Peebles, if he had doubted he was condemned before, now knew he was finished. His only consolation was that all this was happening away from Hove and away from his shop.

"What is this about, Tommy?" Tommy's captain asked.

Reed had lifted his head a fraction and was looking at Peebles closely.

"It comes down to this," Tommy explained. "Mr Peebles was responsible for tampering with Reed's mitt and with a suitable cricket ball which he had ample time to place among the match balls while he was here. When the commotion over the supposed cheating arose, he departed and headed back to his shop, where he pretended, he had been working all afternoon."

"Why would he do that?" Reed asked, his voice filled with hurt.

"More than one reason," Tommy explained. "He was angered the Hove Cricket Bats no longer used his shop and had gone to his rival. He was annoyed that you, Reed, had not chosen to use a local cobbler to create your mitt. But, most importantly, he wanted to revenge himself against Mr Mackintosh, the man he saw as the sum of all his woes. When he learned that Mackintosh was doing repairs on Reed's mitt, he concocted an idea of how he could manipulate the situation to his advantage.

"He broke into Mackintosh's workshop and carefully inserted a magnet in the mitt. The rigged cricket ball he was able to prepare at home. Then all he had to do was be at the cricket match, insert the tampered ball and be ready for someone to spot something was off. I suppose, had it come to it, he would have shouted out an accusation of cheating if no one else spoke up. The result would be the same. The mitt and ball would be examined, Mackintosh would be recognised as the person who had last handled the mitt and would be accused of the alterations. A secondary casualty would be Reed who would be suspected of instigating the crime.

"Peebles did not much care about the impact on Reed. He felt it served him right for not using a Hove cobbler for his mitt. Peebles has spent a lot of time in his empty shop working up resentment towards, well, everyone."

Attention turned to the accused cobbler.

"Don't look at me like that!" he snapped. "You had no care for me, or my business. I could have sunk, and you would not blink. All you care about is this damn game! My shop is the oldest cobblers in the town, and you chose to go to Edinburgh!"

Peebles threw the last words at Reed.

"You might be the oldest, but you are far from the best," Reed responded coldly. He had no sympathy for the man, not after what he had done to him.

Peebles pulled a nasty face.

"You would rather go with this fool and his modern machines!" he pointed an accusing finger at Mackintosh. "You deserved this all, you really did! I just wish you had not all been so bloody curious and had gone with your first assumptions!"

"You have me to blame for the curiosity," Tommy told him nonchalantly. "It didn't quite make sense, you see, and Reed seemed genuinely shocked by the discovery of the magnet. I couldn't just let it go."

Peebles glowered at him.

"I thought, when your wife raised the alarm, it was all over. That I had won."

"Not quite," Tommy replied with a smile.

"There is one thing I am confused about," Hardcastle interrupted. "Why did Mr Peebles go to all that effort only to throw the mitt and the cricket ball into the pond?"

"What?" Peebles asked in horror. "I never did that! As soon as the trouble began, I slipped away. What would be the point of doing that?"

"He is right," Tommy added. "Removing the mitt and ball was completely against what he wished to achieve. Whoever did that was attempting to cover up the crime."

"Don't look at me," Reed said as he sensed their attention returning to him. "I had nothing to do with it."

"Reed was in our sight from the time the accusation was made," Tommy added. "He was wearing the mitt when Annie shouted out."

"But he took it off," Annie said. "He was not wearing it when we were all in this room discussing things. He said it was back in his bag in the changing rooms."

"I only wear the thing when I have to," Reed concurred. "It hurts my wrist like crazy."

"But he never left our sights," Tommy repeated.

"I gave the mitt to someone else," Reed said quickly, seeing that people were still considering him the likeliest suspect for disposing of it. "I asked them to take it to the changing rooms for me while I sorted out this nonsense about cheating. At the time I did not take the matter seriously."

"Who did you give the mitt to?" Tommy asked.

Reed hesitated for just a split second, his teammates had supported him, for the most part, in this matter. At least until the mitt's contents had been revealed and then they had refused to believe his denials. Did he owe them anything for that? Anything at all?

Someone among them had compounded his crime by hiding the mitt. Someone had believed from the moment the accusations were made that he was guilty and had made an effort to cover his trail. The more he thought about it, the more he became incensed that someone had decided he was a cheat before they had even spoken to him.

His reservation disappeared.

"I gave my mitt to Captain Rhodes."

The captain of the Hove Cricket Bats winced at the declaration. No one spoke, but their gazes fell on him with the weight of accusation.

"It is not quite how you are thinking," Captain Rhodes said. "I was trying to, trying to…"

He floundered for an excuse.

"You were trying to cover up a supposed case of cheating," Juniper said, speaking for the first time. Not everyone had noticed his presence until that moment. The sight of the Hove chairman glaring at his team angrily was enough to make most of the Cricket Bats uneasy about their future on the team.

"You believed I was cheating," Reed added, his hurt plain. "You did not ask me or give me the benefit of the doubt, you just assumed it was true. I thought we were friends."

Captain Rhodes cringed at the remark, but he was going to bluster his way out of this, if he could.

"Look, Jim, we all knew you were a compromised player when you came back one-handed. You went on this bizarre journey to have a mitt made that would mean you could continue playing and we accepted that. You even came back a reasonable player, but you were never going to be as good as before and when I saw you playing today, how you were catching, well, I started to think there was a little more than talent behind it."

Reed looked as if he had been physically struck. The comment hit him where he was most vulnerable, and he curled into himself.

"We all saw the way he was catching," Captain Rhodes persisted. "He did not catch like that in practice. I had my suspicions, and I would have spoken to him after the match, but then this lady stepped forward," Rhodes waved a hand in Annie's direction. "I was thinking that if there was something going on with that mitt and it was giving Reed an advantage, we would all be considered responsible, and our team reputation ruined. I had to act fast. It was not hard to suggest Reed give me his mitt to put away while he went inside to straighten things out. It took seconds to pick up the cricket ball too. I had a spare in my pocket, and I just casually swapped them. Everyone was so busy thinking about the accusation, I was not noticed.

"I had to get rid of the mitt and ball as quickly as I could. There was an empty umpire's bag hanging on the back of a chair where it had been left. All I had to do was shove the mitt inside, do up the buckles and then slip it into the pond. I made it look as if it was my bag, if anyone was watching me, and when I put everything in the pond I knelt down and pretended to be tying my shoe. As it happened, no one was watching, and no one noticed I was last to arrive at the meeting room. I know it was rash, and probably not the best of ideas, but it was all that came to me in the moment."

Reed hung his head, a doubly defeated man. One of his teammates reached out and touched his shoulder, finally showing a bit of team spirit. The room was now full of hurt and solemn cricket players. One afternoon that should have been pleasant and good natured had become this mess of accusations and misplaced loyalties.

Mr Peebles started to laugh.

"All this fuss over my little act of sabotage!" he declared, suddenly enjoying the attention. "And after you all decided my stitching was not good enough for you! You never noticed the alteration, did you? Did you?"

"Is that the sort of triumph you want?" Mackintosh asked his rival.

Peebles swung towards him.

"What do you know of it? I showed everyone what I was capable of. You called my work slipshod!"

"I commented on what I saw," Mackintosh huffed. "Maybe if you had put as much effort into your usual work that you put into this stupid mitt business, you would not be struggling."

Peebles did not understand the point he was making, he was just basking in his success.

"None of you guessed, none of you. I made the cricket ball look perfect and I slipped it among the genuine match balls with such ease. I was lucky it was that ball that was chosen for the game, but it was on the top, so I suppose it was obvious."

Peebles was after a response he would not get.

"Don't you see? I have proven myself the better cobbler! Why are you all so dense?"

Chapter Twenty-Eight

Clara was still stuck trying to work out how to discover the person who murdered Gunther. They were close now, the confession being a key piece of evidence, along with the ship number in Gunther's pocket. All of it was pointing at someone who had worked on the Sussex Princess, but that left them with a few too many options.

Clara and the inspector returned to Captain Blowers' cabin to see if they could find a way into this mystery.

"Captain Blowers," Clara said as soon as she saw him sitting at his desk, fingers curled into his short hair as he tried to cope with the nightmare before him, "we have something critical."

She handed him the notebook. Blowers did not at once pick it up. He did not have the energy or interest.

"What is it?" he asked.

"Proof that the Sussex Princess was sunk due to the negligence of the engineering crew, or at least some among them."

Blowers' head jerked up and he grabbed the notebook. Opening it he saw the dense handwriting and groaned to himself. They gave him time to read the material, keeping back while he concentrated on deciphering the small writing. They could tell when he was done from the stunned look that came onto his face.

"This is shocking," he declared. "This means those deaths could have been prevented. It was not Captain Vernon's fault, and it was not some design or construction flaw. It was carelessness by crewmen who should have known better."

"One of them was Gunther," Clara agreed. "But there were others involved and I believe one of them is responsible for the deaths aboard this ship. They are trying to hide their mistakes. I suppose they either did not realise there was a written version of the confession, or they were unable to find it. Matlock had hidden it in his bag."

"We need to know who among your engineering crew was also aboard the Sussex Princess," Park-Coombs added.

"Well, several," Blowers frowned.

"But who would have been in the area when Matlock was killed and, more prudently, when Gunther was shot?" the inspector pressed.

Blowers' frown deepened.

"I am not sure, precisely, but I could suggest a name or two. If I were to draw up a list of those who worked on the Sussex Princess, perhaps we could go through the names?"

"It is worth a try," Clara agreed. Then she paused as an idea came to her. "Did Ernie White work on the Princess?"

Blowers stopped for a second, giving it some thought.

"Yes, now you mention it. He was a senior engineer, I believe, but was demoted after the incident. There was never any blame attached to him for the mishap, but the company needed to make an example and reduced his rank."

Clara exchanged a look with Park-Coombs. He had a strange smile on his face.

"Gunther said Ernie would confirm where he was on the night Matlock was killed. But he didn't. He did quite the opposite," the inspector mused. "Seemed odd that a friend would be so fickle."

"Unless, the friend knew about the confession and had

every reason to want to see Gunther discredited and the confession deemed false," Clara nodded.

"Especially if Ernie White really knew how Matlock died and needed a scapegoat."

Blowers was glancing between them.

"What is this?" he asked.

"If we are right," Clara said, "Ernie White is responsible for not just the deaths of Matlock and Gunther, but for the many deaths he indirectly caused aboard the Sussex Princess. He has been trying to cover his tracks ever since."

"Matlock could have exposed him after he learned the truth, maybe he even intended to. He took down the written confession so that Gunther could not recant it after he was feeling less remorseful."

Blowers was following this closely.

"You mean, Ernie White came here, took my key and shot Gunther?"

"It makes sense. Gunther seemed to know his killer and made no resistance."

Captain Blowers stared into space, countless half-formed thoughts buzzing about his mind at this revelation. He was trying to understand, trying to piece it all together. He was about to speak when there was a knock at his cabin door.

"Enter," Blowers called out absent-mindedly.

A man entered. He was from the search party, and he was carrying something carefully in his hands. He presented it to the captain with a strange look on his face. The object was wrapped in a handkerchief, which he pulled back to reveal a gun.

"Where did you find it?" Blowers asked.

The man pulled a face.

"Lieutenant Harper's cabin. Under his pillow."

Blowers could not have been more shocked had he been told they had found it in his own cabin. He stared and stared at the gun, unable to speak.

"This rather blows our theory out of the water," Park-Coombs said forlornly when no one else spoke. "Harper was never on the Princess, was he?"

Blowers somehow managed to shake his head.

"Even if he was, he would have no responsibility for those watertight doors," Clara said. "This is curious. We need to speak to Harper."

"I did not know he owned a gun," Blowers said, his tongue at last under his command.

"There are a lot of secrets on this ship," Clara told him solemnly. "Summon Harper, Captain."

Blowers obeyed, though he was still in shock and acting without really being aware of what he was doing. Later, he would struggle to recall the details of this debacle. There would be a blank space in his mind where memories of this occasion should have been.

Harper appeared at his cabin within a matter of minutes. Clearly, he had not been far away, even if he had not been involved in the search parties. He had a peculiar look on his face when he appeared, one that hinted at anger. He stood before them all, including the man from the search party who had never found the right moment to leave and was still clutching the gun.

"Is this your gun Harper?" Blowers asked him.

Harper glanced at the gun.

"Yes," he said. "It was my father's service revolver."

"You bring it on a sea voyage?" Park-Coombs asked sharply.

Harper lifted his head, anger making him arrogant.

"You never know when it may be necessary to shoot something or protect the ship. We travel all over and though most waters are safe, there are still mines out there, and even modern pirates. Besides, one never knows when the Germans might start another war," Harper paused to see if they would counter him, he smiled when they did not. "Last time war was announced, I was on a liner in an African port. We came perilously close to being taken prisoner by the Germans. I refuse to allow such a thing to happen again. I have carried the gun ever since."

"That was exceptional circumstances," Blowers

reminded him.

"What is to stop it happening again? Maybe not the Germans, but someone else, anyone else. I won't be caught napping. Anyone tries to take this ship, I shall be ready for them."

Blowers was looking at him strangely, suddenly not so sure he knew the man before him and the paranoia which clearly gripped him.

Inspector Park-Coombs broke the gun barrel open.

"Do you keep this fully loaded?"

"At all times," Harper declared proudly. "You never know what might occur and you could need all those bullets."

"Except there is one missing," Park-Coombs said. "I imagine it is now lodged in Gunther's torso."

Harper froze. The look of shock on his face seemed utterly genuine. Clara watched as this information sunk in and he realised the implication.

"I did not shoot Shaun Gunther," he said. "Why would I?"

"That is a good point," Blowers interjected, his fierce gaze now directed back to Clara and the inspector. "Why would he?"

"I am just going by the evidence of the gun," Park-Coombs shrugged. He rarely became rattled when interrogating suspects, more often he would grow calmer and calmer as the questioning progressed. Clara had learned this was when he was most dangerous as a policeman.

"Gunther had no argument with me, nor I with him," Harper said quickly.

"Where were you this afternoon?" Clara asked him.

Harper blinked, but his answer came quickly.

"Just after dinner, I was on the upper deck playing quoits with some of the guests to distract them. We must have played for a couple of hours, then I was called away to deal with an issue in a guest's cabin. They were complaining that the porthole would not open and though they had been shown repeatedly how it did open, they still protested it would not open for them and wanted to speak to an officer. Thus, I was called. When I was done with that, I came back towards the bridge to ask the captain if there was any news. At which time I was informed of the death of Gunther."

Harper relaxed. He could account for his whereabouts throughout the afternoon and there was no time when he could have slipped away to kill Gunther.

Park-Coombs was thrown. Clara, however, had another idea.

"Who knows about your gun, Lieutenant Harper?"

The lieutenant hesitated.

"Probably more people than really should," he admitted. "I have talked about it among the crew, mainly those who served in the war and remember what it was like."

"You have never mentioned it to me," Blowers rumbled.

"I knew what your reaction would be," Harper shrugged.

There was no way to counter such a comment. Blowers fell silent.

"We can easily confirm where you were," Inspector Park-Coombs told the man in a mildly threatening manner, trying to shake him.

Harper kept calm.

"You will find I have not lied. I should also add that I never lock my cabin. I lost the key some weeks back."

"That is true," Blowers agreed reluctantly. "The key went overboard."

"Then we remain where we began," Clara sighed. "The gun could have been used by anyone who knew of it, then replaced."

"Except, the killer has to have had a motive," Park-Coombs interrupted. "And only a handful of people do. I think we need to consider Ernie White a strong candidate."

"White?" Harper asked, now curious. "You suspect White of murder?"

"Yes," Clara told him. "Potentially of both Gunther and

Matlock."

Harper pursed his lips. Clara sensed there was more he knew.

"What is it, Lieutenant?"

Harper was quiet.

"We need to fetch Ernie here and talk to him," Blowers said when his officer did not respond. "He has a lot to explain, not least his connection with the sinking of the Sussex Princess."

"The Sussex Princess?" Harper said abruptly. "What about it?"

"It appears that Alf Matlock uncovered the secret to the liner's sinking," Clara explained. "He discovered it was not an accident and if we are correct, he was murdered because he knew too much."

"The Sussex Princess was a terrible tragedy that has marred the reputation of the company," Harper declared. "For a while it threatened all our careers. There were many lean months when the company could not fill a ship with passengers. If the war had not come along, we may have never survived."

"It was a hard time," Blowers reflected. "I lost a good friend, but I also saw the potential for my world to spiral out of my control."

"What did Matlock discover?" Harper pressed.

Clara saw no reason to lie.

"He learned that the engineers aboard the liner, including Gunther, were leaving the watertight doors propped open to save time as they moved about the ship. The consequences when the ship hit a mine and sunk were catastrophic."

Harper was so shaken by this news he had to lean out a hand to Blower's desk.

"All those deaths," he whispered to himself.

"It makes the mind boggle," Blowers nodded. "Such carelessness could not be tolerated. Had it been known such a thing had been done, those responsible would have paid a heavy price."

"Instead, every one of the engineers who survived kept silent about it," Clara explained. "They all had something to lose, and their collective guilt was not enough to diminish their collective silence. At least, until Gunther began to feel remorseful. Someone murdered him because he had confessed what had happened to Matlock and the truth was close to coming out."

"They probably murdered Matlock too," Park-Coombs added.

"They stole my gun to commit the murder," Harper had grown pale. "Shift the blame onto me. But what reason would I have to wish Gunther harm?"

No one answered him.

"I think we should summon Ernie White," Clara said to Captain Blowers. "As I said before, there is something curious about him. I sense a secret, but it might have no relevance at all to this case."

"Ernie White was aboard the Sussex Princess," Harper said to himself, then he spoke louder to all of them. "He told me about the sinking, how it was caused by a fault with the doors, but the liner company did not want to hear about it."

"He was lying, though the inquest believed him," Clara remarked. "Gunther's confession makes it plain the doors failed because they had been propped open."

Harper leaned harder against the desk. His face had taken on an ashen aspect, and he seemed unable to comprehend what was occurring. After a moment, he raised his head and spoke directly to his captain.

"A while back, I don't remember the precise date, I had reason to go below decks. As I was walking around, I came across a watertight door that had been prevented from closing by the presence of a heavy chain. I was surprised and also alarmed. As I began to investigate, Ernie White came around a corner and saw me. The look on his face told me he was responsible for the door," Harper flinched as he remembered what he had seen and how he had not had any idea of the significance. "I gave him an earful, told him if I ever came across a watertight door wedged open again, I would hold him personally responsible and see him off the ship. He protested his innocence, naturally, but he was the only person in that area. After that, I made several random patrols of the lower decks to check the doors and never found them wedged open again."

Park-Coombs sniffed thoughtfully.

"Seems to me, Mr White has failed to learn his lesson from the Sussex Princess."

"We need to talk to him," Clara agreed. "Urgently."

She was looking at Captain Blowers. It took him a second to react.

"At once," he said, a grim look on his face.

Chapter Twenty-Nine

They did not want to alert Ernie White to their suspicions if they could help it. Ideally, he would come to them, unwitting that he was now their prime candidate for murder. They headed down to the lower decks and converged in one of the pump rooms and Captain Blowers had a message sent out over the onboard communication pipes that Ernie White was needed to correct a leak. It was not unusual to specify an engineer for a task and with any luck the innocuous message would have Ernie attending to his duties without concern.

"I am still trying to grasp all this," Harper ran a weary hand over his face. His eyeballs felt dry and sore, as if he had stood in a desert. "What we are saying is that two men are dead because of what happened on the Sussex Princess, and the culprit is a man I have known for years."

Harper tried to picture Ernie crushing poor Alf Matlock in a watertight door. The man and the event were too impossible to align.

"Maybe it was someone else?"

"Ernie White is implicated in too many ways," Clara replied to the downcast lieutenant. "He has a lot of explaining to do, at the very least."

They waited and waited, occasionally discussing the matter, and going over the same ground time and time again. Ernie White never appeared. Perplexed, Captain Blowers sent out the message a second time.

"He cannot already know we suspect him, can he?" he asked.

"Well, it would be hard not to notice the search parties we arranged," Inspector Park-Coombs pointed out.

"But, did he suppose they were looking for him?" Blowers scratched at his head. "No, he would assume they were looking for someone else. He is bound to have learned we were looking for a gun. I have no doubt the search parties, despite our instructions to be cautious who they spoke to would have let that slip. If he learned that, well, then he would be thinking that when we found it Lieutenant Harper would be in a lot of trouble, not him. He would feel safe that his plan to shift blame would work."

Silence fell as they considered the situation. The second summons had not brought Ernie White to them.

"He suspects," Park-Coombs sighed. "Smart fellow, after all. He has decided to disappear. Only, we are on a ship in the middle of the ocean, where could he disappear to?"

"Overboard," Harper said darkly.

"White cannot swim, he would never make it to shore," Blowers shook his head. "Not from this far out and against the tide."

"Maybe he does not intend to swim anywhere," Harper replied.

They were unnerved by his sinister tone. Blowers grimaced.

"No. I cannot believe White would go this far just to end it all at the very last. He is a fighter and, if nothing else, he is a survivor."

"Then where is he?" Clara asked the obvious question.

"We need to redirect the search parties, start them looking for a man rather than a gun," Blowers went to one of the speaking pipes near to hand, which would enable him to communicate with the bridge. "Now the game is up, we can involve the crew. Harper, find every man who is free and have them join a search party with instructions to look for Ernie White. I shall have an announcement put out that he must be found urgently."

"Yes Captain," Harper said stoutly, happier now he had some task to perform and that he was no longer under suspicion for murdering Gunther.

He hastened off while Blowers relayed his instructions to the bridge.

"Where shall we go?" Clara asked Park-Coombs.

He twitched his moustache as he pondered the question.

"How many places can there be on this ship to hide?" he said.

"I would hide somewhere no one would think of looking for me," Clara said. "Such as one of the officer's cabins."

Their eyes met as the same idea came to them both at the same time.

"Or a cupboard," Park-Coombs grinned.

They rushed out of the pump room, behind them Blowers was calling out, asking where they were going.

"I suggest you follow, Captain Blowers," Clara called back, though she did not wait to see if he did.

They were breathless as they raced back up the decks, the gangway ladders seeming to get steeper and steeper at each level. When they reached the corridor near the captain's cabin they slowed to a halt and paused to catch their breath. If they were right, they did not want to alert White too soon.

Blowers had decided to follow them, and he appeared a few minutes later. He gave them a curious look, wanting an explanation for their haste, but too out of breath to ask.

Park-Coombs held up a finger to indicate they should be silent, then, still trying to get his breathing back under control, he walked to the large cupboard where a short while earlier they had secured Gunther.

The door had not been locked after the body had been

found. When Park-Coombs placed his hand on the door handle, it depressed easily, and he opened it sharply into the room. For one moment he thought he had surmised wrongly, and the room was empty. The evening was coming on and long shadows filled the space, making it hard to see all the edges. He almost blustered back out when there was a hint of movement at the back corner. He glanced up and looked harder at what had first appeared to have been a set of shelves with an old coat hanging from them – an old coat that had not been there before.

"Ernie White," he declared delighted.

From his corner, Ernie White whimpered then stepped out of the shadows. There was nowhere left to run, and he knew the game was up. Blowers appeared behind Park-Coombs; Clara was at his side.

"I think we need to talk," Park-Coombs said to the engineer. "Preferably in the captain's cabin."

White came from the cupboard without protest. His eyes darted up and down the corridor for a second as he contemplated escape, but he would have to get past either the inspector or his captain. He naively did not consider Clara much of a threat to any escape he attempted. He was just lucky he did not try to make a break for it in her direction. He would have soon learned his error.

He was defeated, for the moment, and he was tired, the last few days having taken a considerable toll on his psyche. Despite the evidence before them, White was not a natural killer and two murders in such a short span of time had taken a chunk out of his soul. He was not even sure why he had committed them anymore. Because he feared some confession? It seemed so ludicrous when he thought about it.

They entered the captain's cabin and Blowers made sure to lock the door behind them and remove the key. White did not look like he was about to make a dash for it, but it was better to be safe than sorry. He was offered a chair before the captain's desk and slumped into it, his head lowered, his shoulders sagging.

"I take it, White, you know why we are looking for you?" Blowers asked, sitting in his own chair with a groan, partly because he felt so ill at the thought of one of his crew being a murderer.

Park-Coombs and Clara flanked the desk either side, so they could see White's face.

"I can hardly fail to know," White sniffed miserably. "It all began to unravel, you see, after Alf's death. I realised things were not going to be as simple as I thought. I just needed it to look like an accident, but everyone was too damn curious."

He clasped his hands tightly together in his lap.

"How much do you know?" he asked.

"We have guessed a good deal," Clara answered him. If he was surprised she was the one who spoke up he did not indicate it. "Shaun Gunther became friends with Alf Matlock, took him under his wing. At some point his conscience over the tragedy of the Sussex Princess and his responsibility for the sinking got too much for him and he told Alf everything."

"Alf reminded Gunther of a lad we had aboard the Princess. He was an apprentice and Gunther felt responsible for him. When the ship started to flood, he went looking for the lad but could not find him. They never did find his body. He must have been trapped somewhere," White pulled back his lips over his teeth at the thought. "Gunther always felt bad about it, felt he was responsible for the lad's death. He took the sinking harder than the rest of us."

"But you were responsible for wedging open the watertight doors?" Blowers asked.

White nodded his head.

"But we could not have known it would be so bad. That we would hit an old mine. It was an accident."

"You disobeyed safety regulations which were laid down for a reason," Blowers told him sternly. "And not a single one of you who survived cared to speak up and explain."

White had no response.

"Why did Gunther confess to Alf?" Clara interjected, trying to get them back on topic.

White sniffed again.

"As I say, Alf reminded him of the lad who perished. Gunther had always been prone to bouts of remorse over the sinking. He would go into these spirals of depression and guilt. You could not talk to him when he was like that. The last one, it was the worst he had suffered, and Alf tried to talk him out of it. Well, that made it even harder, and Gunther could not hold his tongue any longer. He told Alf everything, a full confession and Alf wrote it down! More is the pity. Then Gunther signed the thing!"

White shook his head in despair.

"If that confession got out, every crewman who worked below and survived the Princess tragedy would be hauled into court to determine his level of responsibility for a terrible accident. I mean, if we want to place blame, what about looking at the Admiralty who had all those mines laid in the first place and then failed to clear them? Where is their responsibility? It was an English mine that got us, you know, an English mine!"

"That is hardly the point, White," Blowers said coldly. "To start with we were at war and secondly if the safety procedures had been correctly followed aboard the Princess the sinking would have been delayed, maybe even prevented. The passengers and crew could have been rescued and many lives saved. You cannot remove yourself from the responsibility you bear for those deaths which could have been prevented."

White clearly did not agree, but he did not argue either.

"What happened after Gunther had confessed?" Clara asked.

"Well, he felt better, that was what happened," White snorted indignantly. "Silly fool! If he needed to let vent, why not speak to me or one of the others who knew what had occurred? But no, he had to speak to Alf and then he regretted it and told Alf he did want his secret coming out.

Alf was far too decent, by half. He said if Gunther did not tell the truth about the sinking, he would take the written confession to the maritime authorities. He gave him until the end of this voyage to make up his mind.

"Gunther had no idea what to do, so he came to me, told me what he had done. I swore at him and then I came up with a plan. It wasn't easy to find a way to kill Alf that would make it seem like an accident, but the idea of him being crushed by the watertight door had a certain irony."

Blowers flinched hearing the death of a young man being talked about so glibly. White did not notice.

"We were in on it together, because that seemed the best way and Gunther might have backed out at the last minute alone. Also, we could provide each other with a story as to where we were when it happened. All we had to do then was distract Alf and hold him in the doorway while the door shut on him. It took two of us, but once he was pinned the door just kept pressing him and pressing him."

White's hand tightened over the other, as he recounted the grim last moments of Alf's life.

"It would have been over then, except the police were not satisfied and then Gunther started to have regrets. I told him to focus and look for the written confession. It was in this small notebook. We searched Alf, but we did not find it. All he had in his pocket was a slip of paper with the registry number of the Princess on it. Gunther took that because he did not want anyone to wonder what it meant.

"We searched Alf's belongings too but could not find it and then they were taken to storage and out of our reach. Gunther started to lose his nerve, couldn't face what he had done. Then you were all poking around, and I saw he was on the brink of confessing again. I had to do anything I could to save myself."

"Which is why you denied Gunther's alibi for the night of the murder," Park-Coombs guessed. "You were trying to discredit Gunther."

"I thought it was working too," White chuckled. "But no, you kept looking and looking. Gunther was going to tell you all, I knew it was just a matter of time. I learned where he had been put by the captain and it was not hard to retrieve the spare key or to steal the gun Harper talked about and kept under his pillow. Then I went to Gunther. I was going to talk him out of saying anything, but when we met face to face, I knew it was too late. He was a liability to me and so I…"

White said no more, but they all knew what he had done.

"That makes two murders on your hands, not to mention the many you murdered by negligence aboard the Princess," Blowers said steadily. "It is over now, you understand White? You have nowhere left to hide."

White drew in a shaky breath.

"I knew it was going to come out one day," he said with an ironic smile. "I knew I could not hide from it forever, but I still hoped I might. No one wants to be labelled a murderer, do they."

White looked at his hands which were so taut around one another they had caused the skin of his fingers and palms to lose all colour.

"What happens now?" he asked.

"I arrest you," Park-Coombs answered.

Chapter Thirty

The day had drawn to an unexpected and strange conclusion. Park-Coombs' arrest of Ernie White coincided with the arrival of his constables, which enabled him to promptly remove the man to Brighton. The corpses were also discreetly removed, being now evidence in a murder case. That left Captain Blowers free to continue on his voyage at last. He found it hard to believe, after all this time, that at last he could go home. For a while inertia kicked in and he found himself unable to give the order to carry on. There was so much to consider, so much to come to terms with.

"If your superiors have any heart at all they shall find you utterly blameless in all this," Clara told him as they stood at the railing of the liner and watched White being transported to Brighton. There had not been enough room for Clara in the boat the constables had sailed over in, not with a suspect aboard, so she would have to wait for someone to come and fetch her.

"You could not have known about any of this, you appreciate that?"

Captain Blowers smiled weakly.

"What is true and what the company believes to be true

are often very different," he sighed. "If I need to, might I trouble you to offer your opinion to my superiors about all this?"

"Of course," Clara assured him. "I hope it will not come to that, after all, not only have we resolved the death of Alf Matlock, but we have also revealed the truth about the sinking of the Sussex Princess. You must emphasise that, Captain. You solved a mystery that has plagued the shipping company and threatened their reputation. You have proved it was not their fault, after all. The design of the doors was not to blame, nor the construction of the ship. It was the carelessness of crewmen, which was outside the company's control."

"It was not Captain Vernon's fault either," Blowers agreed. "I wish he was around to hear that."

Sadness came over him and Clara reached out to pat his arm.

"At least his memory is salvaged, for the sake of his family."

"Yes," Blowers said, though not with great conviction. "At least there is that."

Clara arrived home several hours later, having been given a lift on a fishing smack that was coming back into Brighton. She was sure her clothes reeked distinctly of fish, and her shoes glistened from the scales stuck to them. It would be a miracle if Annie could save them.

She entered the house looking forward to a good dinner and a quiet evening sitting in a chair with a book. There was a strong possibility she would doze off in said chair, which was sounding very appealing.

She was somewhat surprised, and a tad annoyed, to find her dining room full of cricket players.

"Tommy?"

"It has been quite an afternoon!" Tommy beamed at her from his place at the head of the table. "There was a terrible moment when Jim Reed was accused of cheating, but thankfully I resolved the whole affair successfully. The game had to be declared void, but we have rescheduled it for next weekend. The lads wanted to celebrate my triumph, so we all came here."

Several cricketers raised their glasses of sherry to Clara. She had a suspicion they were going to make a night of things, so made her excuses and wandered to the kitchen where she could be relatively undisturbed.

Annie had come to a similar idea, the kitchen being somewhat her sanctuary. She gave Clara a weary smile as she appeared.

"Clara, remind me in future not to get involved in a cricket match."

Clara squeezed her shoulder as she went past to sit in a chair.

"I sense there is a story in this I need to be told."

"It is a long story, but the crux of it is simple enough. One man's jealousy of another causing him to do something quite bizarre."

"Is it a crime for the police?"

"It is being referred to the Amateur Cricket Association, they can decide what needs to be done. Though as the culprit is not technically involved in cricket aside from being a spectator, it is difficult to know what the outcome will be."

"They will probably take months over it making a decision," Clara nodded. "What of Jim Reed? Was he involved in the cheating?"

"Not wittingly," Annie explained. "That is going to be quite a complicated matter. The Association is going to have to review his wearing of that mitt and whether it is fair or not. It is all a bit of a mess and, quite frankly, I think Reed was so shaken up he may never be able to face playing cricket again."

"That's a shame," Clara sighed. "But some matters are out of our hands."

"I take it you solved your case?" Annie said. "You disappeared quite sharpish."

"I did," Clara replied, not feeling the strength to explain further. "It is all over and done with."

Annie knew when not to push her for more details. She rose from the table.

"Would you like some dinner?"

"I would love some," Clara groaned. "I am famished."

From the dining room a cheer rose, and male voices began to sing 'for he is a jolly good fellow.'

"This will all go to Tommy's head," Annie tutted. "He shall be unbearable for weeks."

Clara started to smile, until a sudden thought came to her. It had taken a while to creep through her tired mind, but now the notion had arrived it seemed to be screaming for her attention.

Her tiredness evaporated as the thought took hold and filled her with horror. She spluttered out.

"Wait a moment. Tommy took on a case and solved it all without me?"